Born in Lincolnshire in 1912, **Michael Francis Gilbert** was educated in Sussex before entering the University of London where he gained an LL B with honours in 1937. He joined the Royal Horse Artillery during World War II, and served in Europe and North Africa, where he was captured and imprisoned – an experience recalled in *Death in Captivity*. After the war he worked in a law firm as a solicitor, and in 1952 he became partner. Gilbert was a founding member of the British Crime Writers Association, and in 1988 he was named a Grand Master by the Mystery Writers of America – an achievement many thought long overdue. He won the Life Achievement Anthony Award at the 1990 Boucheron in London, and in 1980 he was knighted as a Commander in the Order of the British Empire. Gilbert made his debut in 1947 with *Close Quarters*, and since then has become recognized as one of our most versatile British mystery writers.

FICTION:

THE DANGER WITHIN
BE SHOT FOR SIXPENCE
AFTER THE FINE WEATHER
THE CRACK IN THE TEACUP
THE DUST AND THE HEAT
THE ETRUSCAN NET
FLASH POINT
THE NIGHT OF THE TWELFTH
THE EMPTY HOUSE
THE KILLING OF KATIE STEELSTOCK
THE BLACK SERAPHIM

INSPECTOR HAZLERIGG SERIES:

CLOSE QUARTERS
DEATH HAS DEEP ROOTS
FEAR TO TREAD

PATRICK PETRELLA SERIES:

BLOOD AND JUDGEMENT
GAMES WITHOUT RULES
STAY OF EXECUTION
PETRELLA AT Q
MR CALDERS AND MR BEHRENS
THE YOUNG PETRELLA
ANYTHING FOR A QUIET LIFE

MICHAEL GILBERT

THE DOORS OPEN

HOUSE OF
STRATUS

First published in 1949
Copyright by Michael Gilbert

This edition published in 2004 by House of Stratus, an imprint of
Stratus Books Ltd., 21 Beeching Park, Kelly Bray,
Cornwall, PL17 8QS, UK.

www.houseofstratus.com

Typeset, printed and bound by House of Stratus.

A catalogue record for this book is available from the British Library
and the Library of Congress.

ISBN 0-7551-1146-X

Contents

	Prologue – In Which the Doors Open	vii
1	The Last Hours of an Assistant Cashier	1
2	Paddy Gets Busy	15
3	Introducing a Number of People	31
4	Dinner at the Mogador	47
5	All Trains Go to Waterloo	64
6	Help From Uncle Alfred	79
7	Research in Fleet Street	95
8	Three Parties in Search of a Doctor Potts	111
9	Conferences at Scotland Yard	128
10	A Session at the Green Boy	143
11	The Financial Angle	154
12	The Experiences of a Demagogue	163
13	The Personal Angle	182
14	Assorted Acts of Violence with Surprising Results	198
15	Lord Cedarbrook at Home	216
16	The Political Angle	224
17	Curtains	242

Prologue

In Which the Doors Open

Major Angus McCann, the landlord of The Leopard, does not play a very important part in the matters described in this book. However, he was acquainted with two of the principal actors, and was able, at more than one point, to make good use of a personal friendship with Chief Inspector Hazlerigg. (The origin of this friendship is described elsewhere.)

Thus he was in a unique position to appreciate the shape of the six months' action, from its genesis on a bleak ice-bound January evening down to its startling apotheosis on a fine morning in June.

Seeing it so, and seeing it whole, he was curiously reminded of an experience of his own.

In his early days in London, McCann, who had little money to spare for the more expensive forms of recreation, had used to spend much of his time in walking: finding, when he had learnt to observe it, a great deal of quiet pleasure in the kaleidoscope of the Town.

One afternoon, when the first fog of autumn was touching the air, he had been strolling down a street in that territory of streets which lies between Kentish Town and Camden Town. On his left a line of white wall evidently concealed some considerable warehouse building. It might perhaps have been a depot for one of the large cigarette or catering firms which abound in that district. There was only one door, and that a most massive, double, affair of linked steel rollers, evidently designed for the passage of the largest sort of delivery vans.

This was shut.

As he watched, there came along a small boy, trailing a wooden sword. As he passed the huge door he raised his sword and beat a resounding tattoo on the metal.

And the doors started to open.

There was really nothing to it of course. They were opening because a van was ready to come out. But the incongruity of cause and effect lingered in his mind long after he had forgotten the other details. That brave smack with the wooden sword, the great doors swinging up – and the look on the boy's face. A street Arab, who was also a small Ali Baba.

That was why, when he came to set it out, he believed that there was only one possible title for the history that follows.

Note. Legal readers who may doubt the possibility of the events finally explained in Chapter Sixteen are referred to the case of In Re the City Equitable [1925 ch: 407], the appeal in which was heard almost exactly 25 years ago. This book is in no sense intended as a fictionalization of that case, the personal details of which differ widely. The case is merely cited as an authority to show what can happen in that particular line of country.

1

The Last Hours of
an Assistant Cashier

Patrick Yeatman-Carter ("Paddy" to a wide circle) had spent
the early part of the evening playing squash with a friend, at
Bumpers. And after squash he had drunk a little beer and toyed
with the idea of making a night of it. Then he remembered he
had promised his mother that he would try to get home before
nine. The exact reason escaped him, but he remembered giving
the promise. Being on the whole a dutiful son, he had broken
away from a promising party which was developing round the
famous Fo'c'sle Bar, and eight o'clock found him catching his
train at Waterloo.

The homeward rush of breadwinners had long since ended
and he had no difficulty in finding a carriage to himself, a
circumstance of comfort to a man who topped six foot. He
stretched his legs, lit his pipe, and reflected unimaginatively –
for he was not a very imaginative man – on Life.

Life in the far-off days before the war, when he had been fit
enough to play Rugger for a first-class London side and beer had
been eightpence a pint (good show): and Life during the war
when he had risen (sheer good luck, old boy, not brains – never
had any brains) to command the finest regiment in the finest
Battalion of the finest Infantry regiment in the British army –
and that went for the Brigade of Guards as well (very good
show): and of Life during the succeeding years of peace, first as

an articled clerk, recently as a very junior assistant to a firm of Chartered Accountants (not such a good show, in fact, on the whole, rather a dim show).

The train drew into Richmond, stopped, started again; but without anyone else getting into the carriage. It was certainly no night to encourage travelling – a bleak January with the wind off the ice.

He had nothing against the firm for whom he worked – nothing at all – a very decent crowd, and very well thought of. In a profession which prides itself on its respectability there are few firms more utterly respectable than Messrs Watson & Barrowbridge of Bloomsbury Square, WC (Telephone Chancery 00102 – five lines).

It was just – well, it was just that Life was a bit dull. Things which had amused and excited him before the war no longer quite clicked. And there was not much scope or responsibility in his job, and precious little real chance of advancement. And he wanted to marry Jenny as soon as he could do the thing decently. Here his thoughts entered private channels.

Another station. That must have been Ashford. He was nearly home.

Four hundred yards short of Staines, just before the road bridge, the train passes the long, glass-sided stretch of Messrs Upson and Filliter's Furniture Warehouse – and as often as not, there it stops. The reasons for this halt are buried in the obscure working of the Southern Railway's traffic control system and it may last any length of time from five seconds to five minutes.

Paddy had stood up, buttoned up his coat collar and collected his gloves and briefcase. Now, recognizing the symptoms, he reseated himself patiently.

The train slowed, shuddered twice, and ground its way to a standstill. In the sudden complete silence small sounds became audible: a motor cycle passing over the road bridge, an engine shunting in the distant goods yard.

Sitting in the nearside corner seat, facing the direction in which the train was travelling, Paddy was amused to find that he had an unexpected glimpse into the interior of the next carriage – the dark surface of Messrs Upson and Filliter's windows forming a perfect mirror.

The carriage into which he was looking contained, like his own, just the one occupant and Paddy recognized him at once. He didn't know the name, but had met him often enough on his way to the station in the morning.

"A rum little beggar," he thought, "Strube's 'Little Man' to the life. Wonder if I shall look like that in thirty years' time."

It is always interesting to observe without being observed and Paddy was thoroughly enjoying his God's eye view when the disconcerting thing happened. The man he was watching took something from his pocket. He held it in his right hand and his body, at first, screened it. Then he raised it a few inches and brought it fully into sight.

"Good God," said Paddy, "What the – " With hypnotic slowness the man lifted it higher still. As he did so, he half turned his head and the look on his white face brought Paddy to his feet.

With a crash and a jolt the train sprang into motion, the reflected picture was whisked away, and Paddy, taken unawares, sat backwards on the seat with an undignified bump.

After running for a few seconds they slowed again and the lighted platform of Staines station was sliding towards them.

Almost before the train stopped Paddy had jumped out and hurried forward. As he drew level with the door of the next carriage it swung open and the little man got out.

"He hasn't done it then. Thank God the train started just when it did. Poor little blighter. He must have been screwing up his courage – now he's been put off his stroke. But for how long?" Paddy tried, without much success, to put himself into the shoes of a man intent on self-destruction. The little chap lived alone, he remembered. Then probably that night would be the most dangerous time.

As the crowd shuffled along the platform towards the ticket barrier it occurred to Paddy for the first time that he might have some responsibility in the matter.

3

Attempted suicide. If he did nothing, would he not be guilty of compounding a felony – or something of the sort?

Yet how the devil was he to stop him? He didn't even know his name. Could he denounce him to the police for carrying – No. Hardly cricket. And he had so little evidence. The whole thing might have been a joke.

Paddy then remembered the expression on the man's face as he had seen it in that instant of time. No – it wasn't a joke.

Suppose, then, he did nothing. And was told next morning by some chap on the train – "Heard the latest? Little so-and-so. Yes. Did it last night." Dammit, he'd feel no better than a murderer.

They were passing the barrier and the ticket collector solved one minor problem by saying "Good night, Mr Britten" to the little man, now a few steps ahead of him.

They hurried down the long drab road, bordered by nursery gardens and shuttered summer villas, which leads to the river bank. Here a right turn will take you into the town of Staines.

The crowd thinned and shredded off down the side roads and presently they were alone. Paddy quickened his pace, timing himself to overtake his quarry as they passed under one of the infrequent street lamps.

"Why, if it isn't Mr Britten?"

"I'm sorry," said Mr Britten, his thoughts were evidently far away, "I'm afraid I haven't the pleasure – "

"Carter's the name. Yeatman-Carter. I think we're neighbours in Sunset Avenue."

"Yes – of course. I've seen you on the train, Mr Carter."

"Chilly weather."

"It is indeed."

Paddy noticed, however, that his companion was wearing only the thinnest of threadbare overcoats, without scarf or gloves and was seemingly indifferent to the Arctic wind.

They had reached the black waters of the Thames now, at the point where, in summer, a ferry punt plies to the opposite bank. On the left of the landing stage there is a pleasant little pub, the Pike and Eels.

4

With a gallant attempt at nonchalance Paddy said, "I often stop here for a half-pint on the way home. They have some quite decent whisky, too. I suppose you wouldn't care to join me?"

Mr Britten halted in the road and peered up at his large companion. It was, certainly, a rather unexpected offer from a man who had only introduced himself ninety seconds before.

Apparently, however, he saw nothing to alarm him in Paddy's ingenuous face.

"Well, do you know," he said, "I think that's a very sound suggestion, Mr Carter."

2

"Your very good health, Mr Carter."

"And yours, Mr Britten."

Gracious goodness, thought Paddy, as he watched his little friend splutter over the first mouthful and then gulp the whole of the rest of a double whisky defiantly. Perhaps he's never drunk the stuff before.

"The same again, Mr Carter?"

"Right-ho," said Paddy, finishing his half-pint of bitter – "I think I'll have a stout, this time, if you don't mind. There's more warmth in a stout."

Mr Britten executed the order and seated himself again, though this time he treated his whisky with more discretion. Nevertheless, it went remarkably fast.

"Do you know," said Mr Britten, "when you spoke to me tonight, I was quite surprised. Really, quite surprised – "

"Well," said Paddy lamely, "I thought as we had been neighbours so long – "

"Just so. It was a neighbourly act. The act of a good Samaritan. When you suggested visiting a public house for a drink, my natural reaction was to say – 'Certainly not.' But then, it came to me suddenly, 'Why not?' It's a friendly gesture and what would this world be without friends?"

"The world would be a sad place without friends."

"A sad place, Mr Carter. And a bad place."

"Have one more."

"I don't mind if I do."

"One for the road, eh?"

"To which road do you – oh, an expression. I see. One before we depart. Shall I purchase it?"

"It's my turn," said Paddy.

He made his way to the bar. He thought: If he really hasn't drunk whisky before – though I don't see how any man could reach his age without drinking *some* – and if, as I suspect, he hasn't had anything to eat since lunch, well, one more double whisky ought to do the trick. He'll probably be sick when he gets outside – but that's a lesser evil. And the sort of hangover he'll have tomorrow morning – phew! Anyway, it'll keep his mind off everything else.

"Well, cheers to you, Carter."

"Bungho, Britten."

Most of the third round went down in silence, and then Mr Britten said, "Carter, old man, I want to tell you a story."

"Fire away," said Paddy, "but if it's the one about the curate and the cat, I know it already."

Mr Britten properly ignored this, and after a moment's thought, and a strong effort of concentration, he said –

"Six weeks ago the head of my department was ill. Neuritis, they said. He was away for a week. And that meant that I had to be given Access. I was in charge, you see, so I had to have Access. It should have been young Mountford – he's only a youngster, but they put him over me when he came back from the war. I didn't complain. The job carried a lot of responsibility. But with the chief and young Mountford both away, I should naturally be the person to have Access."

"Access to what?" enquired Paddy reasonably.

"Access to the books, of course. All of them – the Private Ledger and the Distribution Index and the Minute Book. Not the ordinary books – I could see them any day – but the special ones. The books he kept himself. If it had been the ordinary books it wouldn't have mattered. Any of the Cash Books, or the Journals, for example, or the ledger – "

"All right," said Paddy patiently. "I've got hold of that. I'm a sort of accountant myself, you know. Because your chief cashier was away you had access to the private ledgers. That's what you're trying to say, isn't it?"

Mr Britten took another pull at his whisky and nodded.

"That's right," he said, "I couldn't help noticing things. I've been with the firm a long time. A very long time. That's why I couldn't help noticing – "

"Yes – ?"

Mr Britten fumbled inside his tight coat and at last pulled out a wallet. At the third attempt he succeeded in extracting two slips of paper and laying them on the table.

Wondering what secrets he might see, Paddy got to his feet and peered over the little man's shoulder. The result proved disappointing. The two slips were ordinary typed flimsies. Both contained, in three columns, a lot of six-figure numbers. Each column, he noticed, was headed with a different set of three letters.

"I can't make head or tail of them I'm afraid," Paddy reseated himself. "Are both papers the same?"

"No – they are *not*." As he said this, in a most emphatic tone, Mr Britten leaned right forward across the table and added softly, "And that's why I got the sack."

"Good God – and is that why – today you – ?" Paddy found he was running ahead of himself but fortunately his companion noticed nothing.

"Thirty-two years in the company. And then a month's notice – and then, out. Today was my last day. I was hoping – I really was hoping they might reconsider it. I'm over fifty, you know. I shan't find another job – " (It was all coming out now, with the whisky, and the relief of telling it). "There's my little house, but that's mortgaged, of course. And the interest due next month. I never saved much. No insurance, you know. There didn't seem to be any need – I'd only myself to look after."

It was an explanation – yes, it explained a lot. But what to do next? For a few shillings' worth of drink he had surprised the little man's secret. The question was, what to do now? One practical step suggested itself.

"Look here," he said, "I'm damnably sorry. It was a filthy thing to happen – after all those years – and all over some trifling little slip. But may I say – whatever you decide to do – don't use that thing in your pocket."

There was a long silence. Then Mr Britten said weakly, "How did you know about it?"

"As a matter of fact I saw you in the train – you remember, when the train stopped outside the station."

"Yes."

"I saw your reflection in the glass window beside the line and I saw you – did you mean to do it?"

"Yes. Yes, I meant to do it."

"Please," said Paddy, "give it to me. Now – quickly. No one will notice."

Mr Britten made a little move, then checked himself.

"It doesn't solve anything really," went on Paddy, "and besides, it's rather like giving up before you're beaten. It's plain funk."

He managed to invest the last word with all the unconscious contempt which is usually put into them by the strong, the healthy, the nerveless and the well-fed.

The reaction – or the whisky – had brought a hint of firmness into the little man's voice and his weak mouth tightened into something like a line.

"All right," he said, "take it if you like. Take it and – take it and throw it in the river."

He slid the gun across the table. It was a woman's weapon, of miniature calibre, with a mother-of-pearl handle. Paddy picked it up carefully, put on the safety catch, and dropped it into his coat pocket.

"Don't worry about it any more," he said. "I'll get rid of it for you. And I think it's time we had another drink."

He picked up the glasses. They had been sitting in one of the quiet inglenooks which are such a pleasant feature of the smoking-room at the Pike and Eels. Paddy made his way through the connecting door into the saloon bar and pushed through the crowd and up to the serving counter.

The crush was greater now, the noise louder and the atmosphere warmer and thicker. It took him some time to attract the attention of the barmaid and when he looked at the clock he was surprised – even allowing for the well-known habits of public-house clocks – to see that the hands pointed to a quarter past nine.

A thought struck him. He parked his own beer and Mr Britten's whisky under the watchful eye of the barmaid and went out into the front hall. There, as he remembered, between the overflowing umbrella stand and the giant pike in its dusty glass case, might be found a public telephone. And it occurred to him that he ought to let his mother know that he was going to be late.

This mission accomplished, he pushed his way back and collected his drinks. His plans for the rest of the evening were vague.

"If I can get the old boy as tight as a coot," he thought, "then get him home – somehow – and put him to bed – well, by the morning the chances are he'll have thought twice about it all. There's nothing like the morning light for putting a different complexion on these things."

When he reached the comparative calm of the smoking-room a surprise awaited him. Mr Britten had gone. Several plausible explanations presented themselves but when ten minutes had slipped by he began to get alarmed. I wonder if anyone saw the old bird go, he thought. At the next table, as he remembered, had been a rather part-worn middle-aged lady accompanied by two gentlemen friends: but this trio had also departed. In the far corner, the only other occupants of the room, sat a young man and a girl. It was obvious at a glance that they existed for each other and for each other alone. Fat lot of use asking them, he thought, in their present state they wouldn't notice if their own feet were on fire.

He sat for another quarter of an hour, sipping at his beer; then tipped the double whisky gently down on top of it and made his way home. He took the short cut, across Staines footbridge and along the towing path. The river shone like black steel under the cold stars and Paddy shivered a little inside his overcoat.

However, as he stood on his front doorstep feeling for the latch key he was relieved to see a light from between the curtains of Mr Britten's front window.

3

The following evening, having no engagement in town, Paddy caught an earlier train and was home by seven. He found his mother in her favourite chair in front of the fire, talking severely to a pleasant-looking middle-aged man whom she introduced as Divisional Detective Inspector Winterbourne.

"Heavens, Mother," said Paddy, "what have you been up to?"

"It's nothing to joke about," said his mother, "it's poor Mr Britten – "

"Poor Mr Britten, Mother?"

"Yes, he's – "

"Excuse me, ma'am, just a matter of routine. But if you let me do the talking. Thank you. Now, sir, could you let me know when you saw Mr Britten last?"

"Certainly. It was last night at – let me see – about a quarter past nine."

Mrs Yeatman-Carter started to say something but was quenched by a look from the Inspector.

"And where would that have been, sir?"

"At the Pike and Eels. I suppose the landlord told you."

"The information," said the Inspector carefully, "came from the barmaid."

However, it seemed to Paddy that the atmosphere had become, somehow, a little less strained.

"I expect I'd better tell you the whole story," he said. And as honestly as he could, he did so. But it is almost impossible to tell any story whole and it is very difficult not to omit important details, particularly when you have no idea that they are important.

At the end of it the Inspector said:

"Yes. I see. That does rather account for it. What did you do with the gun, by the way?"

"I did what I said I would. I threw it in the river on the way home."

"And the ammunition?"

"There was no ammunition. Except what was in it – I suppose it was loaded."

"You didn't by any chance examine it to see?"

"No," said Paddy, a little impatiently, "Why should I? I knew he'd no right to the thing and I'd no right to it and no use for it either. It seemed safest in the river."

"Quite so, sir," said the Inspector smoothly. "And I expect we should be happier if a lot more firearms which you young gentlemen of the forces brought home as souvenirs and such like were at the bottom of the Thames too. Nothing personal intended. I was just speaking generally."

"Yes," said Paddy. "Now do you mind telling me what it's all about?"

"Well – yes, I can do that, sir. Seeing as you've been so very frank with me. But I'm not saying that all of it's very pleasant hearing for a lady – "

Mrs Yeatman-Carter, in the face of this fairly broad hint, murmured something about an evening meal to see to and departed.

"We found Mr Britten in the river," said the Inspector softly. "Down by the coal barges. Quite an accident that the body was seen at all. It seems that the buckle and belt of his coat must have caught in the mooring ropes as he went past – and that held him up."

"Lord, I feel like kicking myself," said Paddy. "I ought never to have let him out of my sight. And yet – " He thought of the river – as he had seen it the night before, black and secret and ice cold. "I suppose that suicide by drowning is a commonplace to you, Inspector?"

"Ah," said the Inspector, "He wasn't drowned, you know."

"What!"

"Now, don't misunderstand me, sir. I'm not trying to make up a mystery out of it. The Doctor who examined him says he died of shock. Shock from falling in the icy-cold water. I expect the whisky helped, too. It does happen that way, you know."

"I didn't," said Paddy. "I'd no idea – "

"Lord love us, yes. It's what you said – commonplace. Half the people who fall in the water – especially when it's as cold as this – they don't drown. I mean, their lungs aren't full of water. Yes. It's the shock that kills 'em."

"Then if I hadn't filled him up with whisky – "

"Now, now," said the Inspector in his most fatherly voice – though his grey eyes were still hard – "you don't want to go blaming yourself. You acted for the best, I've no doubt."

"Epitaph," said Paddy bitterly.

"And I've no doubt, sir, that he meant to do it. *If* it was the exceptional coldness of the night – or *if* it was a stomach full of whisky – which was the actual cause of decease – well, I can't see that it signifies."

"There was no suggestion" – Paddy felt a curious distaste for the question – "no suggestion of foul play?"

"None in the world, sir. As straightforward a case – now that we've had your story – as straightforward a case as I've ever heard. Here's this chap – getting on in years – losing his job – "

"You've checked up on that, I take it."

"Stalagmite Insurance Corporation. Third cashier. He's made a lot of little mistakes. The last one wasn't such a little one – it cost 'em some money. In fact – I expect I'm stepping out of line in telling you this; but seeing as how you've got well and truly mixed up in it – there was a hint of something more. Sharp practice. No prosecution of course. They don't like trouble, these big businesses. Just a quiet 'Don't come Monday'."

"I see – and your idea is that he threw himself into the river on the way home – after he slipped away from the pub last night – "

"That's right, sir."

"Then," said Paddy, slowly, "what about that light I saw in his front window when I got home?"

"Well – of course, sir, Mr Britten might have forgotten to switch that off – when he left for town that morning."

"Or he might not have committed – I mean, he might have gone home first and done it afterwards – sometime that night."

"You didn't perhaps hear anything to suggest such a thing?"

"Certainly not," said Paddy. "I slept like a log – always do."

"Just so," said the Inspector. "I dare say there's many who wish they could say the same."

"It comes," said Paddy defiantly, "from having a good digestion and a clear conscience."

"Just so," said the Inspector again. "Well, I'll be off."

"By the way" – a thought occurred to Paddy – "when you got Mr Britten out, did you search his pockets?"

The Inspector paused, half in, half out of the door.

"Yes," he said, "we did."

"I suppose you looked in his wallet."

"We didn't find a wallet," said the Inspector. "Good night, sir."

4

In due time a report on the unexciting death of Mr Britten wound its slow way through the channels of the central police organization: for Staines, though twenty miles from the centre of London, forms nevertheless an outlying part of the Metropolitan district.

In the report, as originally printed, Winterbourne had written:

"It did occur to me at one stage to wonder whether Mr Carter might have had some hand in the accident. He seems to have gone out of his way to render Mr Britten intoxicated. The gun, which might have been traced to Mr Britten, and would have formed tangible evidence in support of Mr Carter's story, had most unfortunately been thrown away – etc. etc."

However, Divisional Detective Inspectors are not encouraged to indulge in too much speculation and a heavy senior hand had written in the margin:

"Unlikely. What possible motive could Mr Carter have had for such an act?"

Beneath which no less an authority than the Deputy Commander (Crime) had suggested:

"Schizophrenia. Due to war service?"

"Poor old war," said Chief Inspector Hazlerigg when this came to him. "How she does get blamed for everything."

2

Paddy Gets Busy

"Tell me, Tiny," said Paddy. "What goes on inside that mausoleum?"

He indicated with a thumb the pile of the Stalagmite Insurance Company just visible through the steaming window of the tea shop.

"Honestly, old boy," said Tiny, "I haven't a clue."

"But I thought you worked there. Theo told me – "

"So I do. Yes indeed. Six months come Candlemas."

"Then, surely you must have some idea," said Paddy helplessly.

"It's so big, old boy" – Tiny made a spreading gesture with his fish-knife – "so broad: so many ramifications – so – I beg your pardon, madam. I didn't notice you sitting behind me."

"All right," said Paddy. "It's big, it's wide, it's spreading. There's no need to wave your arms about. But surely you must have some idea of what goes on. Your own department, for instance. What do *you* do?"

It was lunchtime on the day following the events narrated in the previous chapter.

A little research and some telephoning amongst his many acquaintances of the war had produced 'Tiny' Anstruther. ("I believe he's something to do with insurance, old boy. Was a gunner – yes, a mathematical type.")

Paddy remembered him well from an unforgettable course of combined operations on the North Coast of Scotland in 1941.

"Well" – during the interim Tiny had obviously been doing some solid thinking – "it's like this. I sit in a big room with a marble floor and marble pillars – the mixed nougat sort – not unlike that square bit under the dome at St Paul's – and I have a desk and a reading lamp with a rather nice green shade. Don't think I'm exclusive, though. There are thirty-nine other chaps who have desks with reading lamps with green shades, too. We all arrive at nine o'clock and punch a little what-d'you-call-it to show we're there – and then, round about eleven, we trickle out and get a cup of Java and have a bit of gossip. Some of them are good types, you know; some pretty fair shockers, too. I'll tell you who I did meet – Enderby, that Captain in the KRRC – "

"What, not 'Little' Enderby?"

"That's the chap. The one who socked the Town Major – "

"Talking of Town Majors," said Paddy, returning ruthlessly to the matter in hand, "who's the head man?"

"Come again."

"The Boss. The Big White Chief. The man who summons you to a well-appointed inner office and says, 'Tiny, old boy, as a mark of esteem the firm has decided to double your weekly wage' – or more likely 'Tiny, old boy, even the best of friends must part and the time has come that your desk is wanted for another.' "

"That'll be Legate."

"Legate?"

"James Legate. Our manager."

"I see. What's his position? What does he do?"

"He's something halfway between God and a Corps Commander," said Tiny carefully. "I mean, naturally one knows there are powers within powers – people with the ultimate say-so; like our board of titled directors. But Legate is the outward and visible sign of authority."

"What sort of chap is he?"

"Quite decent, I understand. In a rather hard-boiled sort of way. Not that I ever see him to speak to, of course. But what am I among two thousand?"

"Tell me the best way to set about getting to see him," said Paddy.

Tiny finished his coffee, took Paddy's last cigarette and lit it carefully whilst he considered the problem.

"I shouldn't think it would be too terribly difficult," he said at last. "Look here, old boy – what's it all about?"

Paddy said, "I would tell you if I could, Tiny. But it's not my secret."

"All right," said Tiny good-humouredly. "Well, look here. I can give you one tip. Four o'clock in the afternoon's the best time for a snap interview. Send your name in to Miss Pocock. She's Legate's personal yes-woman. She's a very decent little girl. In fact, she and I – well, anyway, send it in."

"Thank you, Tiny," said Paddy gratefully. "That pays for your lunch."

2

The London office of the 'Stalagmite' stands in Fetter Lane, along with other important Insurance Corporations. The style is late nineteenth-century functional, but it has something – a sort of four-square assertive consequence – which saves it from mere ugliness, like an unrepentant old parvenu, thought Paddy, who had acquired, by time alone, a thin veneer of respectability.

Before the war (when manpower was no object), it had taken two employees their whole morning to clean the mighty brass letters of the firm's name which ran from corner to corner across the building.

"Stalagmite Fire and Accident Insurance Corporation", followed by the motto: – "Firm as the Rock Whence it was Hewed", and the corporation's trade mark, a convex boulder with five undeniable stalagmites sprouting from it – a symbol known to two generations of irreverent Londoners as "the inverted udder".

Pushing through the great swing-doors Paddy found himself inside a temple of modern industry. The air was hushed, and if not actually incense-laden was at any rate heavy with the mixed odours of floor polish, brass polish and hot sealing wax which have always distinguished the best city counting houses. Along aisles and transepts hurried acolytes on noiseless feet and over to the left could be seen the sacred enclosure where forty sleek young men bowed their heads beneath forty green reading lamps.

Tiny Anstruther looked up and made what, at that distance, appeared to be the V-sign.

Paddy was aware of a majestic figure standing beside him in a state of interrogation.

"I wish to see Miss Pocock," he said.

"Certainly, sir. Room Number 140. On the first floor – "

It was really surprisingly easy. Miss Pocock, who proved to be a corn-blonde with a crop which would have gladdened the heart of any home trader, showed herself to be all that Tiny had said, and more.

"I've got no sort of an appointment," he had concluded. "But if you'll just tell him that it's about Mr Britten – "

"Why certainly," said Miss Pocock. "This is always a good time of day to see our Mr Legate – before I take him his evening letters to sign. You're a friend of Tiny's aren't you – Mr Anstruther, I should say."

"I think I can qualify for that title. I have put him to bed twice, and I remembered to take his boots off on both occasions."

"You men," said Miss Pocock, tossing her blonde mane and somehow contriving to look both scornful and admiring at the same time. She pattered away.

Paddy was left with his thoughts.

The reasons that had brought him there were obscure, even to himself.

He was not the sort of man to poke his nose readily or willingly into other people's affairs. One of the few things he had learned in four years at an expensive English public school was that it paid, on the whole, to let the other fellow work out his own worries for himself.

On the other hand, he had a proper share of natural inquisitiveness, an active conscience and a strong sense of fair play. And there were certain – well, certain aspects of Mr Britten's decease which rather stuck in his throat.

If it had been an accident – then he was to blame. He and no other had got the poor little man tight. From the best motives, no doubt. But not much comfort in that.

Again – suppose it was suicide. Wasn't that the very thing which he had set out to stop? And which, through sheer inefficiency, he had failed to stop?

His meditations were interrupted by the return of Miss Pocock.

"Mr Legate will be free in a minute," she said. "Across the corridor and the second door on the left. Just go straight in."

"Here, wait a minute," said Paddy, "How shall I know when he's ready?"

"Silly me," said Miss Pocock. "I forgot to tell you. Just watch that panel. The light will come on when Mr Legate's free. Ta-ta for now."

"Ta-ta," said Paddy. "Nice girl." He sat down and tried to pick up his train of thought.

Mr Britten. The River. Accident? Suicide?

A head thrust itself in the door and said, "Have you seen Mr Lindgrum?"

"No," said Paddy truthfully.

"Oh, sorry, I thought you were Bootle." The head withdrew.

The disappearance of the wallet, thought Paddy. Rather a funny coincidence. Just a shade too coincidental, perhaps. The Inspector hadn't made much of it. And then, that matter of the light in the living-room.

The panel flickered and glowed.

Paddy jumped to his feet, opened the door and stepped out into the corridor, and was immediately faced with a difficulty.

There was another door directly opposite. Now Miss Pocock had said, "Across the corridor, the second door on the left." Did she count the one opposite as the first – in which case the next one would be the second. Or did she mean the second along from the one opposite?

All the doors looked equally imposing. Paddy selected the middle one at random. A tall man was sitting at a desk. He was wearing a green shade over his eyes which combined with a hooked nose and an actor's blue chin to give him the appearance of a night editor in an American film. He looked up from a ledger and said, "Yes – what do you want?" in no very pleasant tone of voice.

"Mr Legate?"

"Next door on your left. Have you got an appointment?"

"You'll excuse me saying so, I'm sure," said Paddy, "but I can't see what the hell that's got to do with you."

The man stared at him for a moment, and then returned to his work. Paddy backed out and shut the door quickly.

He knocked at the next door and opened it cautiously. This, he saw at once, was the right place. It was a larger room. Lighter, better furnished – from the grey pile carpet on the floor to the Mornon etching of the North-West Corner of Hyde Park over the mantelpiece. A shortish, square, middle-aged man rose to shake hands with him.

"Mr Yeatman-Carter? Sit down, won't you. I understand that you want to see me about Britten?"

Paddy got several quick initial impressions of Mr Legate from the manner of his speech. He had the unmistakable tight-shaven "executive" face. The easy address of a man who spent his working hours coping with his fellows. He said "Britten" and not "Mr Britten" because he thought of the late cashier as a junior subordinate. But he said it naturally and without affectation. Also he refrained from saying "the late Mr Britten" – or worse "poor Britten". He had no personal feelings in the matter and he pretended to none. On the whole Paddy liked him for it.

"Yes," said Paddy. He was within an ace of saying "Yes, sir," but decided to cling to what little moral advantage he had. "Yes. I was with him the night he – the night he went into the river."

"Then you must be the young man who took him into the public house. The police called you 'Mr Carter'. I wasn't certain."

"You've heard all about it then?"

"Of course," said Mr Legate. "They phoned me immediately."

"Well, in some ways, that makes it easier."

Paddy embarked on his story and found Mr Legate a good listener. Fragments of his conversation with Mr Britten came back readily to his tongue. He had thought it over so often that he could reproduce it almost verbatim. When he came to the incident of the two slips of paper, Mr Legate interrupted him for the first time.

"Can you describe them a little more fully, please?" he said.

Paddy thought back. One of his assets was a good visual memory.

"They were typewritten sheets," he said. "They both looked identical to me – but apparently I was wrong – Britten said so, anyway. On each of them were three columns of numbers – all of them six-figure numbers, and I fancy consecutive, or nearly so."

"You're certain of that?"

"Almost certain. The first four figures were the same in each case. The last two I'm not so sure about."

"And were the columns the same length?"

"Not quite. The middle column, I remember, was shorter. At a rough guess the right and left hand columns contained fifteen numbers each. The centre one, perhaps only a dozen."

"I see. And the numbers stood alone? I mean, they had no letters before or after them."

"No – yes. Wait a minute. There were letters – opposite the first number in each column. I can see them now. I remember what struck me about them. They weren't written consecutively, but one above the other."

"Like this?" Mr Legate scribbled on his blotting-pad.

"Yes – that's it."

"Well, that's one point cleared up. They were fire insurance policy numbers." Mr Legate opened a drawer and took out a printed form – "That's one of our trade marks," he said.

Paddy saw that the number was printed D/K 46702. "That's right," he said. "That's how it was."

"Can you remember anything else about the papers?"

"Only one thing. Each column was headed with three letters – but written in the ordinary way. The first two columns I happen to remember. One was headed ABC, and the other CBA. The same letters but the other way round, you see."

"If I may say so," said Mr Legate, "you did very well. You must have a natural aptitude for observation. After all, by your account you only saw the papers for a few seconds."

He leaned back in his chair, looked at Paddy directly, and without any change in his tone of voice, said, "What's worrying you?"

"Two things," said Paddy. "I'll finish my story and you'll see them for yourself."

"The light in the front window," suggested Mr Legate, when he had done.

"That's one of them. The Inspector thinks that Britten must have left it on, by mistake, when he went to the office in the morning. Now I know that's not possible."

"Expound," said Mr Legate.

"I know his house as well as I know my own. Literally. All those buildings in Sunset Avenue were poured from the same mould. The room which the light came from is the long front living-room. A drawing-room and dining-room combined. It runs into the kitchen at the back – there's a sliding partition and a serving hatch between them. Apart from the entrance hall, and a few cupboards and closets, that makes up the whole of the ground floor. Now the next thing. When I saw the light I saw it as a chink of light between the two curtains. The curtains were drawn. Tell me how a man can come down in the morning and leave the curtains drawn and the light on in his breakfast-room. And even if he skips breakfast there are ninety-nine things which he would have wanted to fetch before going to the office. And even if his breakfast was just a cup of coffee in the kitchen, you can see through into the other room, as I explained."

"Yes. I'm not saying you're wrong. But suppose he came down early – left the house before it was light. He'd have the electric light on for breakfast. He might leave it on when he went."

"No good," said Paddy. "We caught the same train for town – on that and every morning."

"Then you're suggesting – ?"

"*Someone* turned on the light that night. Maybe Mr Britten himself. Well, at any rate that would dispose of the accident theory. But it goes further. I should say, practically, that it would dispose of any idea of suicide, too."

Mr Legate looked up at him quietly and then resumed his study of the blotting-pad.

"You know how it is," Paddy went on – "When you come home with a skinful. At least – I take it you're not a teetotaller."

"You may assume that I have all the ordinary vices," said Mr Legate with a fractional smile. "Carry on."

"Well, then – imagine Mr Britten reaching home in the condition in which I left him – and the night air wouldn't have improved matters – it's a dollar to a dime he would have gone straight to sleep – possibly without even going through the formality of undressing first. Would he have got up, gone out into the bitter night and chucked himself into the river? Not Pygmalion likely. The first thing he'd have known would have been the morning sun, a raging thirst and a head like something halfway between a pneumatic drill and an electric toaster."

"I see you speak from experience," said Mr Legate. "Now let me see if I've got this quite straight," he went on. "Mr Britten lived alone? Quite so. Did his own housework, I take it. A woman came in every weekend? I see. So that his house would normally be empty from the time he left for the office until the time he got back."

"Certainly – and during the daytime my mother would have noticed any visitor. Those houses practically look down each other's throats."

"Very well. And from your knowledge of the structure of his house you say that it's not possible to come down in the morning and leave the curtains drawn and the light on in the living-room without noticing it."

"It's not impossible," said Paddy slowly. "But I think it's so improbable that it calls for some alternative explanation."

"I agree. And from this line of reasoning you infer that, since you saw the light on, someone must have turned it on, and turned it on that night. Did your mother see it, by the way?"

"No," said Paddy. "But you wouldn't from inside the house. It was only a chink of light, between the front curtains. I saw it because I looked for it – you see I was wondering at the time whether – "

"Exactly. Then you go on to say that if Britten turned the light on himself, he must have reached home safely. Therefore he didn't fall into the river by accident."

"Correct."

"And if he once reached home safely, it would be the highest degree unlikely that he would go out again before morning – in the condition he was in."

"Right again."

"Then," said Mr Legate softly, "since your reasoning would seem to show that it was *not* Mr Britten who turned on the light in his living-room – who did?"

"His murderer," said Paddy boldly.

Mr Legate accepted this outrageous statement without visible reactions. Nevertheless he sounded a little shaken as he said,

"Have you got any reason for such an extraordinary assumption?"

"Nothing that would stand up in a court of law," said Paddy. "Except for this. When Mr Britten showed me those papers he took them out of his wallet. And when he'd finished with them he put them back. Now on both occasions I noticed how tight his jacket was, and how difficult he found it to get the wallet out of his inner pocket."

"I see. When the Inspector failed to find the wallet, did he actually suggest to you that it might have slipped out into the river? Was that what he thought?"

"I'm not sure," said Paddy. "He may have done. Or he may simply not have believed me."

"What?"

"Well, you know, I'm not sure that he went for my story at all. I could see it sticking out a mile that he thought I might have pushed the old boy into the river myself."

"You didn't – I take it," said Mr Legate.

It was hard to tell from his candid expression whether he was joking or not.

"No," said Paddy shortly.

"But you suggest that someone else did. Someone who had a motive to conceal or destroy those two papers in the wallet. A motive strong enough to support a murder."

"I know – I know. It sounds horribly unlikely when you put it like that. But yes, that's what I did think."

"And whom, may I ask, had you cast for the role of murderer?"

"I hadn't got quite so far as that," said Paddy, "but one of the villains of the piece was to be your head cashier."

"Good God!" Mr Legate looked genuinely startled for the first time in the interview. "Brandison."

"Is that his name? I didn't know. Mr Britten spoke of the head of his department."

"That's Brandison. William Brandison. Our head cashier. A most respectable man; and, if I may say so, Mr Carter, a most unlikely murderer."

"He mightn't have done it himself. He might have – "

"Hired an assassin," suggested Mr Legate.

"Yes," said Paddy. "It all sounds incredibly naïve when you fetch it out in the light of day. But such things have happened. By the way, was Brandison away from work about – let me see – about five or six weeks ago?"

"Yes, he was. Neuritis, I understand. In fact, since we are on the point, it was during his absence that Britten's shortcomings came to light."

"What had he done? I mean, don't tell me if it's a matter of confidence."

"No – I should hardly call it that. It'll have to come out at the inquest anyway. You probably know that we underwrite a number of our policies. There's a good deal of mutual reinsurance goes on between the big companies in that way. It's one of my jobs to select any potentially hazardous or unsound policies and get them covered. Britten had to do the paperwork. One day he had a list of policies to copy and he made two mistakes – just copying mistakes. The result was that two policies were not covered at all – and as ill luck would have it we had to pay out heavily on both of them. The directors weren't best pleased, of course. They ordered a general investigation of Britten's work. A lot of little errors came to light. None of them definitely dishonest but some of them a little near the bone."

"I see," said Paddy. "That explains the papers, of course. They were probably copies of that list of policies he'd slipped up over."

"Might be," said Mr Legate.

"And there's never been any similar question about Brandison?"

"Never. His record here is absolutely clear. A most reliable man. I mean financially, of course. We haven't the staff or the time to check up the private lives of our employees – though I believe some of the banks do so."

"Then there might, just possibly, have been some private secret of Brandison's which Britten had discovered?"

"It's feasible, of course," said Mr Legate. "We've all got a skeleton tucked away somewhere. But how would you expect Britten to find evidence of it in the books of the firm? I say again, financially Brandison's beyond reproach. He has to be. You know something of this business, Mr Carter. Our weekly dividend turnover is nearly half a million pounds. We can't afford to take any risks with money of that sort. We use the Stassen-Caulfield internal checking system – and our accounts have a full quarterly audit from Broomfields."

Paddy had no idea what the Stassen-Caulfield internal checking system might be but he did know Messrs Broomfields, whose worn brass plate has looked out on the Friars for nearly two hundred years – Messrs Broomfields, who were so efficient and respectable that they had once publicly censured the Treasury for financial incompetence in underwriting a Government bond issue.

"Would you like a word with Brandison?"

"Good God, no," said Paddy. "I've nothing to say to him. He was just a lay figure in my theory of a crime which doesn't seem to have been committed at all. I had made the mistake of imagining that the end might justify the means, without enquiring too closely if the end really existed."

"If you talk like that," said Mr Legate, getting to his feet with a smile, "you'll be mistaken for a Communist."

"Oh, come," said Paddy, "I haven't sunk so low as that."

For a moment a flicker of some emotion showed in Mr Legate's eyes. Then abruptly he held out his hand and said, "Well, thank you for coming along. I may see you at the inquest. Goodbye."

3

The inquest on Arthur Britten of Sunset Avenue, Staines, and late an employee of the Stalagmite Insurance Corporation, was decently devoid of incident. Police witnesses first described the finding of the body, and a faded sister from Kennington spoke to identification. Patrick Yeatman-Carter, also of Sunset Avenue, was then put into the box. He stated that he had been a neighbour of the deceased and had known him slightly. He spoke of a drink taken with the deceased on the way home from the station. No, he was not prepared to swear that the deceased had had too much to drink. He was not pressed on the point. The coroner understood that the deceased had made a communication to Mr Yeatman-Carter indicating that he was in certain financial difficulties. That was so. Then doubtless they would hear more about this aspect of the case from the next witness. Mr Legate took the stand and expressed the official sympathy of the Stalagmite Insurance Corporation for the relatives of the deceased. He indicated briefly the steps which had led to Mr Britten's dismissal. The jury without retiring gave it as their unanimous opinion that Mr Britten had taken his own life whilst the balance of his mind was disturbed.

And that the King be so informed.

It was some three weeks later that Paddy, shortly after arriving at the office in the morning, was surprised to hear that Mr Barrowbridge wished to see him.

The senior partner of Watson and Barrowbridge, and the third generation of that name in the firm, was a chartered accountant, born, nurtured and bred. An irreverent junior once said that he probably struck his first balance sheet between wet nappies and dry nappies. He was small and pompous, and suffered from a slight impediment in his speech.

However, despite these personal failings, he had a professional gift of exposition and Paddy hadn't been two minutes in the room before he was quite clear about one thing.

He was getting the sack.

He heard disconnected portions of Mr Barrowbridge's discourse. "Cutting down our executive staff...opportunities for a young man in a larger firm...glad to recommend him...no complaints about his work...aftermath of war...retrenchment...genuinely sorry..."

It was over in five minutes and then Paddy found himself in the passage. To say that he was startled would be putting it mildly.

Paddy, as has been suggested, was typical of his class. A good regimental officer, with a capacity for hard work, a measure of persistence (witness his dealings with Mr Legate) and a good deal of loyalty towards that institution with which he happened to be connected – whether it was a school, a battalion, or a business house. Not overgifted with brains perhaps – though as far as he knew he had been doing his work well enough. When he had first been articled to the firm it had been understood that a post would be found for him as a qualified man. A subordinate post at first – leading up eventually, possibly, to something rather good. Perhaps even a junior partnership.

Of course there had been nothing in writing. No service contract. But then, in professional firms these things were never expressed in form.

"What the hell," thought Paddy. "What the hell have I gone and done? If I've put my foot in it somehow, I think old Barrows might have had the decency to tell me, instead of just fluffing."

He didn't feel like facing the office for the moment. He supposed he'd have to tell them. There was certain to be a lot of chaff, or worse still, they might be sympathetic.

Paddy thought that a cup of coffee might be a good idea. He'd slip out and get one – not through the general office, there was bound to be a crowd there: out the back way, past the cashiers.

He made his way down the stairs, into the basement, and along the passage. Apart from the cashiers, who had the front office, there were two little rooms at the back used as waiting-rooms or spare conference rooms for clients who wanted to examine accounts.

As Paddy passed the second of these he noticed that the door was ajar and he glanced inside. A man was sitting at the table. He looked up as Paddy went past and showed his teeth in a grin.

Even without the green eyeshade, the hooked nose and the actor's blue chin were unmistakable.

3

Introducing a Number of People

Paddy's long legs had carried him out into the street before the full enormity of the situation suddenly struck him.

"That's the blighter from the Stalagmite," he thought. "Surely he can't have – good God, I wonder if he's been getting at old Barrows? But why in the name of Heaven should he? What's it got to do with him?"

Becoming aware that he was holding up the traffic, he removed himself to the safety of the pavement.

"Of course, if the Stalagmite wanted to do me a bad turn, I suppose they've got a terrific pull with a firm like ours. We get such a lot of work from them."

Common sense here took the opportunity of pointing out that this last fact afforded quite an innocent reason for the presence of an employee of the Stalagmite in the offices of Messrs Watson and Barrowbridge.

Instinct, however, would have none of it.

"Curse it," said Paddy, "he had a bloody shifty look. And what was he doing in our basement? No one ever goes down there. He was probably waiting to be told that I'd received the order of the boot."

His first reaction to this thought was that it would be a good thing to go back and kick someone. The gentleman from the Stalagmite for preference. Or even the venerable Mr Barrowbridge. Fortunately by this time he was far enough away

31

from the office for common sense to prevail. As an alternative method of relieving his feelings he entered the nearest telephone box and rang up his fiancée.

2

Miss Burke was an interesting example of the crimes which can be committed in baptism. Her mother, a devotee of the works of Madame de Staël, had overridden the wishes of her husband, the doctor – as, indeed, she did in most matters – and christened her fourth child Corinne Delphine Burke. Since neither name was at all suitable for nursery usage, her three elder brothers, when they had been moved to address her, had called her Fluff, Nipper, Beany, and other names, less elegant, and immaterial to this narrative. At school, being smallish and not easily suppressed, she had been known as Bunny. On the first day of her first job in London, when asked her Christian name, it had occurred to her that the time had come to strike a blow for personal liberty. "Jennifer," she had announced boldly, "but my friends call me Jenny."

And Jenny it had remained, through a succession of jobs as typist, assistant, and secretary.

She was the possessor of what Paddy, in a rash moment of candour, had once called a serviceable face. Yet a great many men had found her attractive, whilst wondering what on earth it was that attracted them; and if they were of an analytical turn of mind had probably decided in the end that it was the mixture of friendliness, loyalty and unadulterated cheek.

She and Paddy had been friends for a number of years and they had celebrated his promotion to a majority by announcing their engagement. She sat now, in a little Hungarian restaurant at the end of Charlotte Street, listening thoughtfully whilst her husband-to-be blew off steam.

"So that's how it is," Paddy concluded. "It's all utter surmise and guesswork. But if you'd seen the look on that blighter's face, Jenny. He was positively leering."

Jenny scraped the last fragment of crème caramel from her plate before saying, "It might have been stomach-ache, darling. I had an uncle once who suffered from terrible stomach-ache. He always seemed to be leering."

"Well, it might have been stomach-ache," agreed Paddy, "but personally I don't believe it. It's too much of a coincidence. Look at it this way. I stick my nose into the affairs of the Stalagmite, and, what happens? I get the sack for no reason at all. Then I spot this blighter in our office, hiding more or less, in a little room in the basement. What was he doing there? If he wanted to see Barrows, he'd have been up in the waiting-room."

"But how should these Stalagmites be able to do a thing like that? Even if they wanted to."

"We get about three-quarters of our business through them," said Paddy gloomily. "In fact, we're almost a – well, anyway, you can take it from me, that part of it's perfectly possible."

"All right," said Jenny. "What do we do about it?"

Despite the fact that Paddy's unexpected telephone call had brought her out to dinner in her office clothes, with no resources beyond those contained in her two-by-four handbag, she yet contrived to look extremely fetching in a very simple tailored dress of the softest blue angora, worn under a beaver-lamb coat, which effectively kept out the bitter January cold.

"What I want to do," said Paddy, "is to wring someone's neck. Only it all seems so hopeless. There's no sort of proof. It's just my hunch."

"What about Barrows?"

"What do you mean, Jenny?"

"I mean, what about wringing *his* neck? In a nice, legal way of course. Isn't he bound to employ you, as an ex-service man? I believe there's a sort of tribunal you can go to. Or wrongful dismissal. That's it! Let's issue a writ against the firm. Think how old Barrows would hate it."

"Look here," said Paddy. "This working in a solicitor's office isn't doing you any good. It's putting ideas into your head. All the same," he added thoughtfully, "I think you may have something. How shall we set about it?"

"I'll ask our Mr Rumbold," said Jenny. "He's certain to be helpful. He's a sweet thing, and rather keen on me."

"If I catch young Nap casting so much as a fatherly eye at you, let alone a brotherly one," said Paddy, "I'll wring *his* neck."

"Hurry up and finish your coffee," said Jenny, "and we'll be in time for the last house at the Dominion."

3

The gentleman referred to by Jenny as "our Mr Rumbold" and by Paddy as "young Nap", Mr Noel Anthony Pontarlier Rumbold, was sitting in his office. He was the very latest thing in junior partners in his father's firm, Messrs Markby, Wragg and Rumbold, Solicitors, of Coleman Street.

He listened carefully to what his father's secretary had to say and then remarked: "I'll think it out, Jenny. On the face of it I don't think there's much we can do. You see, when Paddy went away he was an articled clerk. Mr Barrowbridge was under an obligation to take him back as that, of course, quite apart from the war. But once he was qualified the obligations would be at an end. At least, I think so. I'll ask the old man. He's had a lot of reinstatement cases lately. Look here, why don't you bring him round to my place for dinner tonight? It's years since I saw him last – "

It was not every young bachelor, in that year of grace, who could ask people round to "his place" for dinner. And Nap owed it to his father's foresight that he possessed a set of chambers in Brick Court, in the Middle Temple. A priceless set of rooms which had last been "renovated" in the year of Dr Johnson's birth and had received a lick of paint and a new door knocker when Dickens was a Parliamentary reporter.

Jenny, though scandalized by some of Nap's housekeeping arrangements, was deeply in love with the apple-green Queen

Anne panelling and after dinner that night she said, without malice, "I expect Patricia is really marrying you for your chambers, Nap."

"Fine set of rooms," agreed Paddy, from the depths of a leather armchair. He was in the comfortable process of settling down to an after-dinner glass of port, the remains of twelve dozen which Mr Rumbold senior had optimistically hoped might cheer his own declining years. "Built for undersized chaps like you, though. I should always be knocking my head on your twiddly little doorways."

"It's divine," said Jenny. "And I think it's got the most beautiful and complicated lavatory in London – if I may mention such a thing in front of a couple of young unmarried men."

Nap lit himself a cigarette and looked at his two guests speculatively. With his absurdly boyish face, light hair and candid blue eyes he looked, as Paddy had once said, "nineteen and devoid of all guile". In fact he was twenty-six and a far from simple soul.

Some of which complication may have resulted from the fact that five-sixteenths of his breeding was French. As to one-sixteenth from his great-grandfather, the Jacobin attorney, Rimbault, who had crossed the Channel with speed and discretion on learning the result of the Battle of Waterloo, and as to the remaining quarter from his grandmother, a Malmaison from Besançon (eighty-one but still hearty).

"All present," he said, "are thanked for their kind remarks on the subject of my apartments. We will now proceed to business. First item on the agenda, possible reprisals against Mr Barrowbridge. I'm afraid you're on a sticky wicket there. What I told you, Jenny, this morning is confirmed by my father."

"I'm not even sure," interrupted Paddy, "that I wish any harm to old Barrows. He's a thundering ass in many ways, and he doesn't think anything exists unless it can be put into a balance sheet, but that's as far as my feelings go, I think he's been got at – by the Stalagmite. They're the people we ought to go for."

"I've heard most of the story from Jenny," said Nap, "but it'll do no harm to have it plainly. What exactly do you suspect?"

"I think," said Paddy slowly, "that someone at the Stalagmite, probably the chief cashier, is up to the neck in some funny business. And there's the bloke with the broken nose and blue chin who looks more like a third-class repertory actor than an insurance operative. He's in it, too. I think that poor old Britten came across something – some secret – he mayn't even have known what it meant."

"All right. That's all possible. What happened next?"

"I don't know. To start with I thought that the people he was interfering with might – well, they might have had him pushed into the river. If there was enough money involved, you know – "

"Don't apologize," said Nap. "People do push other people into rivers even in this highly mechanized age. Your suspicions, I take it, arose chiefly from the disappearance of the wallet."

"Yes. But now I know what the papers were – I told you what Legate said – well, frankly I'm back where I started. It might have been suicide. I don't know what to think."

"But the light – " said Jenny.

"I know, I know. It seemed beautifully watertight when I first worked it out: but perhaps the best explanation is the simple one. Mr Britten, must have been worried stiff, about getting the sack and everything else. Perhaps he *did* leave the light on when he went to work that morning."

"And the curtains drawn?"

"Well – yes. And the curtains drawn."

"Do you know," went on Paddy, "between you and me, when I left the Stalagmite that afternoon, I was absolutely certain that I'd been making a fool of myself. I think if Legate had blustered or bluffed or refused to see me, it might have been different. But he took the whole thing so quietly, and explained what he could, and didn't waste time trying to explain what he couldn't."

Nap said, "Yes, now you're back again where you started – as you said. You just don't know. So let me ask you a simple question. Do you want to find out?"

"What do you mean?"

"Do you want to stir up any more trouble? Mr Britten's dead. A coroner has sat on him. The case is closed."

"No, by God, it isn't," said Paddy. "Look here, if they'd left me alone, I'd have agreed with you. But they went out of their way to kick me. And I'm not going to take that lying down. I don't know what I'm going to do – but I'm going to do something."

"Bravo," said Jenny and clapped her hands softly.

"All right," said Nap, "I was only asking. I never thought you'd climb down. As a matter of fact I've given a good deal of thought to this business and I've got a suggestion to make. Two suggestions."

He fished in the desk behind him and brought out a crumpled copy of a paper.

"Do you know this publication?"

"Why, yes – *The Moorgate Press*. It's a financial rag isn't it? A weekly."

"It's one of the best in the City, in its own quiet way. It carries a high proportion of advertisement, of course, but I'm told that its 'Market Forecast' and Tips to Investors' are quite out of the ordinary. Those who read it swear that it's the next best thing to the oracle at Delphi."

"And where do I come in?"

"Well, as a matter of fact, I know the editor. A very decent bloke, called Cartwright. I happened to see him yesterday and he told me he wanted a legman."

"Don't be so horribly technical," said Paddy; but he sounded interested.

"A man to get around and look at things – interview directors, talk to the Stock Exchange wallahs, attend bankruptcy meetings and make a note of who is doing the buying. Well, as a chartered accountant you've obviously got the financial qualifications. I know you like scribbling – and – in short – I mentioned your name."

"Oh, Paddy – a journalist!"

"Well, why not, Jenny. Dash it, it'll make a change from sitting on my – well, anyway, it'll be a change from Barrows and Co."

"There's this further point," said Nap, "which I think may have escaped you. In your new job, you'll be perfectly situated to investigate the affairs of the Stalagmite – unobtrusively."

"I'm game," said Paddy. "And – it's damned decent of you, Nap."

"There's one other thing. I mention it as a purely practical point. I don't think you're very well situated for either job if you go on living out at Staines. I mean, think of the trailing that head cashier from opium den to opium den along Limehouse Causeway, and then finding you've missed your last train home."

"Curse it," said Paddy, "of course I want to live in London. Who doesn't? But there's nothing to be had except hideous furnished flats in Hampstead at £500 a year."

"I was going to suggest," said Nap calmly, "that you came and lived here, with your legal adviser. There's plenty of room – until the happy event comes off, I mean."

"Nap," said Jenny, "you're a dear." She rose to her feet and kissed him warmly on the tip of his button nose.

Mr Rumbold accepted the salute with an aplomb which Paddy considered must have been due to his French upbringing, and merely said: "Remember, please, that I also am a respectably engaged young man."

4

Living together, as Anne of Cleves was once heard to remark, can be a trial to both parties: but the Rumbold–Yeatman-Carter ménage seemed to stagger along very equally on a basis of mutual misunderstanding.

Nap thought Paddy the most typical Englishman of his acquaintance. Athletic, obstinate, straightforward and (once the ice was broken), eminently "clubbable".

He hadn't the faintest conception of the real thoughts and ambitions which hived inside his friend's untidy head: though he had been near to some of them when he had said, "I know you like scribbling." In fact, Paddy had always wanted to write. He was honest enough to know that he had no flair for creation, but he had a knack of description. Had he not been an accountant he would have made a good reporter.

Paddy, on the other hand, thought Nap pleasant but unstable. Rather French. He had known him when they were lieutenants together in an infantry training battalion in the early days of the war. Nap had not been a good lieutenant. In Paddy's opinion he had lacked the wholehearted enthusiasm which is the basis of good regimental soldiering. In 1941, when Paddy got his captaincy, Nap had disappeared. Friends had reported from time to time that he held some sort of staff job in London. His duties had seemed to take him fairly frequently to the 'Salted Almond' and the 'Berkeley Buttery' and he appeared to keep a permanent room at the Savoy.

On the third morning of his stay in the Inner Temple Paddy got down first to breakfast and sorted out the mail. He had a good laugh over this when he discovered a letter addressed to Lieut. Colonel N Rumbold, DSO. "You've gone up in the world, my lad," he said to Nap, who came in at this moment.

Nap opened the letter without comment and looked at the signature. "Silly young goat," was the only remark he made before starting on his toast.

"Who's the joker?"

"Burtonshaw, at the War Office. Just a note about some arrears of pay."

"What's the idea of – I mean, why did he – good God," said Paddy, as an awful thought struck him. "You aren't all that, are you?"

"Certainly not," said Nap. "And he'd no right to put it. I became plain N Rumbold, Esq., on the day that Group 27 was demobilized."

"But you *were* a loot-colonel?"

"Yes – as a matter of fact – "

"And you *did* get a DSO?"

"I did, yes."

"It must have been a smashing staff job," said Paddy. "Where did you put the marmalade yesterday?"

"In the coal-box," said Nap. "Yes, it was, rather."

Both young men continued to eat their breakfast, but before the silence could become awkward Nap said, "There doesn't seem any point in keeping quiet about it at this stage. I mean, I always thought all the hush-hush business was a bit of a mistake, even at the time. As a matter of fact I meant to tell you, if the occasion cropped up."

"You were in Intelligence?"

"Almost," said Nap. "I did some of that Maquis stuff. On account of my talking French rather well and having a pack of relatives out there. As a matter of fact I spent the last four months before D-day near Besançon, in the Franche Comté."

"Blowing up railway bridges?"

"I never achieved a railway bridge. Though I did once blow up a very tiny part of a synthetic oil-plant. Chiefly it was removing lengths of railroad track, cutting telephone wires and playing the fool generally."

"God," said Paddy enviously, "the luck some people have. An undeserving fellow like you, Nap. Just because you happened to be able to speak the lingo – being allowed to blow up a synthetic oil-plant. I've always wanted to blow up an oil-plant. Never mind – good show all the same. Hello. What's this?"

The letter lying on his plate bore on its triangular flap a sign which he recognized. The trade mark of the Stalagmite Insurance Corporation.

Hardly knowing what to expect he tore it open and looked first at the signature.

"This is from Tiny Anstruther. I didn't know that type could write. Must be in answer to a phone call I sent him. Yes – here we are. 'I have had a good scout round and so has Miss Pocock – etc., etc. – there's only one bloke who looks anything like your description, so far as we can see, and that's Brandison, the chief cashier. He has a room next door to Legate's so it might be the chap you're after – ' Good Lord!"

Paddy and Nap looked at each other.

As when two photographs are placed in a stereoscope the images in them grow suddenly in depth and life, so did the figure of the Chief Cashier spring at them out of the shadows.

Not two people, but one.

The man with the broken nose was the Chief Cashier – the Chief Cashier was the man with the broken nose.

"There's our lead," said Nap. "We ought to be able to do something about this, now."

"Keep an eye on the blighter, eh?"

"That's the sort of thing."

It occurred to Nap that it was time he acquainted *his* fiancée with the state of affairs. He would ask her out to dinner the following night. It was her night off. He sat down and addressed a letter to Nurse Patricia Goodbody, at St Erasmus Hospital.

5

Nurse Goodbody was not in the best of tempers. A large, fair, usually good-tempered girl, she was born to minister calmly and competently to the wants of others. Normally she enjoyed making beds and jiggling mysterious things up and down in small jars and talking to patients about themselves.

Today, however, things had gone wrong. This, inevitably, was due to Sister, who had returned that morning from her weekend off duty. Patricia disliked Sister Faith, who returned the feeling with compound interest.

It was nearly 10.30 before she finished in the ward and crossed the square on her way to her quarters. It was a pleasant place in summer with trees and a fountain, but now it was bleak and perishing cold and she clutched her warm cloak thankfully round her shoulders; wondering, as she passed the pond, how the goldfish kept alive when the surface was covered with ice.

At the post office inside the Nurse's Home entrance she found a letter from Nap and opened it on the spot. "Wonder what he's up to," she thought, "dinner tonight – at the usual place – good." Dinner with Nap would do her a power of good in her present state of mind – whatever wildcat scheme he might have to discuss with her.

"Nurse Goodbody" – it was the Home Sister.

"Blast," said Patricia. "Yes, Sister – coming."

"Telephone call from the ward," said Home Sister. "Sister Faith wants you to do rounds tonight."

Patricia's thoughts on this gratuitous interference with her liberty were fortunately unprintable. "Doing rounds" entailed taking a list of patients to the steward's office, diet-sheets to the kitchens, a visit to the porter at the main gate, and then over to outpatients. Beginning at 6.30 how could she possibly manage to be finished and out to her rendezvous with Nap by 7.30?

Well, with a short cut here and a bit of skimping there, it might be done – just. And so it would have been, but for an unexpected set of X-ray slips which had to be taken up to the third floor.

As it was, she was a quarter of an hour late and found Nap waiting in the rain like a patient cherub.

Over dinner at Pagnanis he told her the story.

"We shall have to follow this man Brandison," he said. "Maybe for days. And I expect that I shall have to do most of the following. Paddy's a dear good chap and as keen on the job as mustard, but the fact of the matter is that his feet are too big."

"Nap," said Patricia, "do be careful. I've got a feeling that something's wrong."

"Of course something's wrong, sweet. And we're going to find out what it is."

"But why should *you* do all this?"

It was an awkward question, and one which Nap had asked himself several times and to which he had found no very convincing answer. The true grounds of the matter was probably incurable romanticism. However, that would never do for Patricia, who was nothing if not a practical girl.

"I reckon," he said, "that it's a sort of public duty. When a person sees that something's wrong, he ought to try to do his best to put it right."

"Well, do be careful."

6

Nap, during his months in France, had been instructed in the arts of street-work by those high-class experts, the French Maquis. Accordingly he trusted, in this case, to his wits and his pedal cycle.

The following day, cutting away early from the office, he changed out of his formal rig into corduroy trousers, a thick polo-necked sweater, a pair of old shoes, and a boy's blue Burberry, by these simple means reducing his apparent age to something in the neighbourhood of seventeen. Stopping only to check the lights on his ancient push-bike, he made off up Chancery Lane, whistling happily. Five o'clock found him ordering a snack in the milkbar opposite the entrance of the Stalagmite building. At five thirty the employees of that Corporation started to emerge: the first ones furtively, with squash racquets tucked under their arms, or dancing pumps sticking from their overcoat pockets; then a steady stream, which by six o'clock thinned away to a trickle.

At six thirty Nap ordered a third cup of washy coffee and began to wonder whether the Stalagmite might not possess a back entrance.

It was nearly seven o'clock when Brandison appeared. He stood, for a second or two, outside the swing door, gave a quick bird-like look to right and left, and then stepped off with his peculiar jerky stride down Fetter Lane in the direction of High Holborn.

Nap paid his bill which he had already bespoken, mounted his bicycle, overtook Brandison, went fifty yards past him and immediately turned at random down the next street to the right. Taking a left turn he paralleled High Holborn for a hundred yards, turned left again and dismounted at the corner where a glass shop front gave him a point of vantage.

A few minutes passed, and Brandison came into sight again under the street lamps, jerking slowly along. In the interval he had bought an evening paper, which he seemed to find interesting, since he kept it glued to his nose as he walked.

Nap repeated his tactics.

At the end of the third repetition both he and his quarry were a few blocks short of the Tottenham Court Road. Nap propped his bicycle against the kerb, withdrew into the porch of a blitzed house, and waited.

Sure enough, within a few minutes, Brandison came into his line of sight at the end of the road. Here he hesitated for a moment, then crossed the street, and went into one of the shops. It was not easy, at that distance, to see what sort of a shop it might be, but Nap thought it looked like a small barber's or perhaps a tobacconist's.

He lit himself a cigarette, huddled down in his raincoat and waited patiently.

A policeman passing on his beat directed a sour and speculative look at him. Nap smiled back happily. The policeman, deciding that his clothes were just sufficiently respectable to pass muster, and that sitting on the top step in the porch of a blitzed house did not, by itself, constitute an indictable offence, went heavily on his way.

It was a quarter to eight when Brandison at last reappeared. Again, almost automatically it seemed, he gave that quick up-and-down look and set off, still westward. Nap allowed him a full fifty yards of start, before taking up the pursuit. Having followed it so long he was confident of recognizing that spare back.

It was the greater surprise, when he reached the open space where Tottenham Court Road meets New Oxford Street, to find that he had missed his quarry. He propped himself on his bicycle for a moment, irresolute, under the Guinness clock. In the Charing Cross Road a figure caught his eye. Surely he recognized that light overcoat, but where was the jerky walk?

As he watched, the figure swung briskly to the right and disappeared. Nap had to make a snap decision. He pedalled quickly down Oxford Street, slipped across the traffic lights, and entered Soho Square from the north. Then, instead of turning left, he moved right-handed and circled clockwise round the square. As he had hoped, this brought him face to face again with the man in the light overcoat.

It was Brandison, all right. But a change seemed to have taken place. He was walking, now, smoothly and firmly. He seemed to have shed his jerky gait. He had the look of a man within distance of his goal.

Nobody, Nap argued, would visit Soho at such a time of night except to eat. It was, therefore, an odds-on chance that the objective was Frith Street or Greek Street.

Greek Street it was, and a minute or two later Brandison had turned in at the doors of the Mogador Club and Restaurant

Here a difficulty arose. Nap felt that his present get-up, admirable though it was for inconspicuous trailing, hardly fitted him for a visit to this particular restaurant. From its gilt frontage and striped awning, its bemedalled doorman and the three or four cars parked outside, it seemed altogether rather a high-hat sort of feeding place.

Happily there stood, immediately opposite, a small café. A glance into its steaming interior reassured him. Here, at least, the standard of his dress would cause no comment. It seemed to be full of out-of-work musicians and their overworked lady friends.

Nap took a seat hear the door, a point from which, through the fronds of a dwarf plant, he could keep a watch on the Mogador and its patrons.

He was feeling peckish himself, by this time, and made a meal of steak (the animal not specified), quantities of greasy chips and a huge mug of surprisingly good coffee. The mug itself was evidently a gift from the Great Western Railway Company.

If the succeeding three hours offered no development of the action, they could yet hardly be described as dull.

Nap never decided whether it was due to his ingenuous appearance or whether it was because he was occupying a particular seat, but the fact remains that during that period he was approached four times by vendors of black-market produce, twice by gentlemen with offers of hashish in cigarette form, and once each by a vendor of suggestive photographs and a motherly looking lady whose offers we shall not here repeat in detail.

All of whom accepted their rebuffs with the greatest of good humour.

At eleven o'clock the café put up its shutters and Nap found himself in the street. There were still lights and sounds of activity in the Mogador; but of Mr Brandison no sign at all.

Discovering that both his bicycle lamps had been stolen, Nap wheeled his machine slowly home through the emptying streets.

On reflection, he was not ill pleased with his night's work.

4

Dinner at the Mogador

It went on like this for three weeks.

Every Friday the Chief Cashier of the Stalagmite followed a routine which was uncannily the same. Observed by Nap, he left the head office, always at the same hour; walked along High Holborn and New Oxford Street; called at the same little shop (subsequent inspection had shown it to be a hairdressing saloon); stayed there about half an hour, then emerged and made straight for the Mogador.

At what hour he left this gilded haunt Nap had as yet been unable to discover, though he waited on the two Fridays following, first in the café opposite and when that closed, in the street, until well after midnight. There was, however, no sign of Brandison on either occasion.

On other nights of the week, the cashier seemed to lead an outstandingly normal existence. Paddy followed him to his suburban home at Warbridge and discovered that he possessed a villa, a garden, a dog and a pallid wife. There were no children in evidence; but there was a maid called Maria, supposed in the neighbourhood to be an Italian. Nap cultivated her acquaintance and spent an evening with her at the Crooked Billet. He soon came to the conclusion that, though her parents or grandparents might have come from Italy, she herself was plain Borough.

It was from her, when a surprising quantity of pink gins had unlocked her pearly lips, that Nap got most of his information about the Brandison household.

It appeared that Mr Brandison was a well-known and respected resident of Warbridge. A vice-president of the Bowls Club and a pillar of the Methodist Church. Later in the evening, becoming more outspoken, she stated openly what she had previously hinted. She did not really like him. He was odd. He had moods. Sometimes very nice, but more often rather "difficult".

Difficult in what way, Nap asked. Did he perhaps make a nuisance of himself to Maria?

Nothing of the sort, said Maria. Why, she wouldn't stay for a minute in a house where that sort of thing went on. Just generally difficult. Frachitty. Irritable. She thought that perhaps Mrs B was the trouble. Anyway, whenever he took a night off in town, which he did regularly every Friday, it always seemed to put him in a better humour – for a day or two. Maria had her own explanation of how Mr Brandison spent his Friday nights and Nap thought it might easily be the right one.

By the time the fourth Friday came round, he had his plan ready. The Mogador, he had discovered, though described as a club, was really an exclusive restaurant of a type not uncommon in Soho: being public to the extent that anyone, in theory, could patronize it, but in reality private, as a place well may be when all tables are reserved by name and in advance.

After some thought, Nap called on an uncle whom he knew to be one of those almost extinct creatures, a man about town, and asked him to reserve a table for him.

"For two, of course, my boy," said his uncle.

"Well, yes – certainly." The cost of the extra cover would be a small price to pay for not having to explain his affairs to Uncle Ambrose. He could always pretend that the girl had stood him up.

"For what time?"

Well, that was the difficulty. How long could one sit over a solitary dinner in a Soho restaurant? If he made it too early he would be forced to leave before Brandison, and would have accomplished nothing. On the other hand, if Brandison had some secondary motive for visiting the Mogador – (Nap found himself thinking for some reason, of private dining-rooms, pink-covered table lights, orchids and polite but formidable head waiters) – well, he might have gone about that business before Nap arrived.

"A quarter to nine," he said at last. "We shall be going to a show first. And by the way, uncle – you know most of these nightspots – "

"Naturally, my boy, naturally."

"Do you know anything about the Mogador? Is it the sort of place I could – er – take a nice young girl to?"

"I've never had very much to do with 'em," said Uncle Ambrose frankly. "But I expect you'll be all right. It's quite a respectable place. Used to be owned by a Greek called Populous, or some such name. Though it's probably changed hands half a dozen times since then."

"And you think you can get me a table?" said Nap.

"My boy," said Uncle Ambrose, "I may be old, and I may be decrepit, but I can still get a table at any restaurant in London."

At a quarter to nine, then, on that Friday night, Nap, looking sleek and seraphic in his best dark lounge suit, entered the Mogador and asked for "Mr Upjohn's" table.

Undoubtedly there was still power to his uncle's name. The doorman summoned a waiter who bowed him into what was clearly one of the best places on the floor – a secluded table for two, halfway along the wall on one side, and commanding a view of most of the room.

"My friend hasn't arrived yet," he said.

"Benissimo," said the waiter. "Will you order now?"

"No," said Nap. "I'll wait."

"To drink whilst you wait."

Nap examined the list. If genuine, the choice was remarkable. He ordered a glass of Bristol Cream and the man took himself off.

The restaurant of the Mogador was not a large one – perhaps thirty tables in all. It was shaped in the form of a rectangle, with the addition of two recesses, one near the door, occupied by a waiter's table and serving door, and another opposite to where he was sitting, forming a sort of annexe with three or four tables in it, none of them yet occupied.

Nap suddenly became aware that Brandison was standing almost at his elbow, looking straight at him. It was an effort not to move – not to let that sign which means recognition come into his eyes. He had followed him so long and studied him so closely that it was difficult to realize that he could still be a stranger to the Chief Cashier.

Brandison passed slowly by. He had a girl on his arm, and at the sight of her Nap began to wonder whether the explanation of those weekly visits might not be the natural if discreditable one suggested by Maria. This girl was clearly of the lowest class. A certain indefinable dime-store elegance seemed to proclaim the pavement. A woman would quickly have picked on a dozen details in her get-up; to Nap she simply looked wrong – wrong from her over-rigged, over-red hair to her black velvet wedge slippers with paste buckles. And she was using a scent which would have anaesthetized a goat-house.

The ill-assorted pair turned into the annexe and sat down at one of the tables half hidden by a pillar. Brandison was virtually out of sight, but the girlfriend was well within Nap's range of vision. She seemed to be finding her escort very attentive, judging by the way she bent forward to listen to him; amusing, too, by the amount of laughter he was provoking. Nap had never thought of him as a squire of dames and wondered what had come over the saturnine head cashier.

He had plenty of time to observe them for the service at the Mogador was not of the brightest. Every course was good, though, when it did at last arrive. And the wine was a first-class

Antinori, so drinkable that Nap felt no compunction at paying what he knew to be twice the controlled price for it.

The last course was eventually cleared: the wicker-covered flask was nearly empty, and Nap was drinking a remarkably good cup of black coffee and doing some thinking.

That girl with the henna hair was pretty obviously an habitué of the place. Careful though the fatherly British police might be, Nap knew that such an arrangement was not uncommon. In a few minutes, when the restaurant was empty, she and Brandison would disappear, he guessed, through that discreetly curtained doorway. He shifted his chair, and received a shock. For the second time the laws of optics were destined to play an important part in this affair.

From where he sat he was looking, as has been explained, directly into the annexe. On its wall, and facing him, there was hanging a framed advertisement for a French aperitif. The shift in his position, combined with the forward tilt of the picture, enabled him to see Brandison's table reflected in the glass.

And Brandison was not there.

His chair was empty. Yet the girl was apparently continuing to talk and laugh, as she had been doing throughout the evening. Look. She was leaning forward now, pretending to say something.

"In a few minutes – when the restaurant was empty – "

In all the human orchestra the shrillest note is the trumpet of sudden danger. During the months that he was working for the French Maquis Nap had kept his ears carefully alert for its unmistakable warnings. Through the clatter of other small noises he heard it now; and the familiar prickling sensation ran up the back of his neck.

A dozen urgent questions called for answers.

Why had Brandison and the girl, alone of all the diners, been allowed to sit in the annexe and been placed at that one table, so that he could see the girl, but not the man? How long had Brandison gone? Where was he now?

And why was the restaurant so empty? His subconscious had been calling his attention to it for some time. Party after party had gone; *but it was a long time since anyone had come in.*

Nap glanced quickly down at his wristwatch.

Half past ten. Yet, when he had been watching the place, he could swear that parties had continued to arrive regularly till eleven o'clock or later. Why were they not doing so tonight?

Had a quiet hand slipped the latch an hour before?

Was the doorman turning people away. "Sorry, sir." "Sorry, madam. We're closed tonight. Yes, closed for redecoration."

And who was going to be redecorated?

The slowness with which his own food had arrived assumed a new significance. He remembered now that a man and girl at the next table, who had come in some time after him, had finished and gone half an hour since.

Nap signalled for his bill and this time the waiter quite palpably ignored him.

These reflections, though they have taken some time to set out, had not actually occupied many seconds. As he was looking round another party had gone out into the vestibule. He heard the doorman saying good night, and the clack of the door closing.

Apart from a scattering of waiters and the girl, who had ceased her charade and was now looking directly at him with undisguised interest, there was only one person visible. This was a large man, who had come in late, he remembered, and was now seated two tables away with his back towards him.

"When that chap goes," he said to himself, "the band will begin to play."

What would happen, he wondered, if he got up and made a dive for the open. One of the waiters was standing beside the inner entrance, which led out into the vestibule. A nasty-looking customer. Most of the waiters, he thought, were Italians or Maltese.

Here it came: the other man was obviously getting ready to leave. He had paid his bill. Now he pushed back his chair and got to his feet.

Then a surprising thing happened.

Instead of making for the door, he swung round, came up to Nap, and sat down beside him.

"Mr Rumbold?"

"Yes?"

"Or 'Pascale' I think it was you called yourself, when I last had the pleasure – "

"Good God," said Nap, with undisguised relief. "It's – wait a jiffy – Angus McCann."

"Right."

"You were the chap in charge of that commando crowd – near Besançon – August 1944 – "

"Right," said McCann again. "And we'll have a good yarn about it later. At the moment, I suppose, you know you're well and truly on the spot."

Nap looked round. The long room was entirely empty. Even the waiters had gone.

"Yes," he said. "Yes. What's the next move?"

"Follow me," said McCann. "Keep close behind me, and never, for one instant, stop praying. Put your hat on – it may save your head. And carry your coat. Drop it at once if anything starts. You'll need both hands."

The two men picked their way down the room towards the vestibule. The silence was unnerving.

The entrance hall of the Mogador was really a small bar. A counter ran up one side. This room, too, was empty, except for a man, who sat on one of the high stools, with his back to the bar, swinging his legs.

"Now look here, Lucy," said McCann. "Be a good chap and open that door. We don't want any trouble."

The man addressed as Lucy – his real name, by the way, was Luciano Capelli – climbed down from his stool, walked slowly up to McCann, and said with venomous distinctness, "You keep outta this, eh."

McCann stood his ground.

"Now listen," he said, and he still sounded anxious to please. "This chap's a friend of mine. A very old friend. Anything that happens to him happens to me, too."

"And if something *does* happen to you, eh?"

"Birdy won't like it, you know."

"I don't give thatta much for Birdy," said Luciano; he accompanied his words with an exceedingly vulgar and expressive gesture. Nevertheless it seemed that a thoughtful look had come into his eye.

But for the fact that the street door was undoubtedly locked, and that he had a feeling that a number of men were at call within the inner Club door, awaiting only the result of the present negotiations, Nap might have found the whole situation amusing. Luciano was a black-haired, intensely virile little Italian with a white face which looked as if it was permanently set in a one-sided grin; closer inspection suggested that this was the result of a long, dry knife-scar running from the side of his cheek, past his mouth and down to his chin. His wavy black head scarcely came up to McCann's massive shoulder.

"You keep outta this," said Luciano again. "No one's gointa hurt your friend. We just wanta word with him, eh."

"Be your age," said McCann. "I've already seen Hoppy and 'Dumb-bell'; they got here just ahead of me. And Tony was in the dining-room. The only talking those lads do, they do with their boots."

During these exchanges neither side so much as looked at Nap who felt exactly like a schoolboy who is being argued over by his father and the headmaster ("Really, sir. Discipline must come first," "But I assure you the boy meant no harm – ").

"Basta," said Luciano with a sudden gleam of anger in his eyes. "I have warned you. If you interfere, you will get hurt perhaps. That is not my fault."

"All right," said McCann. "I hoped we could settle this without hard feelings. Now just help yourself to a look out of the window."

Without taking his eyes off them, Luciano sidled across to the window, then lifted a corner of the lace curtain and shot a quick glance out.

"You see him?" said McCann.

"Yes, I see him," said Luciano mildly. "You're a clever chap, Major. Such a fine, clever chap that it would give me great pleasure to kick you in the guts, eh."

"That goes double, you greasy little ice-cream merchant," said McCann without rancour. "And now will you open the door?"

Luciano must have pressed a bell, for a man appeared with suspicious promptness.

"Unlock the door, Tony," said Luciano, "our guests are leaving us."

"You want to let 'em both go?" said Tony.

"In the circumstances, yes," said Luciano. He glanced again out of the window. "We must not keep the Inspector waiting – such a cold night."

2

Outside in the street stood a short, square-rigged man in a blue overcoat. He regarded them impassively.

"Thank you very much, Inspector," said McCann,

"Any trouble, sir?"

"None at all," said McCann with a grin, "once they spotted you."

"Ah," said the Inspector. "They're very good boys – when I've got my eye on them. But once take it off, and there's no saying what they'll get up to."

"Thank you, anyway," said McCann again. "And Kitty told me to ask if you'd forgotten the way to The Leopard."

"Not much," said the Inspector. "I've been busy. But I'll come round and see you tomorrow. I'd like to hear a little bit more about – that."

He jerked a thumb at the now darkened and innocent-looking frontage of the Mogador.

"I think I'll just run this young man home," said McCann. "I've got my car here."

Nap, who was beginning to feel a little tired of being treated like a pantomime extra, said, "It's quite all right, thank you very much; if it's any trouble I can quite easily walk."

"Not half you couldn't," said Inspector Roberts genially, glancing down the street. "As far as the next corner, I expect – with luck."

Nap gave it up. He climbed without further protest into the back of McCann's ancient saloon car and Inspector Roberts packed in on top of him, saying, "You might drop me off at the West End Central Police Station if you don't mind."

"Right" said McCann. "Let's go."

Midnight was striking from St Clement's-le-Strand when they reached the gates of the Inner Temple. Nap saw from the light in the window that Paddy was waiting up for him. He himself was beginning to feel surprisingly wide awake, and with it came a consciousness that he had been more than a little ungracious to his rescuer.

"Look here," he said. "I haven't started to thank you for what you did tonight."

"Then oblige me," said McCann hastily, "by not starting."

"Don't be alarmed," said Nap. "I'm not going to be embarrassing. What I was going to say was, why not come in and have a drink? There are roughly a million questions I want to ask you. That's to say, if you don't mind – it's a bit late."

"Fine," said McCann. "I'm a late bird. Most publicans are. It's the demoralizing effect of not having to get up before ten o'clock in the morning: Lead on."

They found Paddy stretched in front of the fire reading market reports.

"Where the hell have you been?" he said. "Do you know I was on the point of ringing up the police."

"Then you were on the point of doing something dashed sensible," said Nap. "This is Major McCann, my guardian angel. McCann – Yeatman-Carter. Be a good chap, Paddy, and get out that last bottle of John Haig. I think I put it in the washing basket for safety, but it may be in the broom cupboard under the stairs. Grab a chair, Major, whilst I get some glasses."

The appropriate rites having been performed, Nap proceeded to give both men a summary of the events leading up to that evening.

McCann said, "I'll keep my questions till the end. But I think you had some points you wanted clearing up first. Fire away."

"Who's Lucy?" said Nap briefly. "Who's Birdy? And what is the racket at the Mogador?"

"One thing at a time. 'Lucy' is Luciano Capelli, a Neapolitan by birth, though he took out English nationality back in the early thirties – that was before Mussolini started banging the drum and the FO got so cagey about Wops. I am told that under the compulsion of conscription he even served his new King and Country during the recent hostilities – for one discreditable year in the Army Catering Corps, followed by a spell in the glasshouse for sticking a knife into the backside of the Sergeant Cook."

"Splendid," said Paddy. "Many an army cook would have been the better for it."

"No doubt. The Court were unable to appreciate the purely aesthetic side of the case and gave him nine months rigorous. For there's no doubt that Lucy is an artist – an artist twice over. He's a first class caterer – "

"Agreed," said Nap heartily. "I haven't tasted such food since before the war."

" – and also a first class practitioner with a knife. If he's angry with you, you must never let him get within thirty-six inches – or you've had it."

"I'll bear it in mind," Nap promised him; he thought of the scene in the lobby of the Mogador. As though reading his thoughts McCann said, "I expect you noticed that I was careful to keep well over on his right side tonight. Like most knife-artists he's left-handed. Not that I was in any great danger seeing that I'm a friend of Birdy's."

"Birdy?"

"That's Birdy McLaughlan – a native of Glasgow. Birdy runs the strong-arm side of the food and drink racket. He's a big man in almost every way. No, I don't know why they call him Birdy, except that he always dresses in black like an undertaker and looks rather like an amiable carrion crow. I don't deal with him in the way of business – not on any high moral grounds – simply because I find it easier to run The Leopard honestly. Do you know," he went on, "if people understood the amount of sheer hard work involved in breaking the law, I'm certain that half our criminals would never have embarked on a career of crime. However, that's by the way. Birdy's a personal friend of mine – I was able to do him a good turn once, through a man I know at Scotland Yard."

"And Luciano and Birdy – "

"Well, they're certainly not friends. But they're not open enemies. Neutrals, rather. Polite and powerful neutrals. I don't think they like each other much. But they won't tread on each other's toes if they can avoid it."

"It was lucky you happened to be passing," said Paddy. "I always told young Nap he shouldn't go out to these haunts alone."

"Yes," said Nap. "How *did* you happen to be there? It was mighty opportune."

"The Soho grapevine," said McCann. "It's not a thing which I profess to understand. I can only give you the facts. I knew at half past eight what all the pimps in Shepherds' Market had known much earlier – namely, that there was going to be 'trouble' at the Mogador. Then I heard a name mentioned – Rumbold. I thought that must be you. It's not a very common name, and, of course, you'd been under discussion before."

"Before?"

"Good grief," said McCann. "You can't spend every Friday evening for three weeks at Ma Pinkin's Café without getting a certain amount of publicity in the process. Everybody in that place knows everybody else. As soon as you came in they wondered what your game was."

"And they tried pretty hard to find out," said Nap, with memories of his first trip.

"Well, thinking it might be you, I got my car out and rolled along. Only being a little more cautious – or possibly a little more experienced – I rang up Inspector Roberts first. He's been a very good friend to me and my wife on more than one occasion – he works at the West End Central Station and knows Soho like his own back garden – "

"And if you hadn't turned up," said Nap, "what was the programme?"

"They were going to beat you up," said McCann simply. "And when that crowd beat someone up, they – well, it's just not the sort of thing one wants to happen to one's friends."

"But look here," said Paddy, "how did they think they were going to get away with it – short of killing Nap, I mean."

"I don't think they meant to kill him."

"Then," said Nap, "what was to stop me from going straight round to the police."

"As soon as you could walk – and always supposing you were still able to talk – "

"As soon as I – I say, you do think of the nicest things. Yes, well; sooner or later I must have got in touch with the police. Even if I'd had to crawl there on my hands and knees. That chap Luciano would have been for it – "

"I doubt that," said McCann calmly. "The story would have been that you got very drunk and insulted one of the girls in the café. Her boyfriend very naturally stood up for her. There was a fight – and you lost."

"I see."

"The girl would have been produced. She would have told the court exactly what you said to her and what suggestions you made to her. There would have been at least half a dozen witnesses to support her story. I'm afraid the sympathy of the court would have been with your opponent. He would either have been acquitted or, at the worst, bound over. Luciano might have had to pay a fine for permitting the fight on his premises. I've seen it all happen so often – "

"But," said Paddy incredulously, "these people – don't any of them put up a show. If someone started pawing me about – I mean, I've done a bit of amateur boxing – "

"When I hear you talk like that," said McCann, "I begin to wonder if you really know what you're up against." He paused, then added, "I don't want to sound morbid about it, particularly as it never happened, but have you any idea of the kind of man who was waiting to start on you this evening? 'Dumb-Bell' – so called, I fancy, because his name is Bell and he is, quite literally, dumb. A sort of moron with the body of an all-in wrestler and the brains of a child – rather a nasty child. Or Tony Peroni – he's from Malta, and a handy man with a broken bottle – or his cousin Rudi, who was a meat-porter until he settled a difference of opinion with a market rival with the sharp end of an ice pick. Have you ever seen anyone after they've given him a proper working over? What's the use of talking about amateur boxing? There's only one rule when fighting men like that, and it's a very simple one. Take anything that's coming, but take it on your feet. Die on your feet if necessary. *But don't fall down.* Because no one is ever quite the same again after he's been scientifically kicked in by those beauties."

There was a rather uncomfortable silence: the thoughts of the three men were deflecting towards the same question; but it was not too easy to frame it in words.

It was McCann, again, who spoke.

"Some time ago," he said, "you asked me, what was my connection with these people – the Luciano – McLaughlan crowd. To the best of my ability I've told you. Now let *me* ask you the same question. Where exactly does your line cross theirs?"

"Well, now," said Paddy, "we've explained the set-up as far as we know it – "

"You've explained nothing," said McCann, and looked at Nap, who nodded agreement. "All you've done is to deepen the real mystery. Let me put it this way. You were having trouble with a dishonest cashier in a highly respectable insurance corporation. Maybe only with him, maybe with other members of his firm, too. I didn't follow that part very well. But whatever it is, it's financial jiggery-pokery of some sort. This chap Brandison – he may have been robbing the till and he may have been rigging the stock market – it doesn't alter the fact that he's a black-coated worker."

"And yet," suggested Nap, "he seems to have a firm hand on the strings with Luciano and his boys."

"Right," said McCann. "Somehow he's got contacts with these strong-arm boys. And he's got a pull. A hell of a pull. You saw what happened tonight. Lucy didn't like it much, but at a pinch he was prepared to go ahead with his programme even though I'd warned him it would mean trouble with Birdy. And that says one thing to me. Someone's paying him quite a lot of money for that job. You've got to realize, those boys of his are high-class experts. I don't say they're much to look at. You might pass them up among a crowd in the saloon bar. But when it comes to action, they know their stuff."

"What's Luciano's racket?" asked Paddy.

"He sells his services. I'm not sure what he's doing now but I can probably find out. Prostitution – black market – racing – last year they were on the greyhound tracks."

"If you could find out, it might suggest a lead," said Nap, "though I'm bound to say that on the face of it none of the things you mention fit in very closely with the Brandison we know. However, we've only been watching him for a short time."

"We shall just have to keep pegging away," said Paddy. "When you're pulling down a wall, you have to do it brick by brick. Many a mickle makes a muckle."

"You have got the most comforting and splendid way of saying the most obvious things," said Nap sleepily.

"Good God," said McCann. "It's past three. I'm off. Good night to you both. And thanks for the whisky."

3

Next morning McCann rang up and made an appointment to see his old friend Chief Inspector Hazlerigg in his office at New Scotland Yard. And there and then he told him the whole story.

"It's got points of interest," said the Great Man, when McCann had finished. "I don't think there's anything in it for us though."

"Not yet – but don't you think there may be?"

"Yes. Those two fellows – Rumbold and Carter. Are they all right?"

"Good Lord, yes," said McCann. "They're both honest, if that's what you mean. I don't think Paddy Yeatman-Carter's any great shakes in the way of intellect, but he's quite straight. Young Rumbold's a nice lad, too. I knew him in France. He did a very good job in the Maquis. You could always check up on him through MI5."

"Of course," said Hazlerigg absently. "Yes. I wasn't thinking about him so much as his friend."

"Paddy? I'd stake my week's takings that he was on the level."

"I've no doubt you're quite right," said the Chief Inspector. Official reticence naturally prevented him from saying anything about the Staines report on his desk.

.

5

All Trains Go to Waterloo

"But darling," said Nurse Goodbody, "insurance corporations just don't do things like that. One of my uncles – not really an uncle, but my grandmother's sister's eldest son, is a director of Stalagmite and he's the most respectable person I know, he wears morning dress every morning of his life – not just for weddings – and he sends me the 'Girls Own Annual' for my birthday because he can't grasp that I'm not still twelve years old."

"Which one is that, Pat? Sir Hubert Fosdick?"

"That's the one. Uncle Hubie."

"But I thought he was nearly seventy and quite gaga."

"Well, he's not getting any younger, poor dear, and he is apt to be the tiniest bit absent-minded, but he's certainly not a crook or anything like that."

"I should hope not," said Nap patiently: he found he had often to explain things quite a number of times to Patricia before she grasped them. "It isn't the Stalagmite itself that we're up against. Everyone knows the Stalagmite – they're as solid as the Bank of England. What we think is that their head cashier may be up to some funny business – something to do with his accounts most probably."

"But what has it all got to do with you, darling?"

"Nothing, really," said Nap honestly. "Except by a fluke, or a succession of flukes. It started when Paddy happened to see this man Britten on the night he made away with himself."

"The Junior Cashier."

"That's right. He thought at the time that there might have been something fishy about the very convenient way Britten fell into the river. I don't think he does think so now. But anyway, that's what started him off. He went and saw Mr Legate – that's the general manager – and had a talk with him. Brandison – he's the head cashier – happened to see him go in, and somehow he must have heard what he said. Most probably he simply listened at the door – his room's next to Mr Legate's and he looks the sort of person whose ears are made for keyholes. The next thing Paddy knew, he'd lost his job at Barrowbridge's – and it's a dime to a dollar that Brandison was the chap who wangled it."

"Wasn't that rather mean of Mr Brandison?"

"It was all of that, sweetheart, and it was perishing silly of him, too. You know what Paddy's like. He's a slow old horse, but, like the brigadier's mule and the unexploded bomb, you can definitely kick him once too often. He's got it in for Brandison, well and truly, and I can't say that I should like to be in Brandison's shoes."

"Yes, I understand all that," said Patricia, "But Nap, dear, where do *you* come in?"

"Oh, I'm doing it for fun," said Nap.

"Well, I don't think you ought to get involved," said Patricia. "It's really nothing to do with you, and you know how careful you've got to be. You're a solicitor – "

"Really, Pat, I can look after myself," said Lieut. Colonel Rumbold, DSO, a little irritably, and added, "if anyone ought to be worrying, it's Brandison. We've already found out enough about him to put him right up Queer Street. If we so much as dropped a hint to Mr Legate about how his cashier spends his Friday evenings and the sort of crowd he's running with – I think *he* might be looking for another job, too."

"Then why don't you do that," said Patricia, "and finish off the whole business."

"Well, it would be a sort of revenge – rather a shabby sort. But it's not quite what we're after. We want to find out what he's really up to. After all," went on Nap virtuously, "a great insurance company is almost a public undertaking. It's surely our duty as citizens to look after the public interest."

Whether this specious line of reasoning was entirely convincing to Nurse Goodbody is doubtful. However, being a practical girl she saw that her affianced had made his mind up, and left it at that.

2

The *Moorgate Press* does not, in actual fact, stand in Moorgate at all, but occupies two tall buildings in the no man's land where Finsbury Pavement becomes the City Road.

Life in the offices of a financial weekly paper is not lived at quite the startling rate that it is on the great national dailies; but Paddy was finding it different enough from the white-collared starchiness of a chartered accountant's routine. He liked the general atmosphere of shirtsleeves and strong tea: and after the training he had received from the meticulous Mr Barrowbridge it was a positive relief to enter an office where practically nothing was done in duplicate, important letters were apt to be written on sheets torn from scribbling-blocks and vital documents were always being taken home and lost.

However, he had not been there long before he discovered that the *Moorgate Press* had a business morality of its own quite as strict as that of any professional firm.

"That comes out – all of it," said McAndrews, his copy chief. "Every word. It's nothing but guessing. Intelligent guessing, maybe."

"I got the figures from the secretary," protested Paddy. He liked the old man, and was sorry to have upset him.

"Feegures," said McAndrews, managing to invest this innocent word with quite a remarkable degree of contempt and loathing. "How can you have accurate feegures of future profits? Tell me that. Feegures relate to transactions which have already taken place. Forbye they're not always very credible, even then."

In common with most City firms at that period the *Moorgate Press* was hideously overcrowded and the two men shared a tiny room on the first floor. Nominally their duty was to produce the weekly column entitled 'Tips to Investors', to which reference has already been made: but actually they kept their eyes on a whole group of insurance and production companies.

McAndrews, who had been in the game for nearly forty years, pulled in a four-figure salary and earned every penny of it. It is conceivable that he knew more about the stock market than any man in London, yet he had never in his working life made an investment in anything more exciting than a trustee security. He seemed to understand by a blend of instinct and experience the whims and fancies of that intensely female creature, the public financial conscience. He could differentiate between those events which would cause her illogical extremes of terror and those, equally alarming, which she would ignore. He could sense when the old creature was going to draw her skirts tightly around her, and could even forecast those rarer occasions when she would fling her cap over the moon.

"Give the public the facts," he said to Paddy. "There are few enough papers do that in all conscience. If you draw a legitimate deduction, present it as a deduction. That's our rule. That's why we've a big name in our own line."

This last remark Paddy found to be true.

In his fortnight with the *Moorgate Press* he had already had occasion to visit dozens of firms of stockbrokers, accountants and financial agents of every sort and degree, and he had been received civilly by all, though a doubt existed in his mind as to whether this was due to his own personality, the good name of the paper he worked for, or the fact that McAndrews had in every case given him a personal introduction to the one person who mattered.

"They're a job lot this morning," said the old man, indicating a file of letters which the sorting room had stamped 'Investment Enquiry'. "I can do the greater part of them without stirring myself. There's one here though – would you ever have heard of 'Factory Fitments'?"

The question was purely rhetorical and he went on without waiting for an answer.

"They're an odd concern. I canna quite get the hang of them. For a public company, I'd say they were being just a wee bit coy. I'm told that Moody and Van Bright worked in the flotation. Ask for Philip Van Bright – he'll tell you what he can."

Paddy found the offices of Moody and Van Bright at the top of a large block in Basinghall Street. He had had no previous dealings with them and was interested to see what sort of firm they might be. Experience was already teaching him the little signs which mattered. He was beginning to be able to distinguish between the firm with no work at all (and a terrific air of industry), the firm with a good flow of business and a staff which could cope with it, and a third type of firm – not uncommon in those post-war days – which had inherited a body of custom which it was rapidly dissipating by a mixture of incompetence and optimism.

His first impressions were entirely favourable. His ears told him that the many typists were both busy and efficient, and as he was shown through the outer office he noted the two operators dealing faithfully with a ten-line exchange.

Young Philip Van Bright received him cheerfully, asked after McAndrews' Persian cat – an almost legendary creature, reputed to read the daily financial columns in *The Times* – and asked what he could do for the *Moorgate Press*.

"As a matter of fact," said Paddy, "I want some dope about 'Factory Fitments'."

He was not looking for any particular reaction and was therefore considerably surprised at the result of the simple remark.

It was as if a blind had shut down, suddenly excluding the sun.

(Or was he, perhaps, being oversensitive?)

Van Bright's voice was still courteous, if a little wary, "I'm afraid," he said, "that we don't – that is, what exactly do you want to know?"

"Just your opinion of them," said Paddy easily, "I'm not asking for any breach of professional confidence, of course – " Stick to the usual lines of sales talk, he thought, I believe there's something fishy here – "I'm told you have had most of the dealing in their ordinary shares – "

"Preference shares," said Van Bright automatically. "Yes, we've done a certain amount."

"I understand they deal in all sorts of interior fitting for the normal production job – benches, lathes, machine tools, jigs, overhead transporters and so on."

"That's right."

"Obviously a sound line in these days," said Paddy, "if you can get the necessary permits. What was the public response like?"

"Well – " the stockbroker seemed to be picking his words carefully and his fingers fiddled ceaselessly with a pencil. "Actually, it's difficult to say. They've been fully subscribed of course. With Latham's Steel behind them they were bound to be that – "

"In the present state of the stock market," agreed Paddy, "you'd get full subscription for a company to sell refrigerators to Esquimaux. But I wondered what your experience had been of dealings – "

"There haven't been any dealings," said Van Bright slowly. Sensing Paddy's astonishment he added, "That's what I was telling you. All the shares were taken up by two or three big buyers."

"I see," said Paddy. He knew better than to invite a blank refusal by asking who the buyers were. "Well, that rather accounts for it, doesn't it."

When he reported the gist of this to McAndrews, the Scotsman said, "Much what I thought. They were bought out before the public list opened."

"Is that unusual?" said Paddy. "I mean – there must be lots of nominally public companies which are collared like that. The Bank of England itself couldn't buy preference shares in – " he named two well-known concerns.

"Not now," agreed McAndrews, "all the same, it's not quite as straightforward as you think. Mph'm. We'll see what the gutter press has got to say about them."

He referred in these disrespectful terms to a rival publication, called *Market News* which was not quite so scrupulous as the *Moorgate Press* in its differentiation between fact and surmise, and had therefore a correspondingly wider if less respectable circulation.

At the conclusion of a ten minutes' telephone call which consisted, on his side, largely of "hmps", McAndrews replaced the receiver and said: "So they're back-pedalling, too. If anyone knows anything about 'Factory Fitments', they ought to. They were the people who put me on to Moody and Van Bright – "

3

It was a Friday evening some ten days later and Nap, alone, was dozing in front of the fire. Paddy was out at one of his hearty regimental reunions and unlikely to be home before midnight.

Half of Nap's mind was pursuing the head cashier of an important insurance corporation down the paths of conjecture; the other half was trying to decide whether he loved Patricia well enough to marry her.

Did anybody really love anybody else well enough to want to spend all the rest of their days with them; and was that a thing which you could possibly be certain about before marriage itself? How much of it was reason and how much instinct; or was the whole thing a racket? Was the institution of monogamy just the plain reproductive urge confined to a strait jacket – the bitter pill of necessity coated by layers of saccharine?

The Frenchman in him posed these questions coherently and the Englishman tried to answer them impersonally. Since they remained, naturally, unanswerable, he diverted his attention to more immediate matters.

The difference, as he told himself irritably, between a story-book adventure and a real-life adventure was a matter of focus and selection. In a story everything which happened, mattered: everything was significant. That man who tapped the girl on the shoulder in the crowded street was a friend – or a dark and deadly enemy. His object was to save her or serve her, or even to seduce her. Whereas in real life he would turn out to be a complete stranger whose one desire was to borrow a match or ask the way to Peckham.

Nap had compressed into his four months in occupied France the bits and pieces, the beginning and ends of a dozen adventure stories. He remembered the time that he had saved his life by buying a third-class railway ticket at the last moment instead of a second-class one; the nightmare evening which he had spent giving lessons in English syntax to the Chief of the SS in Besançon; he recalled the occasion on which he had been buried with full military honours and according to the ceremonies of the Roman Catholic Church. And the people he had met. Odd, illogical, incomprehensible characters. The woman who had stood up to six hours of Gestapo questioning and screamed at the sight of a field mouse. The men who were reliable when they were sober, and the men who were only safe when they were drunk, and the glorious blacksmith of Toul who had sworn never again to be sober until the last German had left the Franche Comté (when Nap met him he had been on a fair way to redeeming his vow).

He thought of that occasion on which he and two other agents had sat in an upstairs room in a little house in Dijon and sweated at the sound of purposeful footsteps coming up the stairs; and the door had opened to admit a travelling life insurance agent, touting for custom.

By association, his thoughts turned to Major McCann.

Nap knew him in the vague way that one knew dozens of people in and out of the army. They were something more than acquaintances, something less than friends.

The circumstances of their first meeting had all the elements of drama. Nap and his friends had been leading a tip-and-run existence in one of the little backwaters round which the full tide of the German retreat was swirling. For days they had hoped against hope to see the leading allied troops. All had assumed, for some reason, that these would be Americans,

Then one morning an armoured car had driven quietly down the village street, the pennant of a famous Armoured Division fluttering on its radiator, and halted at the street crossing. A burly figure had leaned out and enquired the road for Belfort in the most atrocious French complicated by a Lowland burr.

Nap, who had been taking a badly needed bath in the mayor's front parlour, had thrust his dripping top half out of the window and said politely, in English, "Straight on to the top of the hill and fork left."

Later he had got to know McCann better.

Now, out of the blue, he had met him again. That was a fortnight ago. Then, after that evening, with its promise of future adventure, a complete hiatus – nothing at all. Indeed, he had had one short note, which he had assumed must be from McCann, since, though unsigned, it had the printed letterhead of The Leopard. It had stated, with bare simplicity – "See if you can find out from your friend Maria what sort of razor Brandison uses." From the beer stains in the corner and the smear of tomato ketchup on the back, he deduced that the Major had written it over a hasty dinner.

Outside, it was blowing up for a wild night, but the little panelled sitting-room was secure and comfortable. Nap sank lower and lower in his chair. A coal fell from the hearth. The soft chimes from one of the City clocks announced eleven. He was very nearly asleep when the telephone bell clamoured urgently.

Lifting the receiver he was considerably surprised to recognize the voice of Paddy's fiancée, the self-possessed Miss Burke.

"Why, Jenny – " he said.

"Nap! Thank God. Listen, the most terrible thing – "

The note of panic came across the wire with startling clearness.

4

"Marriage," said a plethoric Major, "is a state-sponsored swindle designed to relieve the authorities of their proper duty of looking after the womenfolk of this country. A Government which preaches Nationalization should have made it one of its first objects to nationalize the maintenance and upkeep of women."

"Are you going to let the men off?" asked Paddy.

"We should have to contribute, of course. It would have been a form of indirect taxation – an imposition – "

"You've said it," agreed Private Abrahams (the owner of a flourishing barrow business and one of the few real capitalists present). "Just as soon as the clergyman says, 'Do you take this woman?' and you pipe up, like the World's Perishing Mug and say 'I do' – you can hear the old trap go click. Ever after that it's 'pay-pay-pay' – and nothing off for good behaviour."

"It isn't *what* you say," said the gloomy Corporal Botherwick, "it's the way that you say it. You've gotter watch your step, see. First time I took Flo out, we went to a double feature at the local pallay. I'd had a long day on my trolleybus, and before I'd time to see whether we was watching Dorothy Lamour or Donald Duck, I'd shut my eyes and dropped clean orf. I must've kipped a long time, too, cos when I woke up the big picture was nearly over and him and her was going into the last big clinch. I turned to Flo and said 'Gawd, 'ow I wish we was in bed' – not meaning anything, see. But you know how it is once you put an idea into a girl's head – yus, and we was married last month."

"Girls are funny," said a Sergeant from one of the other companies, who seemed to have attached himself to their party. "The other day I took two of 'em to watch a football match – "

One of Paddy's late cooks here thrust more beer into his hand with the result that he lost the thread of this interesting discussion.

"Hear you're getting hitched up," said a Captain.

"That's right," said Paddy.

"Sad," said the Captain, "sad. The outposts falling one by one."

"Take my advice," said the MO – now returned to a Harley Street practice. "If you must marry pick a good cook. Then you've got something to build on. A girl can learn almost anything else given time and patience, but cooks are born – "

'Talking of greyhounds – " said an ex-CSM.

The time was latish in the evening and the occasion a reunion of that ancient and disreputable regiment of the line, the first Hyde Parks. It is sometimes difficult for the uninitiated to gather what pleasure the male sex does get from standing on its feet from six to ten in the evening in barrack-like apartments, filled to overflowing with tobacco smoke, heat, light and the confused noises of pipes being knocked out, beer being pulled and lines being shot; with no exercise beyond that occasioned by a steady lifting of the right elbow; and with a rapidly diminishing grasp of such matters as everyday life, reality and the tune of the Last Train Home.

However, by half past ten or thereabouts the crowd had begun to thin out. Paddy regretfully said his good nights, jotted down half a dozen names and addresses, collected his hat, and pushed forth into the winter's night.

It would be a gross exaggeration to say that he was drunk. He found it very difficult to attain that blissful state on post-war beer; and anyway, in functions of this sort he did more talking than drinking.

As he turned into the street he saw the lanky figure of Corporal Botherwick ahead, and put on speed to catch up with him, at the same time giving him a cheerful hail.

To his surprise the Corporal, though he must have heard him, took not the slightest notice: but actually increased his pace and more than kept his distance.

"Odd," thought Paddy. "What the hell's wrong with him."

The mystery was solved at the next corner where one of the infrequent street lamps shone for a moment on the face of the man ahead.

He was a complete stranger.

Paddy walked on thoughtfully. It was not the most cheerful place imaginable. The streets were still flanked by the uncleared jetsam of the blitz. He passed a cluster of doll's-house prefabs, a row of gaunt, gutted shops, and then an open waste where a mountainous pile of rubble gleamed in the misty moonlight.

As a result of the company he had just left, or the last turn of the conversation, or more probably because it was a philosophical time of night, his mind was running on the mighty twin problems of Love and War. Did he really love Jenny enough? Enough for what? Enough to marry her, naturally. (Don't be a cad, sir, of course you do. Dear little woman.) But wasn't she sometimes a trifle – now what was the exact word? a trifle frivolous. Not quite womanly enough. (Tush, sir, do you want to marry an iceberg?)

Here, turning a corner rather fast, he nearly collided with a small man, whose face was obscured by a checked cap, pulled down over one eye.

This man said, "Look where yer goin', carncher," in such a nasty voice that War ousted Love immediately and Paddy meditated the advisability of giving him a clip over the ear, but before he could come to any decision the small man had disappeared into the surrounding dusk.

The journey home by Underground entailed a change at Leicester Square station, and it was in the Z-shaped, cream-tiled passage which connects the Northern and the Piccadilly routes that Paddy confirmed his earlier impression that he was being followed.

The passageway was almost deserted, for by that time of night the tide of traffic had ceased to run eastward. Ahead of him two women were turning the corner that leads down to the Piccadilly line platform. Behind came an elderly type in evening dress and two soldiers. (Gunners, he saw, from the red and blue arm flashes.)

He stopped to light a cigarette and allowed them all to pass. The short passage was now empty, but he reserved the obstinate impression that he had heard footsteps at the corner behind him, and that the footsteps had stopped when he did. He waited for a full minute and the silence became almost uncomfortable. It was broken by a distant grumbling above his head which he took to signify the arrival of another train on the Northern line, and sure enough in a few minutes the vanguard of a further contingent appeared. A party of three girls, escorted by a sheepish youth, a clergyman, and a man with a trombone.

"Nerves playing tricks," thought Paddy. He moved on and joined the crowd on the east-bound platform. There had evidently been no train for some time and a fair number of people had collected.

Paddy made his way to the far end.

In the distance he heard the roar of an approaching train.

At that moment, away to the left, his eye was suddenly arrested by the sight of a checked cap. He had seen that piece of headgear before, and recently. Unless he was mistaken it belonged to a bad-tempered little man who had bumped into him in the darkened streets of South London.

Suddenly he felt caught. It was as though he was in the centre of an enormous, loosely woven net: a net whose cord had not yet been pulled, but which, if he moved off too far in any direction, would press him gently back towards the centre. Push him –

A rather natural association of ideas, not unconnected with the approach of the train, made him step back hastily from the edge of the platform.

He took a quick look round.

That end of the station was almost empty, and his nearest neighbours looked harmless enough. There were two or three women. Standing next to him was an undernourished little workman. Paddy guessed his trade as fitter or mechanic, from his greasy overalls tight-clipped at wrist and ankle. On the other side of him were an old lady and a couple of shop girls. A soldier stood further back.

He looked up the platform again. The check cap had disappeared. "I'm being a fool," he thought. "Visions of death and destruction." The thought was still in his head as he heard the train coming. The lights shone on the rails, the noise rose to a roar and a presaging draught of cold air drove down the platform. With a final crash the red and gold monster slid into view.

An idea flickered into his mind. Sawdust. Cheese. Coffee. Bacon. He had it! The whole thing was like a monstrous bacon slicer of the sort they used to keep on the grocer's counter at the shop near his home. The red and gold machine, the gleaming steel rail, the irresistible weight and power driving a heavy body across a sharp –

Good God. The workman next to him. He was falling away from him. He put out his hand – or was it already out? – it was difficult to think. He was grasping, pulling.

A woman screamed. He caught a glimpse of the face of the train driver in his green and lighted cab, suddenly and sickeningly white.

Then the workman was on the line and the train had passed over him.

Paddy felt both his arms gripped. The two soldiers who had been standing behind him were shouting. He scarcely found himself able to understand what they were saying.

"You won't get away with it, you bloody murderer."

6

Help From Uncle Alfred

In the charge room at Great Marlborough Street Police Station the clock stood at midnight. The room was crowded. Inspector Hannibal, his voice proclaiming that he resented the unseasonable nature of the proceedings, said brusquely to the station sergeant, "Read over those three statements, please."

"'I am Gunner 1034968 Churchill, A R, Royal Artillery,'" intoned the Sergeant, "'and I was proceeding from Waterloo to Liverpool Street via Leicester Square Underground station. At approximately 10.45 p.m., I was standing on the eastbound platform of the Central Line talking to Gunner 1035655 Roberts, P T, also of my regiment. We observed a man whom I now identify and whose name I now know to be Carter, in front of us, and close to the edge of the platform. Beside him was standing another man whose name I now understand to be Sims. On the approach of an Underground train I observed Carter raise his left arm and push Sims – '"

"That's a lie," said Paddy.

"Quiet, please," said the Station-Inspector. "Go on, Sergeant."

"'– push Sims on to the line in front of the approaching train. I thereupon seized him by the arm and assisted to detain him until the arrival of the police.'"

"Thank you, Sergeant. Now, Gunner Churchill, have you got anything to add to that?"

77

"No, sir."

"What you've just heard is a fair and true account of your recent statement?"

"That's right, sir. Perhaps I ought to have said – "

"Yes?"

"The prisoner, sir – I mean Mr Carter. He seemed to be in a daze. He didn't appear rightly to know what he was doing."

"All right," said the Inspector. "We'll have that added before you sign it. Now read the next one, Sergeant."

" 'I am Gunner 1035655 Roberts, P T – ' "

As Paddy looked round the charge room a very strong feeling of unreality took hold of him. The thing was a dream. In a minute he would wake up. The scene would fade and the puppets of this nightmare would disappear. The little bird-like Inspector, the red-necked beefy constables, the two soldiers, the old lady in bedraggled black seated in the corner. Even Nap, more solid and less dreamlike than any of them, with his brief-case and lawyer's black hat. Jenny was standing beside him, but a new Jenny looking scared and sick.

The sergeant embarked on his third statement, and this was plainly addressed to the elderly party in the corner, who had recently concluded an attack of hysteria and was fighting hard to control an aftermath of hiccoughs.

" 'I am Mrs Laura Jane Oliphant of Carmichael Crescent, Camberwell. I was proceeding – I saw Carter strike Sims in the back – ' "

Paddy opened his mouth to protest again, and felt Nap's hand on his arm. Quite right, better not make a scene. Not now, anyway. After all, it wasn't as if he had *done* anything. This was England. It was the twentieth century. He was quite safe. He had only to sit tight and everything would sort itself out.

The sergeant had finished reading. The old lady signed her statement and retired again to her seat in the corner. There was a momentary pause, a sort of cessation of talk and movement as everyone present looked at Paddy,

The case of the King against Yeatman-Carter.

It was the little Inspector who broke the silence which had become uncomfortable.

"You may make a statement if you wish," he said, and he contrived, as usual, to turn the words into something halfway between a concession and a threat.

"The thing's absurd," said Paddy again. "I never touched the man until – I mean, I had to try and save him. He was falling and I grabbed at him. If he'd been wearing ordinary sort of clothes I might have got hold of him – his coat-tails or his belt or something. But he was wearing a very tight sort of overalls – you saw them. There simply wasn't anything to catch hold of."

"I see, sir," said the Inspector. Something in Paddy's manner had plainly puzzled him. The honesty of the speech was patent. "You say, then, that Sims was actually falling *before* you put out your hand. Do you mean that he had started to throw himself in front of the train?"

"No, not really. It's difficult to explain. If I had been asked I should have said that he might have fainted. It looked more like that. He didn't exactly throw himself. His knees buckled under him and he fell forward. That's the best description I can give."

"And when you saw him going you put your hand out?"

"Naturally."

"I see." He turned to one of the gunners. "Be very careful about this, please," he said. "Does that explanation you have just heard fit in with what you saw?"

"No, it doesn't," said Gunner Churchill obstinately. "I'm sorry, sir, but I was quite near – as close as I am to you now – and I can only say what I saw. This gentleman put out his arm – his left arm, it was – and gave a push. The other man was taken unaware, that I will swear. He tried to resist, like, but he was caught off his balance."

"That's right," said the second Gunner.

The lady in the corner, feeling the eye of the Inspector upon her, gave a moan which could have been taken either for assent or dissent.

Nap felt that it was time for him to intervene. The Inspector was plainly undecided.

"As you know," he said, "I am Major Carter's solicitor, as well as a personal friend. I will undertake on his behalf that he appears in the morning to answer any charge arising out of this incident – by the way, Inspector, what *is* the charge?"

"No charge has yet been preferred," said the Inspector cautiously. "Very fortunately Sims fell between the live rails into the safety trough. The train didn't touch him. He's in hospital suffering from shock."

"Well, then," said Nap, "I expect that if a charge is preferred it will be one of assault. In which case, as you know, you can release Major Carter on my undertaking."

"Perhaps – " began the Inspector. He got no further, for at that moment the telephone rang. It was evident from the Inspector's replies that some considerable authority was talking from the other end. The message, whatever it was, was brief.

At its conclusion the Inspector turned to Nap and said, "We shall have to keep Mr Carter here for tonight."

"On what charge?" asked Nap bluntly.

"On a charge of attempting to inflict grievous bodily harm," said the Inspector equally bluntly.

"I see."

"The charge will be heard in the morning. It will be formal of course. We shall ask for a remand until Sims is fit to make a statement. You will be able to make the usual submission for bail – "

He contrived to imply that he thought it extremely unlikely that it would be granted.

"Yes," said Nap. And to himself, "Damn it, I wish I knew what that phone call was about."

It was one o'clock when they got out of the police station, and by a stroke of luck, found a homing taxi. Nap looked at

Jenny, who was still white and quite silent and said, "I think I'd better see you home, old girl."

"Thank you, Nap," said Jenny.

In the taxi, a comfortable leather-smelling cave of darkness, they sat looking at each other and Jenny's panic was hardly decreased by a feeling that Nap was almost as frightened as she was.

But when he spoke his voice sounded steady enough.

"Jenny," he said, "We're out of our depth. We're clean out of our class. We've got to get help."

"Yes," said Jenny. The terror was plain enough, but there was something more. A note of reserve which had not been there before.

"Jenny," he said.

"Yes, Nap."

"Do you believe that Paddy did it. That he pushed that man under the train."

There is nothing more brutal than truth. When Jenny at last looked up her face was tingling as if it had been slapped.

"No," she said, "I don't really. Not now. Not when you put it like that. But it did look funny. All those people, so honest and so certain."

"What motive on earth could he have had to do such a thing?" said Nap. "It's crazy. He'd be mad – " He broke off as the unfortunate implication of the words came to him. Then he shook his head. "We're getting hysterical," he went on. "I know what's in your mind, and it's in mine too. But honestly it isn't so. It isn't the truth. Paddy didn't push anyone – this chap, or Mr Britten either. He's chivalrous to a fault, and kind and gentle too. It just won't work. He *couldn't* do it. It's mentally and physically impossible."

"War strain," suggested Jenny half-heartedly.

Nap laughed and some of the tension went from the atmosphere. "You're losing your nerve," he said. "Tell me, do you honestly think a chap like Paddy, a roaring raging extrovert like Paddy, found the war a strain? I don't say he didn't see some sticky fighting, but as for suggesting that he's bomb-happy – well, you're engaged to him, and I live with him. Between us we ought to have spotted it by now. It's not a thing that you can keep entirely hidden."

"You're right, of course," said Jenny. "I was just being silly. And here we are."

Nevertheless, late though it was by this time, and tired though she was, she found it difficult to sleep. It was light before her eyes closed.

Nap, on the other hand, slept heavily. But before he got into bed he repeated to himself, with great conviction, something that he had said earlier in the evening.

"We have got to get help."

2

Inland from Blackwall Point and above the Greenwich Marshes and over the railway there lie a few curious streets: streets which rest their eastern or lower extremities in the squalor of Charlton but run out at the western end into the social sunlight of Greenwich; not perhaps quite so aristocratic a district as it was when the houses were built ninety years ago, and the merchants drove their carriages to the City along the Old Kent road. The big, four-storeyed houses had suffered the indignity of subdivision into flats and flat-lets and even into single rooms. The yellow and cream French plaster was dropping from the walls, the bricks were long unpointed, the double window frames peeling, the unglazed fanlights looking out like blind eyes over cavernous doorways.

With one exception Goshawk Road was typical of such thoroughfares. Ninety-nine of its hundred houses were in the last degree of decayed gentility.

Number One, however, the most westerly of all, stood a little withdrawn at the junction of Goshawk Road with Maze Hill. It had, as it were, disassociated itself from its surroundings. Its bricks were freshly pointed, its woodwork soberly new, its upkeep immaculate, from the glass in the highest attic window to the shining brass of its dolphin door knocker.

What this aristocrat of brick and stone was doing among the demi-monde seems to demand an explanation (which will probably not be forthcoming: London possesses hundreds of such paradoxes).

Nap, climbing Maze Hill at nine o'clock on the following morning, thought, not for the first time, how clearly the character of a man might be read in his choice of habitation.

He walked up the short flagged path, mounted the two freshly holy-stoned steps, and jerked the massive iron pull.

Far away in the basement a bell clattered. Slow footsteps advanced along the hall and the door was opened by an ancient white-haired man.

"Good morning, Clutters," said Nap cheerfully. "Is Uncle Alfred up yet?"

"His Lordship breakfasted at hate," said Mr Cluttersley. Although he would never by any chance omit an aspirate he sometimes conscientiously inserted one. "He is now in the morning-room."

Alfred Lord Cedarbrook, eldest son of the aged Marquis of Orso and Trusconnel, is by a long chalk too remarkable a man to be allowed to slip into this account unheralded.

The standard reference books will supply the facts.

Born in 1887, educated at Winchester and at Clare College, Cambridge. A Bachelor of Science, a Fellow of the Royal Society; an Associate of the Royal Geographical Society, etc., etc., etc. In America from 1911–1912 (operating on Wall Street, though the book does not say so). Polar exploration, 1912. Awarded the Arctic Medal, 1913. Served with the 12th Prince of Wales Own Lancers: 1914–1919 (starting as a Farrier-Sergeant's assistant and finishing in command of the regiment). Persia, 1920–1923. Russia, 1923–1924. China 1925–1927. Russia again, 1927–1930, and periodically since. Unmarried.

Those were the bare bones. The living flesh that covered them was even more remarkable.

"The Last Corinthian," old Lady Hevers had said. It was an apt description. For in addition to the taste and the elegance and the exquisite standards he also possessed the two most amiable characteristics of the type. Physical toughness, and the ability to get on with all classes. (Your true Corinthian, you will remember, was as easy in the society of lords and ladies as in the no less exacting company of postillions and bruisers.)

When the Russian position had clarified a little in 1940, both the Foreign Office and the War Office had shouted for Cedarbrook's services.

For His Lordship was not only one of the greatest English experts on modern Russia, not only spoke the Russian language and understood the Russian mind as few Western Europeans have ever done; but in addition, as a legacy of long and active years spent in the country, knew personally a very large number of the surviving Russian statesmen and generals.

He had lived with them, drunk with them, argued with them, quarrelled with them and laughed both with and at them. He had on one never-to-be-forgotten occasion out-drunk in their native vodka five commissars (four male and one female – they went under the table in that order), and on another had lost the top of his left ear in a duel *à l'outrance* with sabres, his opponent being the notorious Russian journalist Ivan Petrov. An escapade for which he had been publicly censured (and privately thanked) by Comrade Stalin himself.

"Just our man," said the Foreign Office.

"Find Cedarbrook," commanded the War Office.

But alas for the vanity of human wishes, Alfred Lord Cedarbrook had disappeared. Enquiries in Goshawk Road had elicited from the imperturbable Cluttersley the information that His Lordship was "from home". Further pressed, he had added that he "might be absent for the duration of the war. He was really unable to say. His Lordship accounted for his movements to no one."

Three more months passed. The Kromisky imbroglio took place. Cripps made his first attempt to cope with a Russian state banquet, and the authorities, in desperation, took a sensible step: a step, indeed, which they might have taken much earlier. They called the family into the search. Young Lieutenant Rumbold, Lord Cedarbrook's nephew on his mother's side, was seconded from his regiment, who were having an exciting time manning a road block in Lincolnshire, and was instructed to find his missing uncle.

By the application of common sense to a knowledge of his uncle's character he performed this task in three days.

First of all he visited the nearest recruiting centre and learned that almost the only active unit which would accept direct recruits of above the normal enlistment age was the Auxiliary Military Pioneer Corps.

"So long as they're fit and willing," said the Sergeant, "we don't worry too much about birth certificates."

Nap had then demanded the locations of all AMPC units in England. No light task, since that tough and spirited corps was apt to be split into small detachments and to go where the job was to be done. Fortune favoured him and at his fifth visit, at Skegness, he had come face to face with his uncle, wearing three stripes, though not much else, and superintending the digging of an aerodrome drainage system.

The old man had been looking superhumanly fit, his face the colour of beaten mahogany, his blacksmith's arms wielding a twenty-eight pound sledge as if it had been a tack-hammer; his flow of language, choicely larded with Russian, Persian and Chinese terms, a joy and a revelation to his squad.

These thoughts and memories passed through Nap's mind in the few seconds that he stood in the library, listening to Cluttersley's decorous footsteps mounting the stairs; hearing the mumble of his uncle's voice; hearing the old man coming down.

He wondered how best to broach the subject of his visit. Lord Cedarbrook saved him the trouble.

"Your father has been on the telephone talking about your troubles," he said. "He gets more long-winded every year. Sit down. What's it all about?"

Nap told him the story. When he had finished everything that he had to say, Lord Cedarbrook proceeded to cross-examine him, and at the end of thirty minutes, Nap began to perceive how much he had left out. At the end of an hour His Lordship was apparently satisfied.

At all events he sat back with a grunt and said, "What do you want me to do?"

Nap had rehearsed his answer to that one, and it came out pat.

"I thought, uncle," he said, "that an independent judgement on the whole matter and a fresh approach – "

"You really mean that? You don't just want me to pull strings and get your friend out?"

"Good Lord, no. That was the last thing in my mind," said Nap untruthfully.

"Hmm. That's a good thing, because there aren't many strings on English justice nowadays – whatever the papers may say. Do you think your friend pushed this man in front of a train?"

"No," said Nap.

"Right. That's something definite. Let's start from there. It means that at least three people are lying."

"The two soldiers and the woman."

"No. The two soldiers and the man who was pushed – what's his name? – Sims. The woman's neither here nor there. Hysterical. Would say anything. Besides, she says your friend struck the man in the back. Both the soldiers say he *pushed* him. They're very precise about it. They both mention that he used his left arm. Significant, hey?"

"Quite so," agreed Nap.

"Now, if the man who was pushed says substantially the same thing, then there will be a strong prima facie suggestion that they were all in it together. Preconcerted story."

"But surely," said Nap, "would anybody take the risk. Being pushed in front of an electric train – "

"Not much risk really," said His Lordship callously. "He fell into the safety trough, didn't he? That's what it's there for. People are always doing it. Look in your papers – it happens once a month. I expect he was well paid. Another thing. You noticed how he was dressed."

Nap turned up his copy of the deposition.

"An overall, belted and clipped at the wrists and ankles. Gym shoes – "

"Precisely. No loose ends to catch on the rails. Rubber-soled shoes. It sticks out a mile, doesn't it? Now listen. You're Carter's lawyer. Can't you insist on being present when Sims makes his statement?"

"Unless he's made it already."

"Two hours ago he hadn't," said His Lordship calmly. "As soon as your father had finished I rang up Rahere's. The matron's a good friend of mine. The man's in a private annexe playing at being shocked. I expect he'll condescend to come round and make a statement sometime today. Insist on being present."

"He's a prosecution witness," said Nap doubtfully. "I don't know that I've any right to be there when his statement is actually being taken."

"All right," said Lord Cedarbrook, "but make a point of demanding it. Then if they refuse we'll get it on the record and it won't look too good at the trial. Creates prejudice. I'll get Hilton-Carver to lead for us – if it ever comes to trial. I don't know anyone in England who's better at creating prejudice. Now, get busy, my boy. There's a lot to do. I'll consider the rest of the story later. It's a very interesting yarn. Great possibilities."

He selected from one of the bookshelves a large red leather volume which appeared to contain press cuttings. The interview was over and Nap retired.

3

That afternoon some surprising things happened in a private ward at Rahere's and elsewhere. They can best be understood if related in chronological order.

At three o'clock Mr Sims sat up in bed, passed a hand over his forehead, blinked once or twice and said in a weak voice, "Where am I?"

A police constable who was sitting beside his bed came mentally to attention and said, "You're in horspital, chum. Er you feeling better?"

"Hospital?" said the man. "What the peeling potato am I doing in hospital?"

"You've been very lucky," said the constable reprovingly. "You fell in front of a chube train."

"Ah, yes, I remember now," said the man. "I was standing – "

"Arf a mo, arf a mo," said the constable. "Inspector wants to hear this."

He stepped heavily from the room and made for the telephone box on the landing. Left to himself, the man sat up in bed. From the look on his face it would appear that he was trying to concentrate. His lips moved soundlessly.

Twenty minutes later Inspector Hannibal was seated by Mr Sims' bed and Mr Sims was talking rapidly and confidentially to him. A shorthand writer took it all down. The Inspector seemed gratified by what he heard. One question, indeed, he repeated, so anxious was he that there should be no mistake about it.

"You felt his hand in the middle of your back pressing you forward? Quite so. He was standing on your right-hand side? Then I take it he must have used his left arm. I mean, he didn't turn towards you. No. I see. Thank you very much, Mr Sims."

"And can I have a copy of that statement, Inspector?"

"Certainly, Mr Rumbold," said the Inspector smoothly. "We have no objection at all. It was at the express – er – request of the Commissioner that you were asked to be present when we took this statement."

"Very civil of him," said Nap.

At four o'clock Nap telephoned Lord Cedarbrook.

At four thirty Lord Cedarbrook called by appointment on a Major-General Rockingham-Hawse at the War Office. He addressed him familiarly as "Rocking Horse" and spent fifteen minutes using his private extension telephone and making a number of enquiries of such authorities as 'Records', 'Discipline' and 'Postings'.

At five thirty an army truck drew up at a small house in a quiet thoroughfare in the residential district behind Liverpool Street Station and a sergeant of military police got out with two of his redcaps in attendance.

At six thirty Mr Sims had a visitor.

At seven o'clock Mr Sims was lying quietly in bed reading an evening paper which one of the nurses had kindly lent to him. He was alone. His statement once taken, it had evidently been considered unnecessary to leave him under surveillance. Indeed, there seemed to be remarkably little wrong with him. He looked very wide awake.

Probationer Larkworthy, a pink and white child, was passing the door when he hailed her.

"Nurse."

"Yes, Mr Sims."

"Where are my clothes?"

The probationer smiled indulgently. "You aren't allowed – really – what do you want?"

"I wonder if you could look in my jacket pockets," he said. "There are a couple of unopened letters. I didn't have a chance to read them."

"Well," said the probationer good-naturedly, "I expect I can find them."

As soon as she was out of the room Mr Sims, displaying remarkable agility for a sick man, jumped noiselessly from his bed, tiptoed to the door and applied an eye to the crack. He saw the probationer go over to one of the lockers in the hallway and open it. He noticed with satisfaction that it was not, apparently, fastened in any way. By the time the probationer returned, he was back in bed again.

"I think you must have been mistaken, Mr Sims," she said. "You can't have put those letters in your jacket pocket. There's no jacket there at all. Just your overalls."

"And my under-alls," said Mr Sims, "eh?"

Probationer Larkworthy thought this remark highly diverting, and laughed quite a lot as she recounted it to her friends at supper that night.

It was as well that she found something to laugh at, in view of what Sister had to say when she made her rounds at nine o'clock and discovered that the jovial Mr Sims had apparently got up, dressed himself, and walked calmly out of the hospital.

4

Chief Inspector Hazlerigg summoned Inspector Roberts from the West End Central Police Station and Inspector Hannibal from Marlborough Street to his office at New Scotland Yard. When he had listened to their stories he was silent for a long time, watching his old friends the gulls scavenging above the Embankment.

He recalled the story which Major McCann had told him, some weeks before. McCann was an old friend, and he knew him to be a cautious man, given to understatement rather than to exaggeration. And he thought of certain reports which were filed in the steel cabinet behind his desk.

"I suppose you've released Carter," he said.

"Lord, yes," said the Inspector. "The case fell through entirely. I've never seen such a flop." He spoke cheerfully, but there was a hint of resentment in his sharp little face.

"What happened exactly?"

"The witnesses all disappeared. Except the old lady. But you couldn't have hung a cat on her testimony."

"Disappeared?"

"Yes. We had the tip from the War Office that both those gunners were bad lads. One was still wanted on a desertion charge. Come to think of it, I've never known the WO move so smartly before. Looks as if someone must have been stirring them up."

"I think someone has," said Hazlerigg. "Go on."

"They sent the CMP round to pick 'em up. But something slipped and they missed 'em. Then the third chap – the one who was playing possum in hospital – he's vamoosed too. Someone got word to him that the gaff had been blown and he evaporated. Picked up his clothes and walked out."

"Did you get a line on him?"

"Yes, sir," said Inspector Hannibal. "We did. And it all fits in rather neatly. In his last job he was employed by a film company – as a tumbler. You know, the chap who takes the place of the hero when he has to drive a car over a cliff or fall off his horse into a pond. I expect that little stunt on the Underground station was toffee to him."

"Hmm. Yes," said Hazlerigg. "Very ingenious."

"What I don't quite see," said Inspector Roberts, "is where Major McCann comes into all this?"

"He doesn't," said Hazlerigg. "Not really. You remember that night you helped him out – at the Mogador – him and Rumbold? Well, Carter's a friend of Rumbold's. He lives with him. The next morning Major McCann came up here, and told me the whole story – as far as he knew it. That was a fluke – a very happy fluke and a very important one. It puts us one ahead of the game. Because when this latest development took place we *already* had the idea that someone – somehow – it was all very vague – might have a good reason for trying to get Rumbold or Carter into trouble. That put us on enquiry. We started asking questions. Then someone else – and I think I know who – started pushing from the other side. Between us we squeezed out the truth pretty quickly."

"As you said, sir, it was ingenious. But do you think it had any real chance of coming off?"

"Yes, I do," said Hazlerigg. "I'll go so far as to say that I think it was very unfortunate not to come off. Tell me this. How often do you make enquiries about the character and antecedents of a *witness*. In a straightforward case, I mean."

"Yes," said Inspector Hannibal slowly. "Yes, I see what you mean."

"And even if we hadn't quite believed the witnesses – if we'd thought, as we might have done, that they'd made a mistake – if there had been enough reasonable doubt for Carter to have got off – don't you see, even then they'd have done most of what they set out to do. As I see it, this chap Carter's got something on them – whether he knows it or not. So they set out to spike his guns. When Carter comes along to see us with some story, we just say, 'Oh, Carter – he's mad. He's the chap who pushes people into rivers and under trains'."

As the other two men were getting up to go, Hazlerigg added:

"I don't think I can ever remember a situation in which I've been more certain that something was wrong and less certain what all the fuss was about. It's got an odd smell about it. Keep your eyes open, both of you. And I'd like you to find out what racket Luciano and his boys are on."

"I can tell you that, sir," said Inspector Roberts. "It's drugs."

7

Research in Fleet Street

"Drugs of course," said Lord Cedarbrook. "It's the only possible solution."

He glanced at Nap and Paddy much as a High Court Judge might regard a couple of recalcitrant jurymen. "If I'd been given the full and proper facts before – "

"I only heard Major McCann's story yesterday," said Nap defensively. "Even so, I don't quite see – "

"Now, listen." His Lordship took his stand on his library hearthrug, his feet falling exactly on the two worn patches which they had obviously occupied a hundred times before. "This cashier – Brandison. He's the fellow we've got our eye on at the moment. So let's start by running through some of the things we know about him – some of the things you have told me. First of all, his habits. Six evenings of the week he spends at home. He leads a normal suburban life. He earns – what? Six hundred and fifty a year? All right – eight hundred. He has a small house at Warbridge – a wife and a servant. He's well thought of locally, a pillar of the church, a cog in the mechanism of local government, a taxpayer and a voter. Now if you were writing a sensational thriller" – he turned accusingly on Paddy – "that's just the sort of man you'd cast as your villain, hey?"

"Well," said Paddy, "I expect – "

"Exactly. He'd be a master criminal – the leader of a gang of thugs and housebreakers – or possibly a receiver of stolen goods.

Despite the fact, as a child could have told you, that since he is under observation every single minute of his day and night it is absolutely impossible for him to be any of these things. A man who lives a family life in a small suburb and works in a large insurance office is living under glass – you see what I mean?"

"You mean he shouldn't throw stones," said Paddy helpfully.

Lord Cedarbrook looked at him for a moment and then nodded his agreement.

"What I mean is," he said, "that it stands to reason that in examining a person of this sort the only points which we need consider are his variations from the normal – if any."

"Friday night?"

"Exactly. Friday night. Now what is Friday night?"

"Bath night," murmured Nap. "Amami night. Pay night."

"Passing over the first two suggestions," said Lord Cedarbrook, "we will concentrate on the third, which has some rudiments of sense in it. Pay night. On a Friday evening Brandison draws his money. He leaves work late. He seems very tired and dispirited. He walks in that jerky way that you have described so graphically and the real significance of which seems to have escaped you entirely. He goes along High Holborn and turns into a small barber's shop. The shop is an old-fashioned one with cubicles for each customer – quite an ordinary arrangement in women's hairdressers, I believe, but rather unusual in male establishments. Brandison, after a short delay, is shown into a cubicle – always the same cubicle, mind. Before going in he makes one or two purchases from the proprietor – a bottle of hair cream, a stick of shaving soap *and* a packet of safety razor blades. Whatever else he buys the last item is invariable. He always purchases one packet of the same brand of safety razor blades. Most of this information, by the way, came from your friend, Major McCann, who's been doing a little investigation on his own – "

"Of course," said Nap, "that accounts for it. He wrote me a strange letter, which I couldn't make head or tail of, asking me to find out whether Brandison used a safety razor – he suggested that I should ask Maria, the Brandison's maid. When I tackled her she was quite definite. He always uses an old-fashioned cut-throat, I see now – "

"Allow me," said Lord Cedarbrook, courteously but firmly. "As I was saying: at the end of half an hour, Brandison comes out of his cubicle. Our observer then notices another curious fact. Nothing actually seems to have been done to him. His hair is no shorter, his chin no smoother – "

The three men contemplated the structure of logic which Lord Cedarbrook's legal mind was building up, and found its conclusions irresistible.

"Sniffs of cocaine done up as razor blades," said Nap. "That's why Brandison looked so frisky when he came out. He'd lost his funny jerky walk, too. Isn't that one of the first effects of cocaine?"

"Why, that explains everything," said Paddy enthusiastically. "No wonder he's such a shady customer. Drugs – I mean to say – "

"I confess that I wish I could be as sanguine as you are," said Lord Cedarbrook. "To my mind, the explanation, satisfactory though it is in itself, would appear only to deepen the mystery."

He walked across to the broad northern window and stared out of it. In the middle distance, between the roofs, the yellow funnels of a tramp steamer could be seen, and as she moved downstream the following wind blew the black smoke ahead of her like a flag. His Lordship seemed to find the sight interesting, for his eyes followed after her and it was a full minute before he spoke again.

"Whatever the cynics tell you," he said, "the vast majority of people in the world are honest. Therefore, whenever you find someone engaged in some shady business – be it financial, political or what-have-you – the first question to ask is – how? How is the ramp being worked? How does the man who's working it do it? And if he isn't doing everything himself, how is he getting hold of his assistants? You see, the honest man who wants to start a career of crime runs up against a big snag straight away. He needs a lot of expert help – and he can't get hold of it. He just doesn't know the ropes. Now in this case you've got someone – we'll stick to the conventions and call him X – who wants to do something dishonest. We don't know exactly *what* it is – probably financial. And he needs some strong-arm stuff. Shall we say, he wants an inconvenient witness put out of the way, or an interfering young idiot whose natural inquisitiveness has outrun his discretion" – Nap smiled politely – "beaten up. X doesn't know any beater-uppers himself. He doesn't move in beating-up circles. But here's where he has a bit of luck. A close friend of his, Brandison, is a drug addict. He knows that Brandison gets his weekly supply from a certain source, and it needs no great effort of the imagination to realize that there must be a number of shady and violent characters involved in such a transaction. So X uses Brandison as a stalking-horse. When he wants a rough job done he gets Brandison to arrange it for him – on his normal Friday outing. And of course" – here Lord Cedarbrook permitted himself a smile – "Brandison can't very well refuse to do what X wants, because X happens to be his employer."

"What?" said Paddy.

"Mr Legate?" said Nap.

"Of course," said Lord Cedarbrook. "Did you really imagine that Brandison was a principal? A man who earns six or eight hundred a year. A man who's so hard up that he can only *afford* to buy his cocaine on pay night. How could a man like that hire the services of a tip-top expensive thug like Luciano Capelli? Why, he couldn't keep him in cab fares. The person we're looking for is a big man, someone who's got some money himself and is in a position to lay his hands on a lot more when he wants it."

"I must admit," said Paddy, "now that you mention it, that it did strike me as a bit queer that Brandison should have been able to get me turfed out of my firm. After all, he's only a cashier."

"Quite so," said Lord Cedarbrook. "As soon as you think about it, it becomes obvious. Incidentally, did it strike you as odd, too, that a cashier should have a private office next door to that of the General Manager? It might have been a coincidence, of course. However – as I said before, this is only part of the answer. There are other parts. There's a 'what' and there's a 'why'. We've got an equation here with at least three unknowns."

"You mean, what is Legate up to, and why is he doing it?"

"Exactly."

"Well, the reason, surely, must be £. s. d."

"Why should it?" said Lord Cedarbrook. "He's a very rich man already. Yes. I'm quite aware that that's not a complete answer. A greedy man is never quite rich enough – and there's the corruption-of-power angle to it, too."

"Is he as rich as all that?" asked Nap. "When all's said and done he's only a salaried employee of the Stalagmite."

"You're speaking without the book," said Lord Cedarbrook. "I know something about Legate because I've made enquiries. It's true that his official position is managing director of the Stalagmite Insurance Corporation. A job which brings in a nominal salary of two thousand five hundred and seventy-five pounds a year – or very much less when the government has had its cut. But there's more to it than that. Legate came into the public eye in 1932. His claim to fame was simply that he foresaw the ending of the 1931 slump about three months before anyone else in the City and had the courage to back his convictions in cash. At the time I'm speaking of he was a partner in a firm of stockbrokers, Moody and Van Bright – "

Paddy stirred in his chair. He was on the point of making an observation so momentous that it might have changed the whole course of this narrative. Unfortunately, however, Lord Cedarbrook chose that moment to give vent to one of his most intimidating coughs, and Paddy relapsed into well-disciplined silence.

"He not only acquired a good deal of money by his foresight – he also earned one of those enviable Lombard Street reputations which are born so silently and die so hard. He was talked about as 'one of the greatest authorities on finance in the City'. He was 'a good chap to watch'. His name became a byword in the markets. And I dare say he deserved a good deal of it. He's certainly a very sound businessman. The Stalagmite wasn't doing too well at the time. I expect they jumped at the idea of getting hold of a first-class man like Legate. He was probably able to name his own price. He's certainly pulled up the Stalagmite's turnover almost a hundred per cent in ten years. Very well, then. Is there anything in all that to suggest to either of you any convincing motive for a career of crime?"

"What about earlier days?" suggested Nap, after some thought. "Before 1931."

"There's nothing much doing there, either," said Lord Cedarbrook, "though our information isn't yet as full as I'd hoped it would be. He had a war record – of sorts. Enlisted in the Royal Flying Corps in January 1915 – never got to France though. Transferred to the RASC and served in various home stations. Then he transferred again – to the Pay Corps this time. He got a commission in 1918 and was demobbed in 1919 and got a job with Buckley and Hobbs – his CO in the Pay Corps was one of their principals, I think – then joined another firm and worked his way up. He was a junior partner by 1931. Then, as I said, he came into his pile, and his name started to mean something."

"Even earlier, then," said Nap. "He must be between fifty and sixty. That would make him – let's see – about twenty-five when the 1914 war broke out."

"That's one of the odd things about the man," said Lord Cedarbrook. "He doesn't seem to have any earlier history. All the facts I've been giving you were easy to come by – War Office records and friends in the City. But when you get back to January 1915 you run up against the wall. I've tried everything, and, quite honestly, I'm at a loss to know where to look next."

"His army records," said Nap. "Don't they give his name and place of birth and his parents and so on."

"They supply a great many facts," said Lord Cedarbrook, "and those which I have been able to check are all, so far as I know, false. For instance, there was no one of the name of Legate registered at Somerset House on the day on which he states he was born, nor is there any record of the marriage of the persons stated to be his father and mother."

Paddy said, "I suppose he must have had some technical training. Have you tried the Institute of Chartered Accountants?"

"Certainly, and every other professional body that keeps records."

"School, then," suggested Nap.

"That's not so easy. But I can tell you another odd thing. If he did go to school – and I suppose he must have done – he seems not to have passed the School Leaving Examinations. The Joint Board and the Universities keep records and there's no Legate in any of the likely years."

"You've certainly put some work in on this case," said Paddy with enthusiasm.

"Uncle," said Nap, "there's more in this than meets the eye. "What does Legate mean in your life?"

"It's funny you should say that," said Lord Cedarbrook, "because until three days ago he meant nothing at all. He was just X, one of the unknowns in your puzzle. I investigated his past as thoroughly as I could, because when I take on a job it amuses me to do it properly. Then, three days ago, an odd thing happened. I called at the Stalagmite, on a pretext, and saw Mr Legate. *And* I recognized him. You see, I'd seen him once before, a long time ago."

If his listeners were expecting a dramatic revelation at this point, then they were disappointed. Lord Cedarbrook added simply, "I can't for the life of me remember where."

"I'm always imagining I've seen people before," said Paddy helpfully. "I remember once in Tunisia in 1943 – "

"You will excuse me for correcting you," said Lord Cedarbrook, "I did not say I imagined I had seen him before. I said that I had seen him before. My mind is quite a reliable instrument – " The look which he directed at Paddy as he said this was more pointed than kind. "It informs me that I have seen Mr Legate before and supplies this additional information. The occasion was in some way connected with the sound of musical instruments, the feeling of water running down the back of my neck and the smell of anaesthetics."

"You only saw him on one single occasion. I connect it also, though, with a photograph I saw afterwards in the papers,"

"A public occasion, then. Was it in the open air? I mean, it sounds rather like an open-air band concert, and someone fainting in the crowd."

"Except that there is very rarely such a big crowd at an open-air band concert – and if it was raining it would hardly be hot enough for people to faint."

"What about a flower show, or a gymkhana," said Paddy, "A big crowd of people jammed together in a leaky marquee."

"Or wait," said Nap, "Why should the water be rain at all? You've done a lot of boxing, haven't you, Uncle?"

"Of course," said the old man – speaking on behalf of a tougher generation.

"Right, then. Here's the picture. You're lying flat on the ground. The voice of a thousand harps is ringing in your ears. One of your seconds is trying to revive you by shoving a wet sponge down the back of your neck. The other is waving a bottle of smelling salts under your nose."

"Quite so," said Lord Cedarbrook. "And where does Legate come in? Was he the referee?"

"The photograph you mentioned," said Paddy. "Was it a photograph of the occasion or a photograph of Legate himself?"

"My recollections of the photograph are even slighter than my recollections of the event. But I think the photograph was some sort of a scene in which Legate was recognizable."

"Some sort of group? A regimental reunion? A house party?"

"One of those candid camera things in a night club – ?"

"I don't think we shall ever get at it by wild and haphazard guessing. The field is too wide. If the photograph was a press photograph – and I think it was – then there is a chance of tracing it."

"There's a chance," said Nap dubiously. "But how on earth would you set about it?"

"I shall go down to Fleet Street," said Uncle Alfred, "and I shall work my way through. I propose to start at the *Daily Record*, where I know the Sports Editor. The Press never throw away a photograph – "

"All the same, it's going to be a devil of a job, isn't it? You've got a choice of at least fifty papers and a period of about fifty years to cover."

"You exaggerate the difficulties. I shall limit my research to the fifteen years between 1910 and 1925. If this thing had happened before 1910 Legate would have been so young that I should hardly have recognized him, and if it happened in the last twenty years I should certainly have been able to remember the details. Also, the field isn't quite as wide as you suggest. Only the top-flight newspapers take their own news pictures. The others all get them from half a dozen agencies."

"Well, I wish you luck," said Nap.

Uncle Alfred was nothing if not a worker, and his contacts in Fleet Street were many and fruitful. Two days later he turned up at Nap's rooms in the evening. His massive shoulders were drooping and his eyes were red-rimmed with fatigue.

"I never knew there were so many damned silly things you could take a photograph of," he grunted as he lowered his great frame into Nap's best chair. "Do you know what the '20s thought about? Racing motorists, bathing belles and trunk murders. The Prince of Wales, Test Matches and the yo-yo. Short skirts and Suzanne Lenglen, the Bunnyhug and the Beggars' Opera, Mussolini and the Immortal Hour."

"Have some whisky," said Nap.

"Certainly," said Lord Cedarbrook, "and not much water. I start on the *Daily Mirror* tomorrow."

Three days later Lord Cedarbrook appeared again, drank the remainder of Nap's whisky, and went to sleep in front of the fire. When roused in time to catch the last train home he said cryptically, "Damn all legs." Nap gathered that he had been working through the illustrated Sunday papers.

Then at last – it was a Friday evening – the telephone rang again and Nap heard his uncle's voice, hoarse with a mixture of fatigue and suppressed triumph.

"Is Carter with you?"

"Paddy – no. But he's due back any moment."

"Hold on to him when he does come. I've got something to show you."

Half an hour later Lord Cedarbrook, Nap and Paddy were poring over a photograph. It had a date inset 18.7.11, and was faded by time but still tolerably clear.

"I found it in the GS Amalgamated files," said Uncle Alfred, "among a lot of stuff they took over from an outfit called 'Topical Shots' which went into liquidation in 1920. The trouble is, there's nothing on the records to show what paper it was actually published in. 'Topical Shots' were a tuppenny-ha'penny little agency who employed two men and a boy and lived from hand to mouth selling news photographs like this to anyone who'd pay for them."

"The eighteenth of July, 1911," said Paddy. "That's a long time ago."

"Quite so," said Lord Cedarbrook. "I wonder how these things occur to you."

"It looks like Hyde Park," said Nap hurriedly. "The north end, by the Marble Arch."

"Right," said Lord Cedarbrook. "As soon as I saw the photograph I remembered it. That very hot summer in 1911. I had just got home from America. We'd been having a heatwave in New York and London wasn't all that much cooler. There was some sort of trouble in the Park. A communist rally bumped up against the police and some heads were broken. That sort of thing was rare enough in those days to make headlines. A lot of people thought that the police had used their truncheons too soon and too hard. I was there, but I wouldn't like to swear to the rights and wrongs of it. You know how it is in a crowd. Then, just as tempers on both sides were flaring, and almost anything might have happened – the floodgates of heaven were opened and down came the blessed rain. A summer thunderstorm. It cooled everyone off marvellously, and ten minutes later the crowds had passed on and there was nothing but a few couples strolling about, listening to the band, which had been patiently playing selections from *Ruddigore*, in the bandstand opposite the gate, throughout the disturbance. The only signs of strife were the St John's Ambulance men attending to the casualties – "

Nap, who was looking at the photograph through a reading glass, said, "That man on the grass is Legate, not a doubt of it. Who's that chap bending over him? He doesn't look like an ambulance man."

"I think he was a doctor. There was a doctor in the crowd, who helped the first-aid people."

"Was Legate one of the communists?" asked Paddy incredulously. "He didn't look much like a Bolshy to me."

"It's marvellous what material prosperity will do for a man's political convictions," said Lord Cedarbrook drily.

"Yes, but was he?" said Nap. "I mean, he might have been a member of the crowd who had got knocked over in the rush."

"Well, he might have been," said Lord Cedarbrook, "but it was my impression that he had been taking some part in the proceedings."

Again a thought, a vague idea, stirred in the depths of Paddy's mind like a sluggish trout in a summer pool.

Again he said nothing.

"The real question is," said Nap, "where do we go from here?"

"To bed," said His Lordship. "I don't know about you two, but I've got some sleep to make up."

It was three evenings later that Lord Cedarbrook arrived unannounced followed by a pale youth, staggering under the weight of what looked like a laundry basket.

"Put 'em down there," he said. "I'll settle up by cheque in the morning."

"Very good, my Lord."

"Now you're going to do some work for a change," said Lord Cedarbrook, as he unstrapped and threw open the wicker lid.

"Golly, what a collection," said Nap. "Where did you get them from, uncle?"

"A press-cutting agency. You'll find in there at least one copy of every paper that was published in the week following that incident in Hyde Park. Some of them probably refer to it. I thought we might get some information – particularly about the victims. Or we might find the name of that doctor! It's not beyond the bounds of possibility that he's still alive. He was quite a young fellow."

Paddy and Nap drew out an armful each and they started to spread papers, periodicals, magazines large and small, slim and fat, over the tables and, when all the tables were full, over the chairs too, and in long lines across the floor.

"Arrange 'em in groups," said Lord Cedarbrook. "Daily papers, comics, technicals – "

"Provincials on the hearthrug," said Nap, "and parish magazines under the sideboard."

They sorted for ten minutes in silence, and when they had finished the room looked like a journalist's nightmare.

The agency had done its work with marvellous efficiency. White, pink, yellow and greenish, a cross-section of the country's forgotten newspapers covered every inch of the room, filling the air with the peculiar, musty smell of stale paper.

"I say," said Paddy with a chuckle, "rather a crude sense of humour they had in those days, don't you think." He was studying the pages of a pink periodical devoted to the Turf and the Stage [well-known to the Edwardian smoking-room, but now mercifully extinct].

"I should confine your researches," said Lord Cedarbrook coldly, "in the first instance, to the daily press of London. After that, the provincial dailies. The humorous periodicals offer, on the whole, a less promising field for enquiry."

They passed a hectic evening.

"I refuse to believe," said Paddy, "that there can ever have been much of a circulation for a paper called *The Rodent-Catchers and Vermin-Destroyers' Weekly –* "

"Just listen to what the Vicar of St Hildegarde's has to say about Suffragettes," said Nap.

"Lord," said Uncle Alfred, "here's a photograph of Flossie Carmichael. I remember that girl falling off a punt at Henley in 1908 and ruining the finish of the Ladies Plate."

Nap broke up the session by announcing that it was three o'clock.

The following night they fell to again and shortly after midnight they had finished. They found that they had acquired a comprehensive knowledge of life as it was lived in the opening years of the reign of his late Majesty, King George the Fifth – but very little else.

Most of the London papers had given some prominence to the happenings in Hyde Park. It was referred to as 'The Hyde Park Incident' – or, in the Leftist papers as 'The Hyde Park Scandal' – and was even honoured by a short and reasonably impartial summary in the columns of the old Thunderer himself.

"*A Procession formed of disaffected workmen*" – (the papers in that year of grace, they noticed, were less mealy-mouthed when discussing trade union activities) – "*drawn principally from engineering works in the area of Charlton and Deptford, yesterday staged a rally and demonstration in Hyde Park. Police reinforcements were called out, and the clash which ensued resulted in a few minor casualties – less, probably, than the organizers had hoped for. One woman was knocked down by the horse of a mounted policeman which got out of control and a few of the demonstrators suffered slight injuries. No ambulances were called out and no one was detained."*

"All very well," grumbled Nap, "but what about a few names."

Nobody, however, had apparently thought it of interest to note the names and addresses of the victims. The personal touch in journalism had not then come into vogue. It was the age of the Common Man.

"No ambulances were called out," said Lord Cedarbrook thoughtfully. "That makes it a waste of time to try hospital registers – even if they went back as far. Blast that policeman. Why couldn't he have hit him a bit harder."

"Always supposing it was Legate he hit," said Paddy.

"And always supposing Legate was one of the communists – not just an innocent bystander."

The warning light flickered again in Paddy's brain: this time it was heeded.

"I meant to mention this before," he said slowly. "I think Legate was a communist. Or, at any rate, I think he sympathized with them."

"What on earth makes you say that, my boy?"

"It's just this, sir. The first time I saw Legate, right at the end of my interview, I made some silly crack about communism – not meaning anything in particular. You know – just for the sake of saying something, and I remember that I caught the tail end of a rather dirty look from Legate. It didn't connect at the time, but thinking back, I'm sure he was bloody annoyed."

"Did he say anything?"

"Not a word. It was just a sort of – well – as I said – a bit of a tired sort of look."

"Well," said Nap, "unless you imagined the whole thing, it means that he must still be a communist. It rather knocks your theory, Uncle, that he was a Red when he was poor but has turned True Blue now that he's acquired some shekels. I mean, you wouldn't get all hot under the collar just because a chap said

something derogatory about a party you'd belonged to twenty-
five years ago and tried hard to forget ever since. But even so, I
can't quite see what it all adds up to. It's like looking for a
needle in a haystack, but without even being certain that it's
a needle that you're looking for."

"There's one person we're forgetting," said Lord Cedarbrook,
"and that is the doctor. He may have written something."

"If he wrote like my doctor," said Nap, "it'd be no use,
because no one would be able to read it."

"It's a chance we mustn't neglect. Of course, if he did write
anything it would possibly be in a medical paper."

"But not in one of these," said Nap. "I know these medical
coves. They need a good deal of time and reflection before they
commit themselves to paper. I don't say that this doctor mightn't
have mentioned his experiences in the Park in some scientific
paper, but the chances are it would have been months, or even
years later."

"Damn it," said Lord Cedarbrook, "if necessary we'll look at
every medical paper from then till now. Third time lucky. I'll get
my press-cutting agency on to it tomorrow."

Curiously enough they struck gold almost immediately. It was
a letter to the editor, in a well-known and highly respectable
organ of medical opinion, and appeared in the February issue of
the year 1912.

"Dear Sir,
    "Referring to your recent and most entertaining article
entitled 'An Examination, Based on Clinical Experience, of
the Effects of Concussion', I had an experience last year
which might interest your readers. I happened to be present
during a political disturbance in Hyde Park and I was able
to be of some assistance to a young man who had the
misfortune to receive a moderately severe blow on the head
– I imagine from a police truncheon – though I can offer no
first-hand evidence on this point and have never enquired.
I rendered first aid, and as he seemed to be still shaky, I put

him into my car and took him back to my surgery. When we got there I told him to lie down on the couch and I administered a sedative. Ten minutes later, when I was working in my dispensary, I was considerably surprised to hear talking. I went in. There was no one there. (No second party, I mean.) The man was talking in an even, conversational voice, sitting upright on the couch, his eyes thrown slightly upwards, showing the whites. I tested his pulse, which was extremely slow (less than 40 if my memory serves me). One interesting feature of the seizure – which was plainly delayed concussion – was the laboured, almost painful coherence of the speech. I wish I had been adept at shorthand transcription, for I would gladly have taken a record for my own edification. I believe that in five minutes I overheard the ambitions, plans and designs of quite an unusual young man. Incidentally I have often wondered what happened to him, and whether the dreams which he outlined so lucidly and so unwittingly to yours truly in 1911 will perhaps come true in 1930 or 1940. '*Qui vivra verra*'.

"I remain, sir, your most obedient servant,

"John Beresford Potts."

"Doctor Potts," said Lord Cedarbrook. "Now we're off!"

8

Three Parties in Search of a Doctor Potts

"When you can buy a horse," as Lord Cedarbrook had so reasonably observed, "why run between the shafts?"

There are four important private detective agencies in London (there were five until last year when The Green Rhomboid got into such trouble over Lady Marshmoreton's frivolous divorce and lost their licence).

"Alberts' Agency, which has pursued its devious and shadowy ways for nearly a hundred years from a set of offices in Ely Place, is as unlike the popular conception of a detective agency as can well be imagined. It doesn't even mention the word "detective" in its note headings which profess to undertake "Enquiries on Credit, the Serving of Summonses and other Confidential Work." It calls its employees "officers" and Alberts' best officers are modest men, hard-working and discreet, if a trifle cynical about human behaviour and liable to suffer from gastric ulcers.

Incidentally, they are not given to violence, nor to inductive analytical reasoning and few of them possess the palate (or the cellar) of a Lord Peter Wimsey. They do most of their work with filing cabinets and a reference library, and when they go out on the job this seldom amounts to anything more exciting than a vigil outside a hotel.

When Lord Cedarbrook decided to ring up a detective agency, it was, as has been explained, less of a coincidence than a rough three-to-one chance that he should have picked on Alberts'. What was a coincidence, and as events were to prove, a rather unfortunate one, was that Alberts' should have put him through to their Mr Gould.

However, the fact was that Lord Cedarbrook usually got the best service that was going and Mr Gould was undeniably one of Alberts' best men. He was flabby and white of face with hair that formed a sandy halo above a pair of grey eyes: eyes which had a disconcerting habit of exhibiting a pinkish gleam when Mr Gould was excited.

Mr Gould listened patiently to what Lord Cedarbrook had to say, made a few notes in a private shorthand and promised his best attention. After Lord Cedarbrook had rung off he sat for a few minutes breathing noisily and rolling a cigarette in a patent gadget.

At the end of this period of gestation he put his hand into the drawer of his desk and took out a locked book. This he opened with a tiny key from his chain.

Having refreshed his memory he drew the telephone towards himself once again, dialled "O" and asked for a private number.

A polite voice at the other end said "Hallo, yes."

"This is Gould."

"Gould who?"

"Gould of Alberts'."

"Oh, yes."

"I did that job for you. Two years ago – you remember?"

"Well, I expect you got your money for it, didn't you?"

"Quite," said Mr Gould. He did not sound upset. Possibly his profession had hardened him to brusquerie. "We've had another client enquiring about the same party. I just thought you might like to know."

"What's that? I'm afraid I didn't hear."

"I said, I've had another enquiry about Doctor Potts."

"Oh. Who's making enquiries?"

"I'm afraid I can't give you his name," said Mr Gould virtuously. "In fact I've probably done more than I should in telling what I have – "

"I see. Yes. Well, it's quite a coincidence, isn't it?"

"I thought so," said Mr Gould.

"Yes. Would you like to earn a hundred pounds?"

"Who wouldn't?" said Mr Gould, his eyes gleaming pinkly.

"Well then, I suggest that you tell Mr What's-'is-name everything that you know about Doctor Potts. Tell him all the stuff you found out when you were working for me. But hold it up for three or four days – longer if possible."

"I expect I can manage that," said Mr Gould.

"I expect you can," said the voice.

That was on Monday.

2

On the Thursday Mr Gould had an odd and rather irritating experience. He got in early to his flat, which was the ground-floor of a quiet house in Fellows Road, and cooked his own modest evening meal. The flat had a number of features which much recommended it to Mr Gould: among them a private side entrance opening on to a little cul-de-sac. This was particularly convenient since it allowed Mr Gould to come and go without disturbing the other flat owners. It also enabled him to receive visitors on the same footing.

From the fact that he put out a second coffee cup and stoked up the fire it was plain that he was expecting a visitor that evening and was prepared to sit up for him.

The hours passed and Mr Gould winked and nodded over his fire. The wireless programmes came to an end and the rare traffic of Fellows Road became rarer still until it finally ceased.

With a nod and a jerk Mr Gould awoke to the fact that it was three o'clock, the fire was out, and he was stiff with cold. It really was most annoying, he reflected, as he climbed into bed. Some people were so inconsiderate. The phone call, which had come that afternoon, from a man for whom he had often done private work, had been quite explicit. It had asked Mr Gould to wait up "if necessary to all hours" since there was "a very promising little proposition" to be discussed. He had waited up to all hours – but there was a limit, even to the patience of a private detective. As he fell asleep Mr Gould reflected that there was a consolation. His job was not one which called for scrupulously regular attendance. He would give himself breakfast in bed the next morning and turn up in Ely Place at midday.

This programme he duly carried out, and a colleague who happened to meet him as he arrived looked at his watch and said jocularly, "Been away to the seaside, Gould?"

"That's right," said Mr Gould, equally jocular, "just back from Eastbourne."

A rather unfortunate remark, as circumstances were to prove.

3

For some reason which he found difficult to explain, Paddy was obsessed by a strong feeling of the futility of things.

There was absolutely no excuse for it.

It was tonic March weather. He had the day off – it was Friday – and he was bound for the Sunny South Coast, on a jaunt which should have been after his own heart.

For Doctor Potts had been located.

Alberts', after four days' silence, had sent a letter by hand. It arrived on the Thursday evening. Opening with a reference to the extreme gratification which Lord Cedarbrook's most esteemed patronage had caused to the firm, etc., etc., it got down to brass tacks with a rush in paragraph two.

"The Subject of your esteemed Enquiry is at present living at Upper Dene, Hindover Road, Seaford, Sussex. He is in practice, but it is thought from our observations that his practice is not a particularly lucrative one. His patients are among bungalow and cottage dweller in the middle-class residential area which lies inland from Seaford. It is believed that he came here in 1930 after a breakdown in health due to overwork in a Midland practice. He has a small car but rarely goes out except on his professional visits. He lives alone."

Paddy turned over this information as his branch-line train trundled out of Lewes and jogged its way southward toward the English Channel. He pictured a fussy, querulous, middle-aged medico with a declining practice and an increasing waistline. What possible key could such a man hold to their puzzle? The end of what thread might be found grasped in those pudgy, nicotine-stained hands: hands which had once belonged to a competent surgeon, but now shook dangerously as they dispensed cough cures and tinctures.

Quite a number of people were getting involved, Paddy reflected, in the business which had started on an evening train from London to Staines, three months before.

"Sea-forrd," called a Sussex voice, and Paddy awoke to the fact that he was at his destination.

He sauntered out into the deserted main street.

Seaford, which boasts a bracing atmosphere, a chalk soil, fifty preparatory schools and one cinema, was, in that season, dead and quiet. The sun, shining genially, brought a deception of warmth to the air, but Paddy gave an involuntary shiver as he paused at the first street crossing. Perhaps there is always something sad about a resort out of season, or perhaps it was just one of those bracing breezes which had wandered in from the sea.

Hindover Road proved to be some distance out of the town. There was a bus; but since this only ran twice a day (three times on Saturdays) and the next departure was scheduled for seven in the evening, Paddy decided to walk. Besides, he felt that the exercise might warm him.

After twenty minutes he found himself leaving the town behind him, and when the road turned to the left, and then bore round to the right, skirting the grounds of one of the biggest of the preparatory schools, it became obvious that he was heading for the open country. A postman on his bicycle obligingly dismounted and made the matter plain.

"Hindover Road," he said. "This is all Hindover Road. It goes right up along." He indicated the white road which turned between the trees, reappeared, and finally went out of sight over the crest. "Hindover they call it. High-and-over, you see. Two or three miles it goes, then you come to Friston." (Paddy gathered he meant Alfriston.) "Dene – that's the village just over the hill – Lower Dene, that lies below it – "

"And Upper Dene, I very much fear, above it," said Paddy, looking at the whalebacked hill.

"That's so," agreed the postman with a certain gloomy relish, "a fair walk is Upper Dene. Nor it isn't so very much when you come to it. Just two houses and the mill."

"I see," said Paddy. It was past one o'clock and the air was making him ravenous. "Is there anywhere I can get a bite to eat, or do I have to go back into the town?"

"Dee-pends what you want," said the postman. "If you were wanting a slap-up meal, in so far as you can get a slap-up meal anywhere nowadays, then you'd have to go back to one of they big hotels on the front. But that's a tidy way back – "

"I'm not fussy," said Paddy, "anything to eat – "

"It's a long walk back," said the postman, who was not to be denied. "And in any case, you see, they big hotels don't open till the beginning of May."

"Well, that does seem to clinch it, doesn't it?"

"Now, if you just want something to eat – well, there's the Fox and Hens."

Ten minutes later Paddy was in the public bar of the Fox and Hens, eating bread and cheese of surprising quality and listening to a man in leather leggings, who looked like a gamekeeper, discussing the mating habits of herons with the landlord and a man called Ted.

When the herons had been brought home to roost there fell a moment's silence, which was broken by the landlord, who stared out of the window and said, apropos of nothing that had gone before, "A fine little old gentleman."

Quite suddenly Paddy knew, beyond any doubt, that the three men were going to talk about Doctor Potts.

"The Eastbourne Summer Show, wasn't it?" said the innkeeper. "A First in the Amateurs and an Honourable Mention in the Open."

"Raspberries?" suggested the man in leggings.

"Raspberries and loganberries."

"There's the soil, of course, there's nothing like chalk for a ground fruit."

"Some of it was soil," said the innkeeper, "but most of it was what you might call the scientific outlook. The same again, Ted?"

"Half-and-half," said Ted. "Now I'll tell you something else about that. All last spring and summer, when that fruit was growing, he never had no trouble with the birds. Fruit that's growing is just natural provender to birds. Then why did they leave it be? Tell me that."

The landlord, feeling unable to answer this, said nothing.

"Netting? No. Scarecrows? No. Wires and guns? Not a bit of it."

"The scientific outlook," suggested the landlord.

"I won't say 'no'," said Ted, "but if the scientific outlook can keep a hungry starling away from a raspberry bed, then it's a powerful great sort of outlook."

"I expect he bewitched 'em," said the man in leggings.

It had occurred to Paddy for some time that he was missing his cues. In theory his course was plain enough. He had to stand a round of drinks, join in the conversation, casually mention the name of Doctor Potts and proceed to pick up some useful bits of information.

"I expect there's a technique in this sort of thing," he thought. "The chaps in the books seem to do it easily enough. Well, here goes."

Climbing to his feet he approached the bar.

"Good morning – or, I should say, good afternoon."

"Good afternoon, sir."

"Another beer, please."

"Pint o' bitter?"

"That's right. And won't you gentlemen join me?"

The gentlemen displayed no undue reluctance and the glasses were charged.

"So far, so good," thought Paddy.

"I couldn't help hearing you talking just now," he said to the landlord. "It sounded as though you must have been talking about an old friend of mine – "

"Yes," said the landlord non-commitally. "One for the road, Ted?"

"No thanks," said Ted. "Must be getting along. Thanks for the drink, mister." He disposed of his beer with surprising speed and disappeared through the door which led to the saloon bar.

When Paddy looked round he saw that the man with the leggings had gone too. The landlord was leaning forward, his thick forearms as brown as the bar counter they rested on, looking through Paddy rather than at him.

The sudden emptying of the room combined with this immobility to produce a slight atmosphere of nightmare.

"I wonder if I really am dreaming all this," thought Paddy. He took a pull at his beer, stared at the landlord and said defiantly:

"Doctor Potts is the name. Doctor Beresford Potts. Perhaps you know him?"

"I should think I ought to," said the landlord, still not moving, "he treated my lumbago these last four winters."

"Does he live near here?"

"His house is down Toms Lane," said the landlord. He seemed to Paddy to be choosing his words rather carefully. "That's a quarter mile up Hindover. You can't miss it. Turn right at the barn – "

"Thank you," said Paddy.

"You're welcome," said the landlord.

As Paddy walked in the afternoon sunlight up the chalk road, he found he had now a different picture of Doctor Potts. This was a kindly little man, who grew raspberries and bewitched the birds of the air. A man who had retired from the busy life of the Midlands and found a resting place under the Downs. A Sussex Saint Francis. This should be an easy and an interesting man to talk with –

"It's no good," thought Paddy. "Stop kidding yourself. You noticed it perfectly well. And all those men knew…"

He turned off the road and strode up the lane and the feeling of futility which had been so strong in the morning came back redoubled.

A little red-backed shrike, the Sussex butcher-bird, sat on a swaying furze top and watched him for a moment with its eyes of jet before it flew about its slaughterer's business. When he saw the garden, the wide, orderly beds, between well-weeded paths, Paddy knew that it had indeed belonged to a garden lover. A pity that the house was so ugly. A modern box of bricks which would not have looked out of place in any suburb. It boasted the usual annexe of a toy garage, and its red brick was an offence.

Paddy walked up the flagged front path.

No smoke came from any of the chimneys. All the windows were shut and a small white cat was sitting in the sun on the porch, looking as if it had been trying in vain to find a way in. As Paddy came up, it arched its back and rubbed against his ankle.

He knocked at the door, but was so certain that he would get no answer that he stopped almost at once, seized the handle, then threw the door back.

He looked into a small, neat, empty hall.

The first door on the right was plainly the parlour, or the main living-room. This too was shut.

Paddy opened it boldly, though he would have been hard put to it to say why he was making so free with a strange house.

When he looked inside the room he got a shock. Seated at the round table which filled the middle of the floor were two men.

One was a uniformed constable. The other was Inspector Roberts of the West End Central Police Station.

4

Chief Inspector Hazlerigg was used to receiving anonymous letters. Some were abusive and threatening, for he had sent a good many men "down" – down from the elevated dock of the Central Criminal Court to the grey depths of penal servitude. Then there were frivolous and leg-pulling letters, for a Chief Inspector, like other celebrities, suffers from his public. But the third, and largest, category were strictly business. It contained information.

"Mr and Mrs Jones, who lives so respectable at 99 Utopia Road were never properly man and wife," or "The stuff from the King's Cross job is in Box 999 at the Westminster and City Safe Deposit. Signed. A Friend of Justice."

Justice has many such friends. All letters came alike to Scotland Yard. None were ever neglected, however unlikely. Most of them lead nowhere, but the hundredth was worth its weight in fine gold.

On the Thursday morning, the day before the above-related happenings, a discreet note was brought to his room by Sergeant Crabbe.

"No prints," said the Sergeant. "No history."

By this he meant that the handwriting or typewriter had never featured before in their anonymous mail.

"Postmark EC2, sir," said Sergeant Crabbe. "That narrows it down to about half a million."

"Well, it's short and to the point anyway," said Hazlerigg.

It was a line and half of typescript on plain paper and it said: "Luciano's boys are after Doctor Beresford Potts. I suggest you get there first."

"How was it addressed?" asked Hazlerigg.

"Just New Scotland Yard, sir."

"Not to me personally?"

"No, sir. But seeing it mentioned that wop Luciano – "

"Quite right. Well, I suppose the first thing to do is to identify this Doctor Beresford Potts. There can't be many of them, with a Christian name like that. We'd better have someone keep an eye on Capelli, too. Get on to West End Central and ask Inspector Roberts if he'd be kind enough to have a word with me – "

Scotland Yard has many and peculiar ways of finding out what it wants to know, and by that evening Hazlerigg had learnt all about Doctor Potts who was living in blameless retirement at Upper Dene near Seaford.

"Luciano doesn't seem to be on the move," said Inspector Roberts, "and all of his regulars are what you might call in situ – that's to say they're doing nothing much, as usual, in a nasty sort of way round Greek and Dean Street."

"All accounted for?"

"I wouldn't say all, because I don't know that I know them all. There's Patsy Conlan. He's been out of sight for a day or two. And there's one or two new boys. They come and go – "

"What does Patsy do?"

"Do," said Inspector Roberts wearily. "None of them ever do anything except make puddling nuisances of themselves. Patsy sometimes drive Luciano's Bentley – when the big boy isn't driving it himself."

"I see. Can you find out if it's missing?"

"What – the Bentley?" Inspector Roberts was faintly surprised. He thought the Chief Inspector was making a fair-sized mountain out of the beginnings of an unpromising molehill: but he knew him too well to let the surprise appear in his voice.

An hour later he wasn't quite so sure. He telephoned Hazlerigg and reported that the Big Bentley was missing from the all-night garage near Piccadilly where Luciano kept it. Patsy Conlan, its driver, was gone too – and it was believed he had taken one of the other boys with him.

"I see," said Hazlerigg. The decision was his. He was well aware that he might be making a fool of himself. The feeling was too commonplace to affect his decision in either direction.

"I'd like you to go down and see this chap Potts," he said at last. "I don't know what you're to ask him. Just a few general questions. You might find out if there is any reason known to him why Luciano should be after him."

"Right, sir."

"It's too late to start tonight. Get off as early as possible tomorrow. I'll fix the necessary permissions."

When Inspector Roberts had rung off, Hazlerigg placed a broad finger on the wooden edge of his desk and added prophetically, "I hope you get there in time."

5

But of course he didn't. Doctor Potts was dead. (As Paddy had realized almost at once when he heard the men in the Public Bar talking about him.)

Inspector Roberts reported back to Hazlerigg that evening, a badly worried man. And it was very little consolation to him to add that Patsy Conlan had been picked up in Eastbourne and was being held.

"On what charge?" said Hazlerigg bluntly.

"Driving to the public danger and refusing to give the requisite particulars when stopped and properly cautioned. Contravention of section 114 – "

"Oh, I've no doubt you're technically covered," said Hazlerigg with a smile. "But unless you find anything else you'll have to let him go within forty-eight hours, you know. Tell me what happened."

"It's the most audacious thing you ever heard of," said Inspector Roberts. "We got the news as we arrived at Seaford Police Station. Apparently the old doctor had a woman who 'did' for him. Well, she arrived this morning at eight o'clock as usual, and found the doctor gone."

"How did she get in?"

"She had a key. She let herself in, went up to wake the doctor and, as I said, found he wasn't in bed. Of course, that didn't upset her. It had happened before. He was often called out at odd hours. The only thing was, he usually left a note, so she'd know what time to get his breakfast, and so on. I think this worried her a bit – not finding a note – and she'd noticed the doctor had been a bit down in the dumps lately – or so she said – she may just have been being wise after the event. Anyhow, in the end – about half past nine – she thought she'd look in the garage to see if the car was out or not. She didn't have to go outside the house – there was a connecting door from the passage at the back of the house – which she found open.

"When she got into the garage, being a bit short-sighted, she went over and opened the big swing doors first. Probably saved her own life. The whole place was full of carbon monoxide. Doctor Potts was there all right – in the car. Very dead. The old lady kept her head wonderfully well, in the circumstances. Didn't try to touch anything – just came straight out and phoned the nearest doctor – then phoned Seaford police station. As I say, we'd just arrived, so we came straight out. We got there at the same time as the doctor. It was obvious at a glance that there was nothing we could do for Potts except bury him. So the doctor, who was a sensible sort of cove, let it alone and spent his time looking after Mrs Farrow, the char, who was having a bad attack of hysteria."

"Well," said Hazlerigg, "that left you a clear field."

"A clear field, an early innings, and no complaints," agreed Inspector Roberts. "And the results were absolutely and entirely negative. I sent the police car back for help, and in three or four hours we'd seen everything, been everywhere and done everything. We took that little house to pieces and shook it – and went over each separate piece with a microscope, as you might say. There wasn't a door handle in the place which didn't have just the right fingerprints on it – Doctor Potts and Mrs Farrow – not to speck too much – or too little of mud on any of the floors – two day's dust on all the window sills – "

"All right, all right," said Hazlerigg. "I don't doubt you did your work properly. You were satisfied that no one had been in the house – no one who shouldn't have been. What about the garage?"

"Well, that's not so easy," said Inspector Roberts. "The front path was stone – the stuff they call crazy-paving, that used to be so popular. A man who picked his step could walk up that without leaving much sign. Then the garage door had a slip-catch lock on the little half-door, and not a very new one at that. Well, you know how much use they are. The London boys open them with a stiff piece of talc and you don't have to touch the handle either. It's the sort of thing they learn at their kindergartens. And once he was in the garage the floor was pretty clean – no oil or petrol. I dare say he could have moved about without leaving much trace. And we did find two things in the garage which might signify. We've been over 'em – " He opened his bag and produced for Hazlerigg's inspection a small key and an oblong block of hard rubber about the size of a matchbox. The key was brand new and not very elaborate – three or four lever apparently, with a pinhole head. The type of thing which opens a good cash box.

"Can't make much of that rubber," said Roberts. "It might be anything – or nothing."

"Yes, I'm afraid you're right." Hazlerigg seemed to find the key more interesting and was squinting at it through a watch-maker's optic. "Would you say this had been used at all?" he asked.

"Two or three times, perhaps. Not more."

"H'm. Where were they exactly?"

"On the floor – in the corner beside the big swing doors."

"They might have belonged to Potts."

"Mrs Farrow didn't think so," said Roberts. "And we searched the house for something to fit the key, but couldn't find a sausage."

"Might have been something he brought years ago and never used," said Hazlerigg. "I think we're getting ahead of ourselves. You'll be making the usual enquiries about the movements of those two men, Patsy Conlan and – who's the other? – Bates.

We'd like to know as much as possible about them. You never know what might help. Past records and everything."

"It's being done," said Inspector Roberts. "I'll let you have a copy of the reports when they come in. I've found out one thing about Conlan already. He had quite a good war record. He was a Sapper – in a Tunnelling Company."

That was Saturday.

6

Next morning Mr Gould received a telephone call at his flat.

He recognized the voice.

"Is that Gould?"

"Yes, Gould speaking."

"Well then, listen," said the voice, "and listen carefully, because I'm not going to repeat myself. I don't like people who write to the police."

"Why – I – "

"Now don't let's tell unnecessary lies," said the voice. "On Thursday morning Scotland Yard got a letter. It wasn't signed. It told them that we were after Doctor Potts. Only one person knew this – and that was you. It is therefore logical to suppose that it was you who sent the letter. You agree?"

Mr Gould started to say something, but thought better of it.

The voice continued.

"We're not complaining. When you deal with a rat you must expect to get your fingers bitten. Very fortunately we had taken certain precautions. And this is what I wanted to tell you. The police found something on the floor of the garage. A key. We put it there for them to find. They know that it didn't belong to Doctor Potts. It's reasonable to suppose that they would be interested to discover its true owner."

"I expect they would," said Mr Gould. He managed to say it defiantly, but there was a crack in his voice.

"Don't interrupt. All you have to do is listen. That key fits a cash box. This cash box is in a safe deposit, in a private renter's safe. There are other things in the safe, and in the box. Papers, receipts, records, pass books. Once they know about this safe deposit it won't take the police long to find out who the safe belongs to. The renter is a Mr Gould. A Mr Gould of Alberts' Detective Agency. Did I hear you say something?"

But Mr Gould was, in fact, past speech.

"Among other things the records in the safe will show that Mr Gould had been receiving cash payments from time to time from a Doctor Beresford Potts of Upper Dene, near Seaford. Significantly enough these cash payments started two years ago – at about the time when you first undertook the job of locating and investigating the circumstances of Dr Potts. I fear this may suggest to the police an obvious solution. It might suggest to them that you had been blackmailing Dr Potts. You and I know that this isn't true, but you know what the police are. I expect the first question they will ask you is where you were on Thursday evening. At home waiting for a friend? Well that isn't much of an alibi, is it? Think it out."

"Look here – " said Mr Gould.

"However," went on the voice cheerfully, "This is all rather hypothetical, isn't it? I mean to say, if the police are never told about this safe deposit, then none of the rest need happen. You follow me? Yes, I'm certain you do."

9

Conferences at Scotland Yard

It must not be imagined that Inspector Roberts had forgotten to tell Chief Inspector Hazlerigg all about Paddy Yeatman-Carter's unexpected arrival at Upper Dene. He had spoken of it at some length. And Hazlerigg had been very interested indeed. But he was a man who did first things first. And he was quite certain in his own mind that Paddy, whatever his sins, had had nothing directly to do with the decease of Dr Potts.

The reason for this certainty was simply that, since the accident in the Underground Railway station, he had had Paddy and Nap watched. Not continuously, the circumstances hardly warranted that. But a discreet eye had been kept on their comings and goings. And he therefore knew that on Thursday night, the night of Doctor Potts' last day on earth, Nap had been with Nurse Goodbody, first at a Symphony Concert and afterwards till a late hour at a night club (the former to please his fiancée, the latter to please himself), whilst Paddy had played some energetic squash at Bumpers, had drunk a lot of beer, returned to the Inner Temple, waited up for Nap till one o'clock; had then got tired of waiting and had gone to bed.

"I suppose, if he had a car hidden somewhere, he *could* just have done it," said Roberts doubtfully. "How long to get to Seaford at night – three hours, or three and a half...?"

"Yes," said Hazlerigg. "But aren't you forgetting that he caught the 8.50 from Victoria for Seaford on Friday morning?

No. He had no hand in this. I'm not saying that his presence at Seaford isn't significant. Unless I'm much mistaken he's going to prove very significant indeed. Do you know, I think the time has come for the putting of a few cards on to the table."

It was becoming increasingly apparent to Hazlerigg that something was going on behind his back and that in the case of the Crown versus Luciano, Brandison, and others, at least two parties were working on parallel lines. One was a professional party, the police, about their business of maintaining the King's peace. The other was an amateur, an irregular and an altogether regrettable party, apparently consisting of a Mr Yeatman-Carter, a Mr Rumbold, and – somewhere in the background – that unpredictable peer, Lord Cedarbrook.

Major McCann was fortuitously connected with it, too. And Major McCann was a man for whom the Chief Inspector had a certain regard.

"There's trouble enough in the natural way," he quoted from his favourite poet, "when it comes to burying human clay. But when you reach a point in a murder investigation where you can't move without stubbing your toes over a pack of amateur helpers – well, it's time to do something about it."

Accordingly he wrote three notes, one to Paddy, one to Nap, and one to Lord Cedarbrook, inviting them to meet him on the following day at eleven in the morning.

Sergeant Crabbe, who carried the notes, found Nap and Paddy without difficulty. At Lord Cedarbrook's residence in Goshawk Road, however, he received a rebuff.

Lord Cedarbrook had disappeared.

Cluttersley, with a back of granite and a face of doom, informed him that His Lordship was not at home, had not been at home for several days and was unlikely to be at home for a considerable period. He could not say how long. When His Lordship departed, about a week previously, he had indicated that he might be away for a month or more. No, he had left no forwarding address.

2

Hazlerigg opened without preamble.

"It's one of our jobs," he said, "to keep an eye on people like Luciano Capelli. Don't imagine, please, that he's an undesirable alien. If he was that, we could get him deported with very little further trouble. He's undesirable as a cold in August, but unfortunately he's a British citizen – by naturalization. He lives and works and does his little bit to help the country of his adoption in the Soho area, and consequently his immediate governor is Inspector Roberts, whom you've both met. I am concerned with him indirectly, because I hold a general watching brief over the food and drink rackets.

"Luciano is proprietor of the Mogador. He owns it and runs it, and turns a respectable, if grimy, penny by doing so. I mean, it's one of the better known Soho restaurants and a very large number of extremely respectable people use it every night, and neither know nor care that its proprietor is a gangster. There's nothing surprising in that, of course. A lot of middle-class Chicago families used to stay at the Lexington when the fourth floor was the headquarters of Al Capone. One of the happy results, from his point of view, is that Luciano is able to keep all his boys together under one roof – and there's no difficulty about their rations and so on."

"Administrative difficulties of a gang leader," said Nap. "What a fascinating thought. It never struck me before that housewives and gangsters might have problems in common."

"This is just to put you both in the picture," went on Hazlerigg. "You've got to understand that we should have been looking after Luciano anyway. It was when he started getting mixed up with that cashier fellow – Brandison, and his insurance company, that it ceased to be a routine job and began to have the smell of a case. And that's where you people started to feature with what I might call almost monotonous regularity. First there was the assistant cashier who fell into the Thames – "

"Primed," agreed Paddy, "with drinks purchased by me."

127

"Then there was the rough-house which didn't quite come off, at the Mogador, on the night of Brandison's visit. You were involved in that – " Hazlerigg turned to Nap.

"I certainly was," said Nap. "If it hadn't been for some extraordinarily smart work by Major McCann I should probably now be adorning your Black Museum, catalogued as the corpse of an incautious diner in Soho."

"I don't think they meant to kill you," said Hazlerigg. "But that's a point I'm coming to in a moment. Next there was the affair of the Underground station – "

"Featuring Yeatman-Carter, in his well-known knockabout act."

"Quite so," agreed Hazlerigg, "And lastly there's the death of Doctor Potts. The body was hardly cold before one of you – it was you, I think, Mr Carter – was on the spot. I may as well tell you straight away that I don't think either of you had anything to do with that – not directly."

"Well, thank goodness you don't," said Nap. "Because as a matter of fact we didn't."

"But that's not to say that you didn't have an indirect connection with it. Otherwise, to put it at its lowest, how did you manage to get on the scene so quickly?"

Paddy looked at Nap and Nap looked at Paddy and said, "Clean breast, I think."

So they told Hazlerigg everything. It took quite a long time.

When it was all over the Chief Inspector said, "Yes. I should like to meet Lord Cedarbrook. I've heard of him, of course. But never having been attached to our Special Branch I haven't had the pleasure of meeting him officially."

Both his hearers looked surprised, and Hazlerigg said, "Didn't you know he worked for MI5 during the war?"

"I knew that he was an expert on Russia," said Nap. "I didn't know that he worked for the Department."

"Where is he now?"

"Honestly I don't know," said Nap. "He went off at the beginning of the week. He didn't say anything to either of us.

Cluttersley may know where he is, but he won't say. He's a confounded graven image."

"Well, I'd certainly like a word with him when he does show up – " The Chief Inspector was silent for a moment and then he added, "Have you ever done any surveying?"

"In a rough sort of way, when we were training in France – " said Nap.

"Orienting the map, and that sort of nonsense," suggested Paddy.

"That's the idea. I'm not an expert on it myself, but you remember the principle of locating an unknown point on the map. It was a particularly useful method when it was a point you couldn't actually get to – in front of your own front line for instance – "

"Yes," said Nap. "I think so. By intersection of rays."

"Quite so. You took a bearing from some spot you could locate – the spot you were standing on, for instance. Then you moved to another spot as far to a flank as possible and took a second bearing. Where those two lines crossed on the map gave you some idea of the rough location of the place. There was a considerable margin of error of course."

"As far as I can remember," said Nap, "if you could, you checked up with a third bearing from a third point."

"Exactly," said Hazlerigg. "You take the words out of my mouth."

"You're thinking of Legate, I take it."

"I'm thinking of Legate. He's up to something or other. We haven't much to go on, you know. Even with what you've given us we haven't got within a mile of the point where we could make a charge against him. But one or two things are beginning to emerge. He's got a lot of ready money behind him. And he's prepared to use it. His particular instruments are Luciano and company. He may have others, of course. If we knew *what* he was trying to do, we might try to stop it. If we even knew how he was setting about it, that'd be a help."

"You say that, so far, our story has given you two lines on him," said Nap. "That, I take it, is what you mean by two intersecting rays."

"Two pointers, yes. The first, of course, was Mr Britten. Rather an intriguing figure, don't you think? A junior cashier at the Stalagmite Insurance Corporation, who got the sack for making a mistake over some insurance policies. And threw himself into the river. Now is that the truth? Or is there more to it than that?"

"Then Doctor Potts – ?"

"Yes. Doctor Potts. A voice out of the past. If Mr Britten was the guilty present, then I have a feeling that Doctor Potts must have been the guilty past. He knew something about Legate or Legate thought he knew something. Either way it proved equally fatal. But there's a much more interesting thing about Doctor Potts and I'm sure it hasn't escaped your notice."

Both Paddy and Nap tried to look intelligent but it was obvious that neither of them knew what was coming.

"Time," said Hazlerigg. "Seconds, minutes, hours and days. The time factor. Put yourself in the shoes of the other side and think for a moment. At the end of last week you three – by a piece of intensive work and research – for which, by the way, accept my heartiest professional congratulations – discovered the existence of Doctor Potts. Up to that moment there was no reason to suppose that anyone necessarily shared your secret. The various press-cutting agencies you employed couldn't know yourselves. Very well. On the Monday you enlisted the help of a member of Alberts' Detective Agency – a very respectable firm, very well known to us – we've nothing against them at all. You are attended by a Mr Gould. On Thursday night of that same week a fairly elaborate plan is put into action. I'll tell you more about it in a minute – but you can take it from me that it's definitely not the sort of thing that could have been worked out in twenty-four hours. You see what I mean? There are two possibilities – either your Mr Gould was thunderingly indiscreet and the other side got wind of his enquiries – and stepped in first. Or – and it's a possibility that's got to be faced – Mr Gould gave you away."

"Have you met Gould before?" asked Nap.

"I've heard of him," said Hazlerigg. "We meet these fellows in court sometimes as professional witnesses. He's got the reputation of being clever, but slippery."

"Do you think the thing is definite enough for you to ask him some questions?"

"Definite or not, I intend to do so," said Hazlerigg. "We can't afford to miss any chances when dealing with this crowd. They're hot stuff. That show on Thursday night was streamlined."

"I suppose," said Paddy cautiously, "I suppose it's just possible that Doctor Potts *did* commit suicide. His housekeeper said he'd been a bit off-colour, you know. His practice wasn't a very paying one. I was asking about it afterwards. He had a few good patients – old ladies he was looking after – but it can't have brought in very much money."

"He *might* have committed suicide," said Hazlerigg. "And so *might* Mr Britten. Both things are equally possible. But do you really believe either of them?"

"That's all very well," said Nap, "but the two cases aren't on the same footing. Britten was drunk and it was a dark night. If Luciano's boys were following him, I agree, they could have pushed him off the towing-path into the river and no trouble. But Potts was sober and in his own house. If they broke in and forced him into the car and held him down, surely they must have left some signs – "

"They left no signs at all – "

"Well, then – "

"I'll tell you what I *think* happened," said Hazlerigg, "because it'll show you the sort of people you're up against. But you must understand that everything I say is pure surmise. I think it happened this way because this is the only way it can have happened. I think that these people knew quite a lot about Doctor Potts and his habits and his practice and his household. I think they must have studied him for some time as a possible subject. But it was only when you three got on to him – got to know of his existence – that he had to be put away."

"You mean that we killed him," said Nap.

"Yes," said Hazlerigg. "I mean just that. Unwittingly, of course. I'm sorry – but you asked for the truth. If it's any consolation to you, I was equally responsible for his death. I knew enough by late on Thursday afternoon to have moved and I delayed till Friday morning. Now let's stop blaming ourselves and try to see what happened.

"Two of Luciano's men drove down to Seaford on Thursday night. They parked the car off the Hindover Road. They went on foot up the lane, and into the garden, keeping to the stone path, and they forced the slip lock of the garage door, and one of them went in – Conlan, I think. The main garage doors were bolted on the inside, but there was the usual little entrance door cut into the big one, as you probably saw, and this was the one they opened. As soon as Conlan was inside the garage, with the doors shut, he switched on the doctor's car and started the engine. Yes – I know what you're going to say. But it's all right. I think he had a mask. Not a gas mask – of course, that wouldn't have been any use to him at all against carbon monoxide – but an oxygen container mask – the sort they issued to the Tunnelling Companies in the Royal Engineers. That was the mob Conlan was in during the war.

"Inspector Roberts found that when he was in Potts' bedroom – which was at the top of the house, on the far side, he could just hear the car engine running in the garage if he listened for it. But Potts was an old man, a bit deaf, and either asleep or very sleepy. Anyway, we may suppose he didn't hear the car running. If he had heard it he'd have come down to investigate and I think he'd have died just the same.

"When Conlan was confident that the level of the carbon monoxide gas in the garage was high enough – a lighted match would have told him – he switched off the car and signalled to the other chap, who went back to the call box outside Dene village and rang up Potts. When Potts answered the phone –

which was in his bedroom, by the way – this chap simply announced that he was the gardener or servant or goodness-knows-what from the big house, and old Mrs Trefusis had been taken powerful bad, and would Doctor Potts hurry over please.

"Well, of course he would. Doctor Potts, as you said, relied on a few special patients, and he couldn't afford to let them down. He got sleepily into his clothes, walked downstairs, and into the garage. Now I don't know why he got into the car before opening the garage doors. It was a cold night – possibly the ignition or the choke wanted adjusting. It makes very little difference. Once he was in the car he couldn't get out. So there he died."

There was silence for a moment in the room, and then Nap said, "It might have made a difference. I know that carbon monoxide works quickly, and is invisible and odourless and so on. But if he had gone straight across and thrown the doors open, mightn't he have saved his life? Or if Conlan wanted to keep him in the garage, that would have meant a struggle, which was just what they wanted to avoid."

"If Potts had gone straight across," said Hazlerigg, "he wouldn't have been *able* to open the door. There were four large sliding bolts and Conlan had wedged all of them with little oblong rubber wedges, cut to fit into the space between the top of the bolt and the back stop. Even if Potts had discovered what was blocking the bolts, he could never have worked them clear in time. One of those wedges was left behind. It was absolutely the only mistake they made."

"If what you say is right," said Paddy, "it all seems to have been carefully worked out."

"That's just it," said Hazlerigg. "It's not the sort of thing that could have been arranged overnight. Those wedges might have been faked up on the spot – but the telephone call wasn't so simple. They'd have to know the names and habits and certain details about the patients to make that bit sound convincing."

"And they must have known a good deal about his household," said Paddy. "That he slept alone, and that his bedroom was on the other side of the house, and that you couldn't hear the car from his bedroom and so on."

"What about the telephone call," said Nap. "Has it been traced?"

"Not a chance," said Hazlerigg. "Seaford's a full automatic exchange. That's a pity, because an operator might easily have remembered a phone call at that time of night."

"Then you haven't a great deal of tangible evidence – "

"There isn't a single shred of positive evidence in the whole thing," said Hazlerigg. "If we dared put those chaps in the dock, a competent counsel would tear it to pieces. He wouldn't even trouble to call evidence for the defence. He'd just claim that there was no case to answer. And he'd be right. So that's how it goes. That's the record to date. Doctor Potts committed suicide – by gassing himself in his own garage. Mr Britten committed suicide by throwing himself in the river."

Seeing the looks on his hearers' faces he added with a smile, "It's all right. I'm not being a defeatist. We shall get them in the end. But this just isn't the peg we're going to hang them on."

"What's your idea of the future then," said Nap.

"That's very difficult. I'm very tempted to tell you to steer clear and keep clear. But that would sound ungrateful after all the good work you've put in. Besides, I no longer think that amateur help means nothing but trouble. If ever I did hold that opinion I was cured of it by an experience I once had with Major McCann. I'll tell you about it some day. And there is a job for you to do. Whatever game Mr Legate is playing, it's a financial game. And most financial games get played in or near the City. Now you both work there, I think. You, Mr Rumbold, are a solicitor, and you, Mr Carter, a chartered accountant – "

"Well, as a matter of fact, I've left the firm of accountants I used to work for – " said Paddy. "I'm with a newspaper."

"The *Moorgate Press*, of Finsbury Square," said Hazlerigg with a smile. "We've been keeping an eye on you, you see. Now you're both well placed for this job – better placed than I am in some ways. I want you to keep your eyes and ears open for every mention or hint or whisper concerning Legate and the Stalagmite Insurance Corporation. Report anything you hear to me at once – however trivial it seems. I'll let you have my private office number. There'll be someone to take a message at whatever time you ring up."

"There's just one thing," said Nap slowly. "How do we know that what we're looking for has anything to do with the Stalagmite? Even if Legate and Brandison are involved in it. It may be a private swindle, something outside of the Stalagmite altogether."

"You're forgetting Britten," said Hazlerigg. "He practically told us that the answer could be found in the books of the firm. The whole trouble started, you remember, when he saw some book or record he wasn't meant to see."

"Then why not take the bull by the horns," said Paddy, "and have the books inspected."

"On what pretext? Do you imagine that the police auditors could find a discrepancy which has escaped the expert eye of Broomfields? I don't think that this thing is necessarily directly financial at all. Besides, we've got to be careful, you know. The Stalagmite are a pretty powerful corporation. Take a look at the names on their board of directors – Lord Stallybrowe, Sir Hubert Fosdick – "

"Nearly seventy and quite gaga," murmured Nap. "All right – I'm just repeating my fiancée's opinion of him. He's her uncle."

"Very well then – Andrew B Chattell – he mayn't be in Debrett, but he's a big name in the insurance world. Charles Bedell Atkinson – he's on the board of the Home Counties Bank. Sir George Burroughs, the shipping man. Hewson-Collet – he'd have been a KC if he'd stayed on at the Bar. That's the sort of men you're up against."

"I know, I know," said Nap. "They don't sound a very likely gang of criminals."

"Not only don't they sound like criminals," said Hazlerigg grimly, "but if we start questioning their business methods and asking for inspection of their books without some very good reason, they'll sound like trouble. They'll sound like Questions in Parliament and the Exit of a Chief Inspector."

"Then we're back where we started," said Nap. "The ramp is being worked from the Stalagmite. But that's not to say the Stalagmite is itself a ramp. What you really want us to do is to see if we can pick up anything discreditable about Legate."

"That's it," said Hazlerigg. "And whilst you're about it, I think you ought to take a few sensible precautions on your own account. Particularly if you discover anything. It can't have escaped you that these people are quite wholehearted in their dislike of interference."

"What do you suggest?" said Paddy.

"Just use your common sense," said the Inspector, with a smile which robbed the suggestion of its usual offensiveness. "Don't go out after dark unnecessarily. And that goes for your fiancées as well – though the danger in their case is much slighter. If you must go out after dark, go in pairs. And keep each other informed of where you're going and what time you expect to be back – that sort of thing. Oh, and I don't think I should dine in Soho. If there's going to be a fixture, you might as well play it on your own ground."

It was, on the whole, two rather subdued young men who left New Scotland Yard and made, without a word being spoken, for Bumpers Fo'c'sle Bar. Here two pints of bitter, and again two more, were disposed of in quick succession.

"Do you feel an overmastering desire to look over your shoulder the whole time," said Nap, "to see if you're being followed?"

"I do," said Paddy.

"Well, you're right, you are," said Nap. "That's Buttonshaw, just come in now. I can see by the look in his eye that he's dying to tell us his famous story of how he won the Battle of the Ardennes and what he said to the American Brigadier."

"Come and have a game of squash," said Paddy.

3

On the following morning Chief Inspector Hazlerigg summoned Mr Gould from Alberts' Detective Agency to have a few words with him in his room at New Scotland Yard.

Mr Gould obeyed reluctantly. A private detective, working on official sufferance, does not disregard the lightest request of a Chief Inspector. Nevertheless the summons caused him no pleasure at all. And he took certain precautions in obeying it.

First, he paid a visit to his club in Whitehall Court. This had three entrances. The front one in Whitehall Court itself, a side one in Court Street, and a service door into Court Alley. He went in at the front entrance, walked straight through the club and out at the service exit, moved smartly down to the Embankment, under the arch, up Villiers Street, and in at the side entrance to Charing Cross Station. From here he took an Underground train to Waterloo, went out of the main exit and caught a bus which took him back on his tracks, across Westminster Bridge. At the traffic lights at the top of Bridge Street he jumped off the bus and strolled into the Yard by the Cannon Row approach.

"Sit down, Mr Gould," said Hazlerigg. "Thank you for being so punctual. We are both busy men, so I'll try not to detain you any longer than I can help."

"I am always happy to oblige," said Mr Gould. "The gentlemen of the Metropolitan force and I have always got on very well together."

"Quite so, Mr Gould. Quite so. And I expect we always shall," said Hazlerigg. "Sometimes I am asked why, if we have such a competent and efficient police force, we should allow firms of private detectives to exist at all. But that is a point of view with which I have no sympathy. I am convinced that there are different forms of work suited to both of us. We pursue our course, you pursue yours. There is no need for us to interfere with each other."

"Exactly," said Mr Gould more happily. He surmised that his original fears had been groundless. The wild thought occurred to him that the Chief Inspector might want a bit of private and confidential work done. Well, why not? Even Chief Inspectors have wives.

"Our dealings with your firm," went on Hazlerigg, "have always been very happy in the past."

"I think I may say the same," said Mr Gould.

"Have you ever heard of Doctor Potts?" said Hazlerigg. The sudden ring of steel was almost audible.

"Have I ever – I beg your pardon. What was that?"

"You heard perfectly," said Hazlerigg. All affability had gone from his voice.

"Doctor Potts – I seem to know the name – "

"You know the name damned well," said Hazlerigg. "You made enquiries about him for Lord Cedarbrook less than a week ago. Come man, your memory can't be as bad as all that."

"You will realize," said Mr Gould with an attempt at dignity, "that all enquiries which I make are confidential."

"That's what I want to find out," said Hazlerigg coldly. "Was the result of your enquiry treated as confidential."

"I don't quite follow you?"

"Then you aren't trying. I'll be even plainer. When you had made those enquiries did you pass the information on to anyone else besides Lord Cedarbrook?"

"No," said Mr Gould. "I didn't pass any information on." Under the grey eyes of the Chief Inspector he was glad, for once, to be able to tell the literal truth.

"I see. Mr Gould, have you ever met a man called Legate?"

This time it was quite obvious that the shot had gone home. Mr Gould tried to speak, failed, and remained for a time dismally silent.

In an instant Hazlerigg had changed his tactics. The affability was back in his voice, and he sounded quite genuinely friendly.

"Why not speak frankly," he said.

This, as he was well aware, was the first real chance he had had of breaking into the case. Mr Gould knew a great deal of what was going on behind the scenes. He was an actor in the shadow play, of which they, the audience, were seeing only the carefully distorted fragments.

But now Mr Gould was silent – and Hazlerigg guessed at the reason, and came very near to guessing it correctly.

"You know Luciano Capelli," he said. His voice was still friendly.

"I know of him," said Mr Gould.

"He's a dangerous man? An awkward customer? A nasty chap to cross?"

Mr Gould nodded. There was no point in denying the obvious.

"Well let me do my best to assure you," went on Chief Inspector Hazlerigg very gently, "that I am more dangerous than him. In the long run, far more awkward to cross."

Mr Gould nodded again. He was in fact between the devil and the deep sea.

But being so placed he decided that the only policy was to say as little as possible.

So Hazlerigg let him go.

10

A Session at the Green Boy

April passed quietly.

In the absence of a single positive piece of evidence to connect them with the death of Doctor Potts, Conlan and Bates were dismissed with something bordering on an apology, and returned to prop up the corner of Frith and Old Compton Streets, in the intervals between playing endless games of seven-ball in the pool room underneath the Mogador.

Mr Legate and Brandison continued to serve the Stalagmite Insurance Corporation, each in his respective capacity, and 'Tiny' Anstruther announced his engagement to Miss Pocock. The other members of his department subscribed to buy him a silver cigarette box with the crest of the Stalagmite engraved on the lid, and Mr Legate handed him a small cheque with the best wishes of the directors.

Hazlerigg did a lot of work, mostly on other cases, and Inspector Roberts continued to watch Luciano ceaselessly. Possibly to show his appreciation of these efforts Luciano led a model life and sent the Inspector a case of 1926 Champagne Grand Prix on the occasion of his birthday – a present which Inspector Roberts had regretfully to decline.

Lord Cedarbrook remained continuously absent and Cluttersley, for the seventh week in succession, drew the house-keeping money from the bank and placed on the growing pile on the library table yet another unopened copy of *The Times*.

Nap and Paddy both worked hard at their jobs and kept their eyes and ears wide open – and learned nothing at all.

And so it went on, until the first week in May, when Paddy, in the course of his daily routine, happened to visit a financial pirate who had his office in a cul-de-sac at the Bank of England end of King William Street.

The pirate, whose name was Stacey Loveless, was a jolly, tubby little man, with a button nose, ruthless light blue eyes, and a nice round bald pink patch on the top of his head. His office was his poop deck and his Spanish Main stretched from Lombard Street to the Stock Exchange. (He does not feature very prominently in this particular story and we will therefore only mention here in passing that he was resourceful, amoral and entirely parasitic, and that no well-ordered Socialist state should have tolerated his continued existence for a moment. He made a very comfortable living out of other people's mistakes.)

Paddy had often had occasion to visit him and had never found him doing anything very much at all – though once when he himself had been kept late, he had happened to pass Stacey's office at seven o'clock at night and had seen the lights still on in every window. But then Stacey's employees were unlikely to complain, since he paid them twice as much as any other employer in the City of London, exacting in return complete silence and discretion about his affairs.

When Paddy had finished his business with him – it was an enquiry about a South American railway which possessed little permanent way, less rolling stock, and absolutely no paid-up capital – Stacey Loveless made his customary suggestion.

"All right," said Paddy, who was becoming hardened to this aspect of City life. "Where?"

"The Green Boy."

"OK," said Paddy. "Only it's always so infernally crowded."

"Not if you set about it in the right way," said the pirate, slamming on a bowler hat and seizing an umbrella as if it had been a cutlass or a boarding axe. "Come on. I'll be back in half an hour, Miss Greig."

"No you won't," said Miss Greig.

"If that call comes from Newcastle tell them there's nothing doing,"

"Very well, Mr Loveless."

"And if Buster calls tell him where I've gone."

"Very well, Mr Loveless."

"Marvellous girl," said Mr Loveless. "When she first came I said, 'Why do you look at me like that? Are you expecting me to seduce you?' and she said without batting an eyelid, 'Well, you're paying me so much more than I'm worth, Mr Loveless, that I couldn't help wondering'."

Mr Loveless roared with laughter, dodged in front of a bus, and pushed his way into the bar of the Green Boy.

The place was absolutely crowded and it was only by dint of some pretty ruthless work with his umbrella that Mr Loveless got through to the back. Here he seized Paddy by the arm and pushed him through a door marked "Private. Management Only". Inside, in a small parlour furnished in the exquisitely uncomfortable style of the 1890s, three men were sitting at a table drinking out of half-pint glasses something which looked to Paddy uncommonly like turpentine.

"Hullo, Stacey."

"What cheer, soaks," said Mr Loveless. "Introduce a friend of mine – "

"Pleased to meet you – take a seat – have a drink," said the man who had first spoken. He was one of the fattest men Paddy had ever seen outside of a circus.

"What is it?" asked Paddy, seating himself cautiously on a black horsehair sofa, crenellated in mahogany.

"Bullocks' blood," said a dapper party in striped trousers. "Strong ale and rum – extremely costive."

"What's new, Stacey?" said the fat man.

"Nothing you don't know," said Mr Loveless with a grin. "Heavy industrials are down. The market remains quiet."

"You don't say," said the fat man. "It must be the weather. The same again all round, please, miss. Have you heard the story that's going round about the Divorce Court Judge and the lady tightrope walker – ?"

No one appeared to have heard the story, which had in fact only been passed for publication by the Stock Exchange that morning. It was therefore duly told and a fresh round of drinks was ordered,

"I hope you've all unloaded your cotton," said a red-faced, military-looking gentleman who had not yet spoken.

"I never carry cotton," said Mr Loveless – nevertheless Paddy thought he looked interested. "What's in the wind, Major."

"Nothing's in the wind," said the Major. "Only I see that old Gold is booked to speak at Liverpool tomorrow. You know what he's like – he can't open his mouth without taking a running jump at private enterprise. Well, I reckon it's a dime to a dollar he can't speak to a Liverpool audience without saying something pretty shocking about cotton. And you know what delicate nerves they've got on the Mersey."

Everyone laughed except Paddy, who had rather lost the point of the conversation, and was trying to calculate whether the one-pound note and two half-crowns which represented his entire liquid assets at that moment would be equal to the strain of paying for five glasses of bullocks' blood.

Stacey Loveless unwittingly saved the situation by announcing,

"I'm sick of this muck, for God's sake let's have some decent bitter."

The fat man discovered at this point that Paddy was a friend and acquaintance of the celebrated McAndrews and took the opportunity of telling him two new stories about Scotsmen and reciting a limerick dealing with a rather improbable episode in the life of the Dean of Chichester.

Paddy had just finished the laugh which custom demanded, when he heard the dapper party (whose name appeared to be Gordon – though whether this was his Christian or surname was not apparent), say to Mr Loveless: "I fancy Bairsted's on his way out, Stacey?"

"No fancy about it," said Mr Loveless. "He's finished – kaput – done for. The petition's on the file already."

"It's a damn shame," said the fat man. "It was a perfectly sound set-up and Henry was a perfectly sound chap – he used to be with Impeys, the steel people, you remember."

"Well, if he was as sound as all that," said the Major, "why's he headed for a receiving order? Don't tell me he's been got at."

"Of course he's been got at," said Gordon. "It's the oldest game in the world. They lent him money on his factory – an ordinary mortgage, of course. Very accommodating. Now they're suddenly asking for their money back. Everyone knows Bairsted could pay if they gave him time. He just happens to be short of capital. You're bound to lose money in the first year or two at a game like that. I tell you, that business of his is as sound as the Bank of England."

"It's all very well," said the Major. "But if that's so why doesn't somebody else take over the mortgage. God knows there's enough loose money floating round at four per cent these days – "

"No one's going to lend him a penny at four per cent or forty per cent," said Gordon. "Not after Stalagmite cancelled his policies. It must have cost them a thousand pounds to buy back the cover. They wouldn't have done that without inside information."

"H'm," said the fat man. "I expect you're right. They're a lousy tight-fisted crowd of grasping baskets who'd skin their own grandmothers if they could see a percentage in it – but they undoubtedly know their business."

"I'm not so sure," said Stacey.

"What do y'mean, Stacey?" said the fat man.

"Come on, Stacey," said the Major. "You can't start knocking the insurance companies. That's hearsay."

"What's on your mind?" asked Gordon.

"Oh, nothing much," said Mr Loveless. "I was just thinking of the Stalagmite – "

"What's wrong with 'em," said the fat man. "Legate knows his stuff. I should have said he was the pick of the bunch."

"Shut up, Charley," said Gordon kindly. "C'mon, Stacey, old boy, spill the beans to your pals. What d'you know about the Stalagmite."

"I don't *know* anything," said Stacey Loveless. "So you can all stop looking so confoundedly ghoulish. You're not going to hear any dirt. It's just that twice in the last month I've got the impression that they were – well, if anyone else had done it I should have used the expression 'playing the fool'."

"Seriously?" asked the Major. He suddenly seemed to be several degrees more sober.

"Not seriously enough to shake the sort of credit they've got – no. But first of all, I heard at fourth or fifth hand that they put up most of the money for Factory Fitments – "

Gordon whistled. "That's not playing the fool. That's just plain dirty," he said. "Legitimate of course, but dirty."

"Why?" said the fat man.

"Factory Fitments are the chief competitors – almost the only real competition – to Bairsted Enterprises. They both specialize in the same type of factory equipment."

"I see," said the fat man. "Yes, that is a bit Prussian, isn't it. First they float Factory Fitments, then kick Bairsted's show downstairs by withdrawing their insurance."

"All right," said Stacey Loveless. "That's dirty but not silly. Now what about this – I also heard from the same source – somebody who got it from somebody who got it from somebody else who got it, I think, from Pip – that the Stalagmite had bought a controlling interest in Syn-ol."

The information clearly meant nothing to most of those present.

"What about it?" said Gordon.

"They're quite a good little company."

"Who says so?"

"*Market News*, among others. They gave them a good write-up last month."

145

"Then it only confirms my opinion of *Market News*," said Stacey coldly. "How *can* a concern be sound when its one and only object is the making of synthetic fats from vegetable products."

"Isn't that exactly what – "

"Of course it is. The government-sponsored scheme's started already. What hope in hell do you think a private company would have of operating in competition. They won't be able to keep their prices in the same street. The stuff they produce will be half the quality and twice the price. Why dammit," said Stacey, "you might just as well set out to operate a rival Post Office."

Catching sight of the barmaid he relieved his feelings by ordering a double whisky all round.

"It sounds a bit odd when you put it that way," agreed the Major thoughtfully. "But it doesn't mean that they're tottering."

"Of course they aren't tottering. I just said I'd run across two instances recently of them playing the fool. One of them was a bit dirty, but may have been profitable. The other was plain loony."

"Unless," said Gordon, "they had reason to believe the official body would buy them out – it's been done, you know."

"Maybe," said Stacey. "And if they'd been a set of mushroom jobbers I'd have believed it. But it just didn't seem like normal behaviour for one of our biggest insurance corporations. It's like – dash it, it's like catching a bishop filling in football pools."

"So what?" said the fat man. "I knew a Dean once who doubled his stipend in the year Applejack won the Oaks."

"Charley," said Gordon, "some of the Deans you've known must have been surprising characters." Paddy found himself in a dilemma.

He knew – indeed, it did not need a great degree of perspicacity to see – that he was near the heart of the perplexity. Gathered together in that room, purely by chance, were four men. None of them had anything directly to do with the matter in hand. But all of them had a very special knowledge and experience of the world he and his friends were investigating. The dapper man called Gordon was, he gathered, an outside broker. The Major was apparently an accountant who specialized in company matters. Stacey, he knew, could be described as a financial operator. The fat man, too, belonged to the circle though he found it difficult to place him. However, he felt convinced that these four men between them could answer all the questions that were puzzling him and his friends. And the deadly part of it was that he simply dared not put a single question – in fact, he hardly dared to show that he was interested at all.

At the moment they were talking shop – and talking it freely, the result of a good many drinks, a strong community of interests and the fact that they could see no reason to be cautious. He knew well enough, however, that one unconsidered word by him would dry them up at once.

There was, moreover, a further complication. He was getting infernally drunk.

Somehow two full glasses of whisky had lined up in front of him and he had a third, half filled, in his hand.

And it was most emphatically a school in which one did not sit out a round.

"In my way of thinking," said the fat man, "all insurance companies are swindles. It's like the pools. You pay a lot in and they pay three-quarters of it back. It's money for old rope."

"They get stung sometimes," said the Major. "Look at Rosenberg's claim against the UP. That must have cost them a quarter of a million to settle."

"What's a quarter of a million to an insurance company," said Gordon. "They add a tenth per cent to the premium rate for that particular risk and it all balances out at the next audit."

"Besides," said Stacey, "it serves them right for accepting insurance on such damn silly risks."

"There's nothing you can't insure against if you try," said the fat man. "A friend of mine – he was a farmer – insured against rain on his holiday. Went to Manchester, and stayed a fortnight. Sun never stopped shining once."

"A friend of mine," said Stacey, "he was a farmer, too, insured against daughters."

"Against daughters?"

"Yes – said they represented a financial loss. Be no use to him on the farm. Perfectly normal arrangement. He got a thousand pounds if the child was a girl. Fifty per cent premium. He had to pay out five hundred if it was a boy."

"What happened?" asked the fat man.

"He had triplets," said Stacey. "Two boys and a girl, so he finished up all square."

"Stacey," said the Major, "are you telling the strict truth?"

"Any man who calls me a liar," said Mr Loveless with dignity, "stands me a drink."

"Then you must live in a permanent state of intoxication," said the Major.

The conversation seemed to have drifted away for the moment from purely financial topics. The fat man was embarked on a series of reminiscences involving most of the senior members of the Bench by name, and Paddy seized the opportunity of pushing one of the full whisky glasses in front of Stacey Loveless. The other he had perforce to begin drinking. It seemed to go surprisingly quickly.

"Stacey ol' boy," he said – and the words seemed curiously difficult to form; yet when he had formed them they seemed excruciatingly funny, so much so that he repeated them again with a giggle.

"Hullo," said Mr Loveless, "you still here?"

"Stacey ol' boy," said Paddy, "I'm absolutely broke – cleaned out. I think it's time I stood another round. I'm a round behind – two rounds behind. Can you lend me some money?"

"Never mind about that," said Mr Loveless. "I brought you here. Have the next one on me."

It was definitely the next one – a liqueur brandy – that did the trick. Paddy ceased to have any noticeable grip on reality. The faces of the four men elongated and widened and distorted in the frowsy atmosphere. The fat man shone like an enormous jovial sun; the dapper man grew so thin and tenuous that he hardly seemed to exist at all. The Major, on the other hand, became curiously more and more like Paddy's Commanding Officer in the Hyde Parks.

He confided the coincidence to the Major who laughed, whereupon Paddy laughed too, and suddenly everybody seemed to be laughing.

Fragments of conversation still came to him. At one point in the proceedings plates of bread and cheese appeared on the table – they were drinking stout at the time – and in one of the spasmodic moments of mental clarity brought about by the introduction of this solid matter he clearly heard the dapper man say, "Were you serious about the Stalagmite, Stacey?" to which Mr Loveless answered. "Of course not, Gordon. I'm never serious."

"You don't think it's going to be another You and Me smash – " The mists of alcohol rolled back before Paddy could get the answer to this.

At some indefinite period later he found himself involved in an acrimonious argument with the fat man, from which Stacey rescued him, seizing him by the arm and propelling him across the floor.

"Musn't slang your host, ol' boy," he said. "I think it's time we took the road."

"Watchermeanmyhost, didn't I stand 'm a drink," said Paddy indignantly.

"It's all right ol' boy, he owns the place," said Stacey.

Further time passed and Paddy found himself in the Bank Underground Station.

He was violently sick at the foot of the emergency stairs – but fortunately no one appeared to notice. Slightly sobered he climbed on to a Central Line train and fell asleep, waking again momentarily at Ealing Broadway. He recognized himself to be off course but decided to sit tight. Sure enough, next time he opened his eyes he was back at the Bank again. How long he would have continued to shuttle backwards and forwards on the Central Line is problematical, but fortunately at this point Nap, who was coming home early from the office, happened to find him. Taking in the situation with a practised eye he steered Paddy home and put him to bed.

11

The Financial Angle

"Mac," said Paddy next morning, "I need your help, and I need it badly."

"What you look as if you need is a large alka-seltzer and a packet of aspirin," said McAndrews in an unprejudiced sort of way. "What happened to you yesterday?"

"I got tight, Mac. Beautifully, uproariously tight. All in the line of duty."

"Nae doot," said McAndrews. "You rang me up at five o'clock last night and urged me to buy cotton. You said, so far as I could very well understand you, that you had inside information that the Government was planning to blow up the Liverpool Cotton Exchange."

"Did I?" said Paddy guiltily – "That must have been after I got home. But never mind all that now. What I want you to do, Mac, is to answer some questions and not ask me why I'm asking them – if you see what I mean?"

"Oh, ay," said McAndrews.

"First of all then," said Paddy, "have you heard of Bairsted Enterprises?"

"If you were thinking of putting money into them it's too late," said McAndrews. "They're sunk."

"I know. But do you know who sunk them?"

"So far as I know," said McAndrews cautiously, "they sunk themselves, by a process of under-production and over-expenditure."

"That's what you were meant to think," said Paddy. "But it isn't true. They were scuppered – by the Stalagmite Insurance Corporation."

"And why would the Stalagmite Insurance Corporation want to do that?" asked Mac. He sounded more interested than surprised.

"Because they had put up the money for a rival show – Factory Fitments. You remember, some time ago, you asked me to look into them, and I found out that they had been bought up at issue – well the Stalagmite did that. Then they set out to wreck Bairsteds. They lent them money on mortgage and called in the mortgage at a time when they knew that Bairsteds couldn't pay up. Then they did something or other with insurance policies – I didn't quite follow that bit – and destroyed their credit in the City so that no one else would take up the mortgages."

"That first bit's true enough," said McAndrews thoughtfully. "They cancelled their policies. The big companies have a 'get out' clause, ye ken, in some of their commaircial policies. They retain the option to cancel the policy at short notice. It costs them money of course."

"It cost them a thousand pounds," said Paddy.

"Very likely. Where did you pick up all this?"

"Some of it from Stacey Loveless – some from a little man called Gordon – "

"Ay – that'll be Gordon Epps – you've been moving in high society. So the Stalagmite are behind Factory Fitments – that's verra interesting. What else did you pick up?"

"Look here," said Paddy. "You're not meant to be asking me questions. I'm meant to be picking your brains. And I'm telling you this in confidence."

"It shall go no fairther than these walls," said McAndrews with a solemn grin. "Ask your questions."

"Well then, who is Bairsted?"

"Henry Bairsted. He used to work for Impeys, the Deptford steel people. He's been with them since the year dot. Then he started out on his own, manufacturing factory equipment – about three years ago. You know as much about the rest as I do."

"I see. Next question. Who is Pip?"

"He might be different people in different places. In what precise context did you happen to hear him mentioned?"

"Someone said that the Stalagmite was behind a firm which made vegetable fat – synthetic stuff. I didn't quite catch the name – something like syncol."

McAndrews gave a long whistle. "Syn-ol," he said. "That's a verra surprising idea. Verra surprising indeed. You're sure you're not mistaken."

"No. Syn-ol. That was it."

"The only Pip likely to know a thing like that," said McAndrews slowly, "would be Philip Van Bright."

"Philip Van Bright," repeated Paddy. "Moody and Van Bright." It seemed to him that the information was significant, but for the life of him he couldn't quite see how. His head was not in the best condition for thinking.

"They seem to feature quite prominently in this affair," went on McAndrews. "You'll recollect that they acted in the flotation of Factory Fitments, Ltd."

"Yes," said Paddy. "And as far as I can recollect Stacey said that *both* his bits of information about the Stalagmite came from Pip – that's from Philip Van Bright. Both the bit about Factory Fitments and the bit about Syn-ol – "

"If you're not sure, why don't you ask him?"

"Because he wouldn't tell me," said Paddy. "He only mentioned it yesterday because he was tight – well, not tight exactly – but anyway I'm sure that if I said anything about it to him this morning he'd dry up like a tap – "

"I expect you're right," agreed McAndrews. "Was there anything else?"

"No – there was a bit about Gold – the MP – talking at Liverpool – but I think that was a joke. And then – oh yes. What was the 'You and Me smash' – ?"

A curious change came over McAndrews. For a moment all movement ceased; then, when he turned to face Paddy, he had the look of a man who has seen a ghost.

"The You and Me smash – " he whispered. "You're certain – yes, of course."

"Why, Mac, what is it? What's it all about?"

"The You and Me smash," said McAndrews slowly, "was the biggest private financial disaster that I can ever remember. The 'You and Me' Mutual Insurance Company – you'll be too young to remember the name, but it was a big name, a name to juggle with, in the early years of this century. They were one of the most important half-dozen firms specializing in life insurance. Then, just after the war – the First World War I mean – they crashed."

"Why?" asked Paddy.

"Do you understand how an insurance company works," asked McAndrews.

"Yes. No – not really. It's just one of those things you rather take for granted. How does it work, Mac?"

"An insurance company," said McAndrews – he seemed to have recovered his equanimity, "like all truly great institutions, is a meeracle of simplicity. A great deal of money goes in at one end – that's the premium, ye ken – and a good deal, though not quite so much – comes out at the other – that's the payments to the insured. The only difficulty they experience is what to do with the money in the interim. When you realize that they may be receiving something like a hundred thousand pounds in a day – "

"Good God," said Paddy, "what's difficult about that? If anyone gave me a hundred thousand pounds I'd be happy enough. Can't they invest it?"

"That's precisely the trouble," said McAndrews. "You can't go down to the Stock Exchange with that sort of money in your pocket and get rid of it as easily as putting five pounds into the Post Office Savings Bank. It needs the most judeecious handling."

"All right," said Paddy. "I see that."

"It's the General Manager who controls the investments. That's why he has to be such a sound man. Well, the General Manager of this particular Company was not a good man. He was an out and out bad one."

"A crook?"

"Yes. Or criminally foolish. The distinction so far as he was consairned was purely theoretical. He was jailed. The company, it was found, had succeeded, under his guidance, in turning a million and a half of profit into a two million loss. Some of the money was gone for ever – in foreign stock, which was hardly worth the paper it was printed on. Some had been directly embezzled – by this man and his associate."

"So he was put into clink – and serve him right," said Paddy.

"He was, as I say, jailed. But that was not the most interesting point. After the criminal proceedings were over, the Attorney-General, on behalf of the shareholders, instituted two actions – one against the directors and one against the firm of chartered accountants who had been auditing the accounts. *Both actions failed.*"

"I see," said Paddy. He was in fact beginning to see dimly what McAndrews was driving at. "That was before the old Company Act."

"Yes. I'd almost say that certain sections of the Company Act were aimed at that decision. The directors were just the ordinary crowd – not guinea pigs, by any means. But not financial experts either. They attended board meetings and signed the cheques – and left the investment to Cummins – that was the name of the general manager."

"But the man in the street didn't like the directors getting off scot-free?"

"There was a lot of public feeling about it," agreed McAndrews. "And then the Company Act was passed – and now this new one. I haven't just studied it closely, but I fancy it doesn't make a director's responsibility any lighter."

"I see," said Paddy. "So you think that if there was a *new* 'You and Me' smash it might be the directors who got it in the neck?"

"The general manager wouldn't escape, of course," said McAndrews. "But I think that if the liabilities were on the scale you are contemplating – well, the general manager might be at the Old Bailey, but the directors would be in Carey Street."

"H'm. But the Stalagmite directors – they're not fools, are they? They must know all this."

"They're sairtainly not fools," agreed McAndrews. "Stallybrowe and Sir Hubert Fosdick are a bit long in the tooth. And Sir George Burroughs has got so many irons in the fire that he wouldn't have time to pay very close attention to the routine details of what was going on. But Charles Atkinson and Andrew B Chattell are a different proposition. They're both trained accountants and they've been in insurance all their working lives – yes, what is it?"

"Dammit," said Paddy, "every time you mention those two names together, it rings a bell. I've heard them before, I know. Not precisely in this connection, either. When Hazlerigg was talking about them the other day I had exactly the same impression – "

"And who may Hazlerigg be?"

"Never mind that," said Paddy hastily, "go on with what you were saying."

"Well then – there's Hewson-Collet, too. He's primarily a lawyer, but that doesn't mean he's a fool about finance."

"Quite," said Paddy. "Then what it amounts to is this. Any managing director nowadays who hoped to do what that other chap – Cummins – did for his Insurance Company would have to be pretty circumspect. He's in a position of authority so far as the rest of the corporation are concerned. They are his subordinates.

So the ordinary checks won't catch them. They're designed to prevent the office boy stealing the stamps or the junior ledger clerk making a commission on the side by undercharging their friends. But they're no use where the fellow at the top's concerned."

"Right," said McAndrews. "You know the saying. 'Any branch manager can rob his own branch.' It's only the outside checks which catch him."

"And in the case of an insurance company, the outside checks are the directors – and their auditors."

"Yes. And between you and me, laddie, with directors like Chattell and Hewson-Collet and Atkinson I don't see anyone getting away with anything – not permanently – not even for very long."

"One other question," said Paddy. "These investments of the Stalagmite that we have unearthed – Factory Fitments, and the Syn-ol outfit. There's nothing odd in that, is there? I mean, insurance companies don't always put their money into gilt-edged securities – "

"Preserve us, no," said McAndrews. "There isn't enough gilt-edged to go round. If you can call anything gilt-edged today. No. They'll go for anything with a reasonable prospect in it. You'd be surprised how often you dine out or go to the theatre or watch a cabaret as the guest of one of our great insurance companies. You know that the Consequential own a first division football team?"

"I didn't," said Paddy. "Are you joking?"

"Indeed not," said McAndrews. "And now, Patrick, if ye've done with your questions, I've one for you."

"All right. I guess what it is."

"Then perhaps you'll answer it. What's this all about?"

"That's just it. I can't tell you."

"Is it a police matter?"

"Yes," said Paddy. "Yes. The police are interested. But they aren't playing a hand yet. Look here, Mac, I'll make you a promise. When I'm certain that something is going to break, I'll let you in on it first."

"Fair enough," said McAndrews. "In return I have in mind a little investigation which I will make on your behalf. A professional enquiry."

So the matter rested for two days.

In the morning of the third day, which was a Saturday, McAndrews spoke to Paddy just before they both left the office at midday.

"About that matter we were discussing," he said, with a casualness so elaborate that it would not have deceived a schoolboy.

"Yes," said Paddy.

"You might be interested to know," said the old man, "that your friend Mr Legate is a man of parts. Ay, indeed, a man of many parts. Beside his job at the Stalagmite, he owns a newspaper. Not a very good one, or a very big one, but a newspaper none the less."

"The *Market News*," said Paddy with a premonition.

"The same," admitted McAndrews. "But here's something else for your private ear. And it's a thing which not more than six people in the whole of the City could have told you. He has also a controlling interest in the firm of Moody and Van Bright."

The announcement was so unexpected that it did not immediately penetrate Paddy's consciousness. When he suddenly grasped its implications he opened his eyes very wide indeed.

McAndrews, having dropped his bombshell, went placidly on his way.

Paddy went to Twickenham. He always went to watch the final day of the seven-a-side competition. It was usually a great gathering of the clans. But on this occasion Paddy avoided the crowds and went to sit on the emptier benches at the open end of the ground. There, in the sun, with the green turf in front of him, he really started to think for the first time about the affair in which he had become entangled.

He saw a brick wall, high and solid. And as he gazed at it a little crack appeared in the top left-hand corner and started to run diagonally downwards, splitting the wall as it went, And it grew wider and wider, and whole bricks came tumbling down; and now it was so wide that he could see the light shining through the crack.

12

The Experiences of a Demagogue

In the spring of that year the crowds who listen to London's street-corner speakers began to notice a new figure.

He appeared on Tower Hill and in Finsbury Square, and once, but once only, he addressed the Sunday audiences in Hyde Park. His favourite pitch seemed to be the south-east corner of Lincoln's Inn Fields.

The employees of the Land Registry, who have a dress-circle view of this latter forum, christened him the Lion of Scotland: and the name was so obviously appropriate that it stuck. For there was the thick tawny mane of hair, the pug nose, the pendulous, slightly unshaven jowl, and above all there was the great roaring voice, which would not have disgraced the King of Beasts at his kill. The accent was a sort of Clydeside.

The Lion of Scotland made a spectacular first appearance on this stage.

By a species of gentleman's agreement not uncommon in public oratorical circles, the platform had been reserved on that particular day for a speaker from a religious brotherhood – (the ones who believe in the transmigration of souls and the ending of the world at midnight on the thirty-first of December in the year AD 2000).

The Lion, arriving ten minutes before the Prophet, took possession of his rostrum and began to speak.

The prophet, when he did show up, proved to be quite a militant type, and proceedings opened with a free fight, won by the Lion on points. A police constable who was called on to intervene showed that British genius for compromise by relegating religion to one end of the platform and politics to the other.

Since the platform in question was simply a small stone pediment (designed to serve as the base for a drinking fountain) it was obvious that victory was going to depend, in the long run, less on audience appeal than on plain lung-power. And here, as we have indicated, the gentleman from Glasgow had it every time.

The crowd at his end of the rostrum grew accordingly, whilst the prophet's audience shrank, until in the end it comprised only one professional supporter (with a banner), one small girl, and a Chancery judge who happened to be passing and appeared to be much attracted by the prophet's theories on the Book of Isaiah.

The Lion of Scotland, in contrast, based his appeal on the broadest popular lines. For appeal he undoubtedly had, though it was difficult to define exactly where it lay. To a certain extent it was noticeable that he suited his style to his audience, being incendiary on Tower Hill, plausibly financial in Finsbury, and verging on the forensic in Lincoln's Inn. But those who listened to all his utterances – and to a small band of the faithful appeared to follow him from place to place – remarked one idiosyncrasy which many more reputable demagogues might well have copied. He never wasted very much time over theory.

"Get at the facts," seemed to be his motto, "and if you can't find facts, go hard for the personalities.

"Twa' days syn at Clurkenwell polis court," he informed his audience at Lincoln's Inn (it would be hopeless to attempt really to reproduce his accent phonetically, so we will abandon all but the barest indications), "a puir office boy was sent to preeson. And what was his offence? Not working? No sir, though I can well imagine that such a suggestion would come verra readily to your mind" (Discomfiture of interrupter). "His offence was that he stole twa' shillin fra' the cash box. If justice had been done that lad would have been rewarded, whilst his employers would have been sent to jail. And why? Because they were making – at that verra time – an undeclared profit of more than twelve thousand pounds per year. They were defrauding the revenue in surtax and profit tax of more than twelve thousand pounds per annum. In short they were stealing a thousand pounds a month fra' the pocket of the working man. They were picking my pocket and your pocket, yet they remained free to live in luxury, to eat of the fat of the land, to ride to their offices each morning in their Rolls Royce motter cars, whilst this puir lad, the representative of the working man, was sent to jail for the crime of taking back twenty-four pence. And in case you think I'm leeing," roared the Lion in a voice which fluttered the pennants over Lincoln's Inn Chapel, "I'll tell you the name of that firm – and I have no objection if you write it down and make a note of it – "

Whereupon he proceeded to slander in detail a well-known firm of fountain-pen manufacturers, to the enormous delight of the crowd, who, of course, lapped it up and asked for more out of the same dish.

Which, in days to come, they duly got.

(It is, on the face of it, obviously improbable that the Lion could have any real sources of inside information. Nevertheless, a few days later, newspaper readers noted a paragraph which indicated that the Investigators of the Commissioners of Inland Revenue were asking for a special audit of the books of the firm in question, and that developments were expected. Fluke or not, this did nothing to decrease the growing reputation of the Lion of Scotland.)

But the misdoings of commercial firms was by no means his only topic. Many of his favourite illustrations of the inequality of the capitalist system and the tyranny of the man at the top were drawn from service life. This was not in itself unpopular with his audience – most of whom had suffered at one time or another in the ranks of the Army or Air Force and were by no means averse from hearing their recent lords and masters taking a knock. But when, inevitably, he descended from the general to the particular, a degree of partisan spirit began to manifest itself.

One of his favourite examples was a certain Corporal Collins, of the RAF, who had apparently suffered martyrdom in various stations in England and abroad, his only offences being the trifling ones of insubordination, sedition and incitement to mutiny.

The first occasion on which the Lion encountered any serious opposition was over Corporal Collins.

As soon as he mentioned his name a small group of ex-servicemen in the front row of the crowd began to show signs of interest.

"Well I remember him," said one of them loudly.

The Lion never objected to a discussion with a member of his audience. His talks, in fact, were usually well spiced with these dialogues.

"So you remember Corporal Collins," he observed. "One of the unsung heroes of the war. What do you remember about him?"

"I remember him getting thrown out of the Corporals' Mess – the wee runt."

The crowd shouted their unmistakable delight, and the Lion moved on hastily to less delicate ground.

But it did not always pass off so easily.

One morning he was letting himself go on what he described as "Sairtain widespread and well-justified revolts" which had taken place in the previous year in a well-known RAF station in the Middle East, and had, in fact, caused a good deal of embarrassment to all concerned.

As usual he drove straight for the personalities.

"The gentleman," he announced, "who happened at that time to be officer in command of this station – if such a man had any right to call himself either an officer or a gentleman, was a sairtain – bullying – swaggering – foul-mouthed – tyrannical – beast" (on sequences like this, the Lion achieved a very effective sort of drumbeat rallentando), "who would have been more fitting had he been adorning the dock at Nuremberg than ill-treating and blackguarding men whose boots he was hardly fit to pullish – "

"And that's a lie," observed a loud voice from the front row.

The Lion said something that sounded like "Harrarsch" and enquired "A friend of yours perhaps?"

"And what if he was, you long-haired, bandy-legged son of Ananias," said the voice affably.

The Lion of Scotland now took time off from the subject of the Commanding Officer and begged to tell his interrupter – whom he quickly identified as "an agent-provocateur of the upper middle class" – a few home truths about himself. To which the Voice, who appeared to be quite unabashed by his sudden prominence, replied in kind, even gaining a point or two in the exchanges by describing the Lion as a blaggarding down-at-heels keelie.

Stung possibly by this salvo – for 'Keelie' is a word which no Glaswegian loves – the Lion made the fatal mistake of stepping down from his platform.

It was not that the Voice – who turned out, on closer inspection, to be a very small man with a very large "Flying Officer Kite" moustache – showed any undue signs of truculence. Nor, indeed, that there was ever any real likelihood of violence. The crowd were enjoying this unrehearsed interlude far too much to permit of any such crude exchanges, particularly between two opponents so ill-matched in size. A number of the brighter spirits on the fringe shouted "Oh, I say, I rather go for that, what," and a few of the Lion's old friends advised the Lion to "eat him up". But tempers were well under control.

What was unfortunate was that by stepping down from his rostrum the Lion had, as it were, shifted the centre of gravity of his audience outwards, away from the quiet corner formed by the fountain and the pavement, and out into the main road.

Thus there was presently added to the cries and counter-cries of the crowd, the roaring of the Lion and the trumpet tones of his adversary, the hooting of angry horns as motorists going about their lawful business found themselves unable to pass.

This, of course, at once put a very different complexion on matters.

Constable Burt was by nature a tolerant man. In the course of his duties he had to listen day by day to the most revolutionary, incendiary, not to say nonsensical discourses from a succession of orators and usually did no more than smile at the odd passions which Theory seems to excite in the mind of man. He was a practical believer in the freedom of speech. But this was quite different. This was a Common Nuisance on the Highway, and an unwarrantable obstruction, too, of the Flow of Traffic. He was not at all sure that it did not verge on a Disturbance of the Peace.

Removing his thumbs from his belt he strode vigorously forward and the crowd parted in front of him. "Now then," he said firmly. "We can't have this. I'll have to ask you to move along."

The Lion said something which sounded like "Move your Aunt Fanny", but passion combined with a Glasgow accent made it difficult to be certain. The sense, however, was plainly negative.

"Then I'll have to ask you to come along with me," said Constable Burt.

Which was how the Lion happened, next morning, to climb into the dock of a Central London police court and face the candid gaze of Mr Blinkhorn, the kindliest and wisest of our Metropolitan magistrates.

The Lion, whose name appeared from the records to be James Watson, glared round the court in the manner of a practised actor assessing the reactions of a first night audience and pleaded not guilty.

Mr Blinkhorn invited Constable Burt to take the stand and to put him in possession of the facts; which Constable Burt obligingly did.

Mr Blinkhorn then turned to the prisoner and asked him if he had anything to say.

"Sairtainly," said the prisoner. "It's a lee."

"What is a lie?" asked Mr Blinkhorn patiently.

"What that pullisman says. It's nothing but a lee. I'd be black ashamed to tell such a lee in a court of law. I never caused any obstruction. If the crowd obstructed the traffic," concluded the prisoner reasonably, "is it my fault?"

Apparently Mr Blinkhorn thought it was, and proceeded to explain to the prisoner some of the intricacies of the English Law of Nuisance.

At the end of which he formally found James Watson guilty as charged and enquired of the prosecution whether anything was known about the prisoner.

It was then that something rather unexpected happened – unexpected by Mr Blinkhorn, to whose experienced eye Mr Watson had not the look of an habitual criminal; equally unexpected, apparently, by the prisoner himself.

A quiet man, hitherto unnoticed, got to his feet, entered the box, took the oath in a practised manner, and introduced himself to the court as Colonel Smith-Wright, attached to the Adjutant-General's Department. He said respectfully:

"In view of the fact, sir, that this man's previous convictions have been by Courts Martial, I have been asked to produce the records. So far as I know he has no civil convictions."

"I see," said Mr Blinkhorn; he was clearly at a loss. "Yes. I suppose I can hear this. If it's relevant."

"That's for you to say," said Colonel Smith-Wright non-committally and without further ado he proceeded to relate the story of Private James Watson as derived from his army records.

It was quite an impressive recital.

"I see," said Mr Blinkhorn. "Three times under section forty. Then three times for assault – and once for mutiny." He turned to the prisoner and said, "You don't seem to have had a very happy time in the army, do you? I think I'll remand you in custody for a week."

"I protest," said the Lion in his most leonine voice.

"Your protest is noted," said Mr Blinkhorn gently.

For a moment there was a curious little battle of wills. Then the Lion turned round and allowed himself to be led back to his cell.

Harry Hyde, who wrote a column on the Courts for one of the left-wing weeklies (in imitation of the sort of thing produced by the evening papers), scribbled desperately. The scene had appealed to him. And he sniffed at the story behind it. It had news value. And would appeal greatly to his particular editor. Something odd about that, he said to himself. I've never heard military convictions used in a police court before. And old Blinkhorn isn't a country JP. He knows his stuff all right.

Also he had a conviction that he had seen the prisoner before.

The surprises of the morning were not over.

As the journalist was leaving the court, one of the policemen who was acting as usher tapped him on the shoulder and said,

"Step in here, would you Mr Hyde."

"Certainly. What is it, Groves? A pinch."

"No, no, Mr Hyde. A gentleman wants a word with you."

He led the way into the clerk's office.

Inside was a medium-sized, heavily-built man, with a grizzled moustache and light-blue eyes, who introduced himself – quite unnecessarily as it happened. He said: "Just a word in season, Mr Hyde. We always get on very well with you gentlemen of the press. We do our best to help you and you do your best to help us."

"Certainly," said Mr Hyde.

"Then I'm sure we understand each other."

"You don't want anything in the papers about that case this morning?"

"That's right. I happened to notice you were the only representative of the Press in court. And I may say I was considerably relieved. You see I knew we could rely on *you*."

"Of course," said Mr Hyde.

Nevertheless he left the Court a badly puzzled man. For he was an experienced newspaperman and he knew enough about the workings of the Metropolitan Police to realize that it could hardly be an ordinary case which brought the head of the Special Branch down to a magistrate's court.

He went back to his office in Fleet Street and sat for ten minutes scribbling on his blotting-pad and thinking furiously. Then he unhooked the telephone receiver and asked for an outside line. And talked long and earnestly.

A week later he sat in the same court. But if he had expected fireworks he was disappointed.

Mr Blinkhorn addressed the Lion in his usual urbane and conversational way.

"At the previous hearing," he said, "we listened to a list of your army convictions. I do not propose to go into the question – the rather vexed question – of whether these should be admissible against you as evidence in a criminal court. To my mind the question does not arise. Not that I approve of the line of conduct you appear to have adopted in the army. It reflects, if I may say so, little credit either on your character or your patriotism. But that is as may be. When I examine the charge which is at present being brought against you, I observe that it is one of obstructing the traffic. Now I cannot see that this has any possible connection with assault, violence and sedition – which were the charges made against you by the military authorities. If the charge on which you are in front of me had been one of assault, I might have thought differently. As it is I shall find you guilty as charged and fine you forty shillings. Do you understand?"

The prisoner appeared to have grasped the basic point.

"You mean I can go for two pund?"

"Yes," said Mr Blinkhorn. "That is exactly what I mean."

"How can I pay two pund," enquired the prisoner, "when all my money has been snatched by the polis?"

"They will now give it back to you," said Mr Blinkhorn patiently. "How much had he on him when you arrested him!"

"Three pounds sixteen and fourpence, sir."

"Very well. Give him the balance. I take it you elect to pay? Yes. Well don't let me see you here again, Mr Watson. Good morning."

If Mr Watson thought it was a good morning he refrained from saying so.

Thereafter, with the most curious consistency, the Lion seemed to encounter trouble.

At first it was no more than ordinary heckling – with which he was competent to deal. But as time went on it seemed to become both more personal and more organized. Had such an outrageous thought been possible, it might even have been supposed that the police had taken to heart the remarks made by Mr Blinkhorn in his summing up and were determined that the next time that James Watson was arrested it *should* be for assault.

(That is to say, in any less well regulated country than England, the thought might have occurred.)

Be that as it may, there is a limit to everything – even to the patience of a Lion.

It was again in Lincoln's Inn Fields that the unfortunate incident took place. It was difficult, even in the light of after-knowledge, to sort out exactly what happened. Everyone is agreed that the Lion stepped down from his platform to reason with a heckler. Then someone pushed someone else, someone else hit someone, and bingo! Before anyone knew quite what was happening a fight had started.

Police Constable Burt blew his whistle, and went in resignedly to break it up.

Which was how James Watson again came to face Mr Blinkhorn.

Mr Blinkhorn was not amused.

169

"Twice in three weeks," he observed. "You know, you're becoming a bit of a nuisance. Not guilty, I suppose. Quite so. Let's hear the witnesses."

Once again, more in sorrow than in anger, Police Constable Burt gave his evidence. It seemed that James Watson, not content with haranguing his audience, had on this occasion resorted to more direct arguments and had struck one of His Majesty's lieges, William Bird, causing him bodily harm. To whit a black eye. William Bird was present and would both testify to the facts and exhibit the damage to the court.

"All right," said Mr Blinkhorn. "One thing at a time."

He turned to the prisoner and asked him if he would like to question Police Constable Burt.

"The prisoner is represented," said a voice genially, but firmly, from the solicitors' bench.

Mr Blinkhorn looked, for a moment, like a pedestrian, who, proceeding along a pavement in the dark, impales himself on an unsuspected scaffolding pole.

Recovering, he said, "Certainly, I'm sorry, Mr Rubinstein. I didn't know that you were in this case – "

Mr Rubinstein smiled genially. He was the most experienced criminal lawyer in London, and Mr Blinkhorn knew it, and Police Constable Burt knew it, and Mr Rubinstein sometimes even suspected it himself.

"Now, constable," he said briskly, "I should just like to take you over your statement once more. You say that you actually *saw* the prisoner strike Mr Bird."

"Yes, sir."

"I feel it is only fair to warn you that I am calling a number of witnesses – people of unimpeachable veracity who were actually in the crowd – who will state quite unequivocally that the prisoner was *not* the man who struck Mr Bird – "

"Well, sir, I can only say what I saw – "

"Quite so. Or what you imagined you saw, eh? Now how near were you standing?"

And so on, and so on.

170

It was really child's play for Mr Rubinstein who had done it all hundreds of times before.

In five minutes Constable Burt was not quite sure what he had seen himself and in ten minutes no one believed he had seen anything.

Thirty minutes later James Watson was leaving the Court without a stain on his character.

He seemed slightly dazed.

In the foyer he overtook Mr Rubinstein and stopped him. The Lawyer was obviously in a hurry, but he inclined his head courteously and listened whilst his humble client expressed his thanks.

"No trouble," he said. "No trouble at all. I enjoyed it. Now I really must be off – "

"But who – " said Mr Watson. "I mean. It was very good of you. But I didn't – "

"Quite so," said Mr Rubinstein. "You want to know who instructed me on your behalf. It was a friend of yours. A close friend. A Mr Jones. I really must be going now. Conference in chambers. I'm sure you understand."

An impartial observer would have doubted the truth of these last words. As the busy lawyer pattered away a look of the deepest puzzlement overspread Mr Watson's face.

And as Mr Watson went on his way towards his little bed sitting-room in Acton, this puzzlement seemed to grow.

Mr Watson, in fact, had the look of a man who is in the toils.

He seemed to be the sport of contending powers, powerful but unseen; like the royal baby in the fairy story, round whose christening there circled a potent host of fairy godmothers bringing unpredictable gifts of good and evil.

Or possibly it was simpler than that. He may merely have been wondering who the hell Mr Jones was.

When he reached his house he let himself in and set the table for lunch. He spread a clean sheet of newspaper on the table, turned up the gas ring under the kettle, cut some bread and margarine and brought out some slices of cold sausage from a paper bag in the corner cupboard. A jar of pickles and a small and rather stale square of cheese completed the repast. When the kettle was boiling he made tea, straight into a big mug, using an infuser.

Brown sugar and condensed milk went into the tea.

The meal seemed to revive Mr Watson. When the last flake of cheese had been washed down with the third mug of tea he took out a cigarette, belched comfortably, and sat down with his feet on the guard in front of the hob.

An occasional coal dropped in the grate, the old alarm clock ticked on the mantelpiece and outside in the street the cries of the children and the bells of the errand boys' bicycles sounded faintly through the tightly closed window.

Mr Watson might well have dropped off to sleep, but it is a fact that he did not. As the room grew darker the fire flickered up and its light was reflected from his open brown eyes. He looked like a man who is waiting for something to happen, without being very sure what it may be.

A double knock on the outside door and the flip of the letter box announced the arrival of the evening post and brought the landlady down into the hall. Evidently one of the letters was for him, for with a perfunctory knock she came in, apologizing when she saw him in the room."

"One for you, Mr Watson," she said. "A twopenny-half-penny."

"Indeed," said Mr Watson gravely.

He waited until she had gone and then opened the envelope neatly with his cheese knife. It was typescript, as was the letter inside.

This was on glossy paper, with a black and expensive looking heading "A and D Jones. Theatrical and Literary Agents, 105 Henrietta Street."

The note was short, and indicated that Mr Jones (or possibly both Mr Joneses) would be very grateful if Mr Watson could see his way to calling on them at two o'clock on the next day.

The offices of A and D Jones, as viewed by Mr Watson from the outside, on the following afternoon, hardly lived up to their notepaper.

Number 105 was a moderate-sized block of what might once, a very long time ago, have been respectable shop premises. A wooden indicator board inside the front door showed that it was now given over to a surprising number of professional and commercial enterprises. Messrs A and D Jones occupied two rooms at the back of the third floor: the principal drawback to which, as rooms, seemed to be the fact that they possessed no outside windows at all. The outer one was occupied by a pale young man, who received Mr Watson without interest and asked him to sit down.

Mr Watson sat patiently on the edge of a chair.

Presently a buzzer sounded and the pale youth climbed to his feet and opened an inner door. Evidently his reception was encouraging, for he looked back at Mr Watson and said, "He'll see yer now."

Mr Watson said nothing, but got up heavily and moved through the door which the youth held open just sufficiently for him to insert his bulk. A paunchy-looking man rose to greet him. His wavy black hair was so thickly greased that it had something of the solidity of marble – but, quite frankly, this was the only thing about Mr Jones which in any way suggested a classical stature.

As he extended a plump hand Mr Watson was able to count five gold rings glittering thereon – two on the index finger and one each on the other three. No doubt had he been able to find one big enough, he would have worn one on the thumb as well. He said, "Glad you were able to get here, Mr Watson."

"Look here," said Mr Watson directly, "What's it all about?"

"I'm afraid I don't know what you mean?"

"You know fine what I mean," said Mr Watson. "Why did you write to me? Who told you where I was living? And that felly at the polis court – "

173

"Mr Rubinstein. Yes? A very good lawyer, I'm told. A little expensive perhaps. But you always have to pay for competence."

"Aye – but who paid?" said Mr Watson, going, as usual, straight to the point.

"Well," said Mr Jones, "I don't know that I'm bound to account to you for all my good deeds – but as a matter of fact I don't mind telling you. It's a little organization of which I have the honour to be the representative. A philanthropical organization, one of whose objects is to help those who are in trouble – "

"Am I in trouble?"

"My friend," said Mr Jones, "You certainly are. You're in trouble with the police. You're in trouble with the Special Branch. You're in trouble with the War Office. In fact, I've rarely met anyone who was in more trouble – "

"What for would they want to trouble with me," asked Mr Watson slowly.

"That's what I want to find out. To start with, perhaps you'll excuse a personal question – "

"Perhaps," said Mr Watson in an unpromising sort of voice.

"Is your real name Watson?"

"No – it isn't."

"Would it perhaps be – Wilson?"

"It might be."

"Any relation to Angus Wilson – who got into such trouble last year, owing to the stupid suspicions of the security police at the Government Research Station in Bedfordshire?"

"Angus was my brother," admitted Mr Wilson, alias Watson.

"I see – I thought I recognized a slight resemblance from the photographs – he was younger than you, of course."

"Angus is my youngest brother. There's no harm in him at all. He was framed – "

"Of course," said Mr Jones. "Of course. Just as they are trying to frame you."

Mr Wilson looked so genuinely surprised at this that Mr Jones almost permitted himself a smile, at any rate, he parted his lips a fraction and two or three gold teeth glittered genially in the light of the lamp.

"Do you mean to say," he said, "that you didn't realize *that*. Really, Mr Wilson, such simplicity is refreshing. That little man with the large moustache at your meeting three weeks ago – he's a police agent – and all those gentlemen who have been patiently following you about ever since – did it never strike you that their efforts were directed – rather crudely directed, I might say, into getting you into trouble?"

Mr Wilson seemed to be taking this in rather slowly. But again he went to the heart of the matter.

"What for would they want to get me into trouble," he said.

"Well," said Mr Jones reasonably, "in one way and another you have caused them quite a lot of trouble in the past few years, haven't you?"

"I have spoken as the spirit moved me," admitted Mr Wilson.

"I'll say you have. And that brings me to the point. This organization for which I work can use a man like you, Mr Wilson. So far your efforts have been uncoordinated and, if I may say so, unrewarded. We can change all that – "

He leaned forward confidentially and talked.

There was no doubt of Mr Wilson's interest. Indeed, as he listened with his mouth open, he seemed to be following every word with desperate concentration. But at one point his attention was diverted. He had a very keen sense of smell, and it was not difficult to detect that a cigarette of a particular and expensive Mid-European blend had been smoked in the room and smoked quite recently. Mr Jones did not look at all like the sort of man who smoked expensive Mid-European cigarettes. Nor was there an ashtray on his desk.

But there was a curtain in the corner, and Mr Wilson surmised that it might cover a door – possible a private exit.

He brought his mind back to what Mr Jones was saying.

"And this other felly," he enquired. "The one you say will be putting up the money. Would you be wishing me to see him."

"He'll certainly want to see you."

"Where?"

"He's not very certain of his movements in the next few days," said Mr Jones, "but if you'll be so good as to call back here tomorrow, I'll make all the arrangements."

As Mr Wilson turned to go a last thought struck him.

"What's the felly's name," he said, "the one I'll be seeing tomorrow."

"Rose, Mr Bernard Rose."

The following day, in the most perfect weather, Mr Wilson accompanied Mr Jones on a short journey. It was one of those unbelievable days that sometimes graces the end of May or the beginning of June, when the sky is blue and the sun warm, but not too warm, and every breeze seems to have blown straight from the Garden of Paradise.

Even the prosaic landscape of North London as seen from a tube train seemed to take on its own beauty.

The Edgware train took the two men sedately out into the open at Finchley, and slid quietly northwards. It was midday, and the carriages were empty, and station after station almost deserted.

They finally got out at Burnt Oak; and when the automatic door had hissed shut and the train had gone on its way they had the world to themselves.

"Do we meet him here?" said Mr Wilson in some surprise.

"Yes." Mr Jones' manner had grown appreciably shorter. He seemed almost nervous.

"It seems an odd sort of place for a meeting," said Mr Wilson.

"Why? Can you think of a quieter one."

"No. It's quiet enough. How will he come?"

"By train. Did you think he was going to – " Whatever Mr Jones had meant to say, he evidently thought better of it. After a minute he went on more amiably.

"He'll be arriving in a train from Edgware. We can sit in the waiting-room, if it's empty. Or if not, then we can walk along the platform. It won't take long. He just wants to ask you a few questions."

"He's paying the money," said Mr Wilson agreeably.

Two trains had come from the direction of Edgware, and passed on their way without incident, before Mr Jones looked at his watch and said "This will be the one. He'll be in the end carriage. Come on."

Both men moved up to the far end of the platform.

The train slowed, and then stopped. The doors slid open.

A slim, grey-haired man stepped out.

For a moment he stared at Mr Wilson, and for a long moment Mr Wilson stared back at him.

"Stand away," shouted the guard.

As if the cry had broken the spell the slim man jumped back. The doors closed. The train gathered speed, rounded the bend of the cutting and disappeared.

Mr Wilson was breathing as if he had been running. He turned to look at Mr Jones, and it was noticeable that his hand was in his jacket pocket.

Mr Jones, however, was in no state to contemplate violence. He was clearly frightened out of his wits, and the heat of the sun was insufficient to explain the great beads of perspiration which were standing out on his face.

When he spoke he sounded very old.

"You knew him," he said. "He knew you."

"Yes," said Mr Wilson, alias Watson, very gently. "Yes. We knew each other."

13

The Personal Angle

"Who the Devil is Henry Bairsted, Jenny?" said Nap, breaking off the dictation of a complicated letter on Death Duties.

"I don't know. Isn't he someone Paddy keeps talking about. Some financial person – "

"That's it. I knew I'd heard the name."

"What makes you ask?"

"I've had a phone message," said Nap. "It's from someone who got it from someone who got it from someone else, but I think it came originally from Uncle Alfred."

"Lord Cedarbrook?"

"Yes. It was a bit cryptic, like most of his messages, particularly at fourth hand. But I gather he thinks it important that either Paddy or myself should attend at the Bankruptcy Court this afternoon."

"Is that where this Mr Bairsted is being tried?"

"It isn't called a trial," said Nap, "though it amounts to about that. It's a Public Examination in Bankruptcy. Have you ever heard one? Well, come along too, then. You can always pretend to be there on business. Take some notes or something."

It was glorious weather still. Nap was in his shirtsleeves and Jenny was wearing a low-cut print frock, which had caused Mr Rumbold senior – on catching sight of it in the passage that morning – to reflect that solicitors' offices had changed since he was an articled clerk.

Nap and Jenny had been seeing a good deal of each other during the past few weeks. In fact, ever since Hazlerigg's warning he had taken the precaution of seeing her home in the evenings.

And a very sensible precaution, too, thought Jenny. That's what men were for. To look after women. And since the two of them worked in the same office, and Paddy was usually busy in the evenings and couldn't get away, what could be more natural than that Nap should undertake this duty. Exactly and quite so.

Jenny frowned at her shorthand notebook, and drew a pentagonal sign with three loops and a tail which stood, apparently, for "the residuary personality of the deceased".

The telephone rang. It was Paddy.

"I got your message," he said. "Look here, old boy, I can't possibly make it. Can you get along?"

"I think so," said Nap. "I was just suggesting to Jenny that I'd take her along too."

"Splendid," said Paddy. "You do that. I'll try and get there towards the final curtain. What time does a thing like that finish?"

"It all depends. I suppose they usually rise at about four."

"What's it all about?"

"I haven't the faintest idea," said Nap. "Maybe we shall know when we get there."

2

The Court in the Bankruptcy Buildings in Carey Street (there used to be two such rooms, but one of them failed to survive the Blitz), is a small, not very dignified, rectangular, yellow-plaster box. It is designed on the lines of a bearpit.

The bankrupt stands chained, in a manner of speaking, to the stake in a small enclosure, upon which converge triple lines of benches. Apart from the short side benches, which are used by the ushers, law reporters and odd functionaries of the Court, there are three long lateral pews. In the front one sit the

Counsel (there is no distinction in this court between "silk" and junior). In the second bench are the solicitors and their clerks. In the back one are the hangers-on, the law students, and the occasional members of the public who look in on this legal bear-baiting.

When Nap arrived the proceedings had begun and were already going with a swing.

He identified Mr Bloom, one of the Official Receivers in Bankruptcy, a large man who sported a menacing pair of pebble glasses; Mr Collinshaw, an old and extremely bitter barrister who sat on Mr Bloom's right; and to his right again a thin barrister with a contralto voice whose name he did not know, but which turned out appropriately enough to be Tinkle.

"Now, Mr Bairsted," said Mr Bloom, consulting a paper on which he evidently had it all written down. "You were, I believe, for many years with Messrs Impeys, the Deptford engineering firm?"

"That is so."

"You were with them a great number of years."

"Yes. I joined them in 1904."

"Then you have had over forty years experience in the manufacture of steel goods."

"That is not quite accurate. Until 1914 I was on the personnel side at Impeys. From that time on I have been concerned in the production and selling of commercial steel."

"Quite so. Why did you leave Impeys, Mr Bairsted?"

"I'm afraid I can't answer that exactly. I suppose I thought that it was time I branched out on my own."

"But wasn't 1944 a rather curious time to take such a step?"

"I don't follow you."

"I mean, Mr Bairsted, with your knowledge of the commercial steel market – a knowledge which covered two European wars – were you not aware that a post-war period is a very difficult time for such an enterprise?"

"I didn't know when the war was going to end."

"You mean that you were reckoning on war contracts continuing for some time."

"No – yes – good Heavens, I don't know. You have to take a chance sometimes."

"When you are only risking your own money, Mr Bairsted," said the Registrar, "you may take what chances your fancy dictates. Where other people's money is involved it is the duty of this court to see that the project you undertook had a reasonable commercial chance of succeeding, and was not one of rash and hazardous speculation."

"Yes. I suppose so," said Mr Bairsted wearily.

"If you please, your honour – ?"

"Certainly, Mr Collinshaw."

Counsel half rose from the bench, directed a viperish look at the box and said, "Mr Bairsted, when you took this extra-ordinary step to which my learned friend has just alluded – that is to say, when you left the firm with which you had been associated for so many years – was it as a result of a personal difference with the Management?"

"Certainly not."

"It wasn't because the Management had come to the conclusion that you were too old for your post and wished to move you down to one of – er – less responsibility."

"It was nothing of the sort – I – "

"I see."

Mr Collinshaw resumed his seat.

"It's no good saying 'I see', as if you didn't believe a word of it," said Mr Bairsted with some spirit. "I repeat that I left Impeys of my own free will in order to start my own firm."

"Your remarks have been noted, Mr Bairsted," said the Registrar.

"Now, Mr Bairsted," said Mr Bloom, jumping up to resume the attack, "I see here in your statement of affairs that the premises which are occupied by your firm are subject to a mortgage – quite a large mortgage. Just over eight thousand pounds, when we include unpaid interest. The lender is a Mr Symonds. Is he known to you personally?"

"So far as I know I've never met him."

"Then how were the arrangements for the mortgage made?"

"Through my solicitors."

"And they introduced you to Mr Symonds – "

"They didn't introduce me," said Mr Bairsted. "I've just told you. I've never met him."

"I used the term in a commercial sense. Let me put it to you another way. You needed this money, and they found a client who had it. Is that right?"

"I suppose so," said Mr Bairsted.

"And you subsequently gave Mr Symonds an absolute bill of sale on your trade machinery and stock, to cover a further advance of three thousand pounds."

"But that was later. You see I needed – "

"One moment, please. Confine yourself to the question. Yes or No?"

"Yes."

"So that Mr Symonds – whom you have never met – became your principal creditor, in an amount of more than eleven thousand pounds?"

"Yes."

"If you stood so far in debt to a *secured* creditor, did it not strike you as imprudent, Mr Bairsted, to run up further large unpaid accounts – with Messrs Thomas Jamieson & Co., for instance, who supplied you with sheet metal?"

"Everybody in the trade buys their sheet metal on credit terms."

"Fortunately," said Mr Bloom, "everybody in the trade is not subject to secured debts which exactly equal their assets."

"I'm afraid that the matter didn't appear to me in that light," said Mr Bairsted.

"Quite so," said Mr Bloom.

"Your Honour?"

"Certainly, Mr Collinshaw."

"Mr Bairsted, you are a businessman?"

"Yes."

"You understand facts and figures?"

"I think so."

"You knew what your premises and fixed machinery and stock-in-trade were worth?"

"Yes. They were valued every year for the purposes – "

"Please. I am not talking about valuations. We all know how valuations are made. I am asking you if you knew what they were worth?"

"Yes."

"And how much were they worth?"

"About eleven thousand pounds."

"Quite so. Your total realizable assets were worth eleven thousand pounds, and your secured debts amounted to eleven thousand pounds. In other words, your unsecured creditors – of whom my clients, Messrs Thomas Jamieson & Co., were very much the largest, could expect exactly nothing."

"I suppose so."

"You said a moment ago, in answer to a question on the same point put to you by my learned friend, that the matter did not appear to you in that light. In exactly what light *did* the matter appear to you, Mr Bairsted?"

"I don't know," said Mr Bairsted. He was an old man and he looked his full age, and he looked very tired. "I don't know. At the time that I did it, it seemed quite a natural thing. I just didn't expect that the mortgage would be called in."

"This bill of sale, Mr Bloom," said the Registrar. "It was absolute and not by way of security only."

"That was exactly my point, your Honour," said Mr Bloom.

Thereupon ensued a very learned discussion about a recent decision referred to by all concerned as "re Ginger" – a discussion which was obviously much enjoyed by Mr Bloom and Mr Collinshaw and the Registrar, and not understood very much by anyone else.

"Now Mr Bairsted," said Bloom, at the end of it all, "the point which his Honour has just outlined to you, I expect you realize how important it is in your case – "

"I'm afraid I didn't quite follow it all," said Mr Bairsted.

"I shall try to make it plain to you, then. This Mr Symonds, whom we have heard about, not only held a mortgage on your real property, that is to say on the land and buildings, but he had also an absolute bill of sale – not a bill by way of security only, but an absolute bill of sale on your machinery stock and other trade assets. The result of this is that they do not pass to your trustee in bankruptcy. Though to all appearances you were the owner of a prosperous business – and it was no doubt for this reason that Messrs Thomas Jamieson and other firms extended you their credit – yet in fact, in actual fact" – Mr Bloom placed an enormous forefinger on the edge of the pew and leant on it until the top joint stood backwards almost at right angles? – "you had nothing?"

"I suppose that is so."

"In that event, everything has gone to this secured creditor, Mr Symonds?"

"Yes – if you put it that way – I suppose it has."

"Mr Bairsted," said Mr Bloom, "are you quite sure that you were not acquainted with Mr Symonds?"

For some seconds Mr Bairsted did not appear to see the implications of this last question. When it got home to him, he jerked his head back as though he had been struck in the face.

"I didn't," he began – "certainly I didn't. I've told you. He was a complete stranger."

"A very accommodating stranger," observed Mr Collinshaw.

"Your Honour," said Mr Tinkle, appearing to come out of a deep trance, "on behalf of my client I must object to such an insinuation."

"I think the suggestion is one which arises quite naturally from the evidence, Mr Tinkle," said the Registrar.

"Then I defer to your judgement," said Mr Tinkle. He had already had some very rough treatment from Mr Collinshaw and had been caught out by Mr Bloom, citing the wrong section of the Bankruptcy Act.

He subsided gratefully.

"Now Mr Bairsted," said the Registrar, "I should be glad if you would deal with Mr Bloom's question."

"I didn't hear any question."

"Then I will put it to you again. Was not your whole arrangement with Mr Symonds a collusive one?"

"No."

"Is it not obvious that when you started this business, you realized that you might lose money. And that you installed your friend Mr Symonds as a convenient cover – someone who could take over the valuable assets and enable you to step out, leaving your trade creditors in the cold?"

"Certainly not, I told you before, I have never even met Mr Symonds."

"And I suggest that on the face of it that is a very unlikely statement."

"I can't help what you suggest," said Mr Bairsted desperately. "It's not true. I have never met him."

A middle-aged man, sitting on Nap's left, here made a smacking noise with his lips as if he had just emptied a nice pint of draught beer. One member of the public at least was evidently relishing Mr Bairsted's discomfort.

"On a point of order, Mr Registrar," said a new voice.

A scholarly looking barrister, his rather prominent blue eyes emphasized by square-lensed glasses, had seated himself silently at the end of the front bench, on Mr Tinkle's right. The rustle of silk proclaimed a leader. Attention had been so focused on the unhappy Mr Bairsted that no one seemed to have noticed the arrival of the newcomer.

"Certainly, Mr Hilton-Carver," said the Registrar. "Do you appear?"

"Yes, your Honour. I was about to say, your Honour, that as I understand the matter – I am open to correction – Mr Symonds, who is here a secured creditor, has not entered his proof. There is, of course, no reason why he should do so. But in the circumstances it is surely not open to us to question Mr Bairsted about him. I need hardly remind the court that questions should be confined to matters which arise directly out of the statement of affairs and the claims of *proving* creditors."

"H'mm." The Registrar evidently knew his Hilton-Carver. "I think the point is within my discretion as arising out of the Debtor's conduct. However, Mr Bairsted in any event has denied all knowledge of Mr Symonds. There is, perhaps, no need to press the question."

"If you please," said Mr Hilton-Carver. He had, in fact, achieved his objective, which was to take some of the impetus out of Mr Bloom's assault.

"Might I ask for whom my learned friend appears in this matter?" enquired Mr Collinshaw acidly. "I was under the impression that *my* clients, Messrs Jamieson and Co., were the only proving creditors."

"Then I am afraid my learned friend's impression was an erroneous one," said Mr Hilton-Carver courteously. "I represent Messrs Jeffereys, who have proved for a small account rendered of twenty-three pounds, and I hold a watching brief for Office Cleaners Limited, seventeen pounds three shillings, and the Fluorescent and Incandescent Overhead Lighting Corporation, twelve pounds eighteen and fourpence."

"I stand corrected," said Mr Collingshaw. "I should have said that I represented the only substantial proving creditor."

"As to the substance of your *clients*," said Mr Hilton-Carver smoothly, "there can of course be no question."

The Court were still working this one out when the Registrar intervened.

"We are out of order," he said. "Mr Bloom, if you please."

Mr Bloom picked up his papers and continued his examination. It was noticeable, however, that a good deal of animosity had gone out of his voice. It was all right, thought Nap, for him to bully old Bairsted when he only had Tinkle up against him, but it was rather a different proposition under the eye of Hilton-

Carver who was not only a personal friend of the Chancellor, but was notoriously a snip for the Bench himself at next reshuffle.

Why a leader of his eminence should be in the Bankruptcy Court at all, let alone representing three creditors whose total debts would hardly have sufficed to cover his brief for a morning's work, was just one further puzzle in a puzzling business.

At this moment Nap became aware that someone had sat down beside him, and looking up he saw Lord Cedarbrook. His Lordship looked remarkably fit and wore the smile of a successful impresario.

Nap was not certain whether he was intended to know his uncle or not. Since Lord Cedarbrook took no notice of him he decided that probably he wasn't.

Mr Hilton-Carver was now on his feet.

"Mr Bairsted, there is one point in connection with these proceedings that I am far from clear about. When the mysterious Mr Symonds entered into his arrangement with you, by which he was to lend you eight thousand pounds on a mortgage of your business premises, was this mortgage intended to be a permanent one?"

"I thought so," said Mr Bairsted.

"Was anything said about this?"

"Not in writing. No. But I understood that it was to be a long-term arrangement."

"And were your premises valued for the purpose of this loan?"

"Yes, of course. By Messrs Garney & Percy."

"And what was the valuation figure?"

"Eight thousand pounds."

"Really! And did it not strike you as remarkable that a businessman – I suppose Mr Symonds was a businessman – should be prepared to lend you up to the *whole* of the valuation."

"I certainly thought it was more usual to leave a margin."

"But you didn't object?"

"It was his own money. I imagined he could do as he liked."

"I am not questioning your motives in accepting the money," said Mr Hilton-Carver smoothly. "Rather I am questioning Mr Symonds' motives in lending it."

The Court sat up. The Registrar frowned and Mr Bloom started a hurried search in his file.

"Well then, let us go on to the moment when Mr Symonds decided to call in this rather improvident loan. When this happened, why did you not go elsewhere for the money?"

"I did try, but I couldn't find a lender."

"Not for the full eight thousand," agreed Mr Hilton-Carver, "but surely your premises would have been ample security for, say, six thousand?"

"There were two reasons," said Mr Bairsted slowly, "why no lender in his senses would advance me anything. One was that Symonds refused to release the bill of sale. And no one fancied a mortgage of business premises with a third party retaining an unpaid bill of sale on the machinery and contents. The second reason was that the Insurance Company chose that moment to cancel my policies."

"That would be the Stalagmite Insurance Corporation?"

"Yes."

"And the policies?"

"A comprehensive, a workman's compensation and a three-year trading loss policy."

"And they cancelled all three?"

"Yes."

"Without giving any reason?"

"They hadn't got to give any reason. There was a clause in the policies allowing them to get out on payment of a certain sum. I thought it was purely a nominal arrangement. I never thought it would be used."

"If you don't mind me saying so, Mr Bairsted, your judgement – or perhaps your luck – seems to have let you down twice rather badly. You told us that you imagined that Mr Symonds would not call in his mortgage. He did so. You imagined that the Stalagmite would never cancel their policies. They did so."

"Yes."

There was something in Mr Hilton-Carver's manner which his listeners found difficult to understand. Although his questions were straightforward enough, and were put to the man in the box, there seemed to be some purpose behind them. It was almost as though, in fact, they were not being addressed to Mr Bairsted at all.

"I will put it to you another way," said Mr Hilton-Carver. "Mr Symonds and the Stalagmite Insurance Corporation between them seem to have been too much for you."

"Really – " said Mr Bloom.

"Your Honour – " began Mr Collinshaw.

"Mr Hilton-Carver," protested the Registrar, "are you serious in the allegation you have just seen fit to make? Are you suggesting that Mr Symonds was able to influence the Insurance Corporation?"

"Certainly not, your Honour. I am suggesting that the Stalagmite Insurance Company influenced Mr Symonds. That Mr Symonds was in fact a nominee of the Stalagmite Insurance Corporation."

"But Mr Hilton-Carver. What possible motive could an Insurance Company – a Company, that is, of the standing of the Stalagmite – have for doing such a thing?"

"I think we are a little outside the scope of our enquiry," said Mr Hilton-Carver, "but if you invite me, then I could make one or two suggestions. It might be that the Stalagmite Insurance Corporation was interested in some business in direct opposition to Mr Bairsted's, which would, of course, profit from the extinction of a competitor."

"Surely," said Mr Bloom, "on ethical grounds alone that is a highly improbable suggestion."

"I am afraid that I am not as conversant as my learned friend with the morals of an insurance company, but it should be borne in mind that I did not say that this was the explanation. I said that it might be. Actually, if it is proper to enquire into the motives behind the actions which had led up to this bankruptcy, I think we should find that they were more – er – personal than financial."

In the silence which followed, the spectators seemed to become aware for the first time of some of the undischarged artillery in the atmosphere. Nap felt a savage jerk, and looking down in alarm saw that the middle-aged man on his left (whom he had noticed before) was grasping the bar in front of the benches so tightly that it was quivering like the rail of a ship at speed.

The Registrar said very seriously: "Mr Hilton-Carver, I think I need not remind you of the professional relationship in which you stand towards this court – and therefore I need not ask you if the suggestion you have just made is a serious one. It is hardly in my province to criticize the line you have seen fit to take. However, have you any other questions which you wish to put to the debtor?"

"With your Honour's permission," said Mr Hilton-Carver, "I have a few further questions. The suggestion I put forward was a perfectly serious one, and the questions I have to ask bear on it."

"Very well."

"Mr Bairsted. You have told the court that when you worked as Messrs Impeys, the engineering firm, you started in the personnel department."

"Yes."

"You were in that department in 1911?"

"Yes."

"What was your job exactly?"

"I was in charge of postings."

"So that if an employee of the firm had to be taken on, or dismissed, the orders would come from you."

"Well – not exactly."

"I don't mean that you would decide the policy behind the orders. I simply mean that you would implement the order –

interview the man concerned, decide the amount of wages to which a man might be entitled in lieu of notice, and so on."

"That is correct."

"Not a job which would be likely to make you very popular."

"No. That, in fact, is why I eventually asked for a change and transferred to the production side."

"Quite so. But that was not until 1914. I would like to direct your attention to the year 1911. Can you recall any untoward incidents in that particular year? Incidents which led to dismissals?"

"Yes," said Mr Bairsted. "Yes. I can. That was the year of the labour agitation. We had to get rid of a number of men."

"I should like to recall to your memory one of the men to whom you were instrumental in giving the order of dismissal. I think you will remember him, since he was one of your promising young technicians – a Herbert Lake – "

"Bless my soul," said Mr Bairsted. " 'Crimson' Lake."

"I beg your pardon!"

"I'm sorry. The expression slipped out. His friends used to call him 'Crimson'. Crimson Lake, you see. It was a sort of joke. He was a very earnest communist."

"Do you think such a man would be likely to nurse a grudge against you in particular."

"Yes," said Mr Bairsted. "I suppose he might. There was a very unpleasant scene when – yes."

"Your reticence does you credit, Mr Bairsted, but I think the court should have the facts. When you informed Lake that he was to be dismissed for his share in a Union demonstration, there was an unpleasant scene in your office?"

"Yes."

"Lake attacked you?"

"Yes. But I don't think it was as bad as it seemed on the face of it. We found afterwards that he had been hit on the head during an incident in Hyde Park and was suffering from delayed concussion – "

"Nevertheless, he assaulted you."

"Yes."

"And the police had to be brought in?"

"Yes. And then he wounded a constable. I don't think he knew what he was doing."

"That can hardly have been the view of the court," said Mr Hilton-Carver, "since he was sentenced to six months' imprisonment without the option of paying a fine."

"I suppose not."

"Then I put it to you again, that you have in Herbert Lake a man with every personal reason for a grievance against yourself."

"Yes."

"I take it then, Mr Bairsted, that you were not aware, when you entered into these business arrangements, that Herbert Lake changed his name after he came out of prison and is now the managing director of the Stalagmite Insurance Corporation."

A genuine and perfectly timed *coup de théâtre* often affects the actors as well as the audience. As Mr Hilton-Carver touched off his meticulously prepared bomb-shell the court sat for an appreciable moment as if turned to stone.

Then the silence was broken from an unexpected quarter.

The man sitting next to Nap climbed to his feet and stumbled out towards the door. Since no one else was either speaking or moving all eyes turned for a moment on him.

Then the Registrar resumed command of the situation.

"I understand, Mr Hilton-Carver, that the line you are taking is that this was a forced bankruptcy."

"That is so, m'lud."

"In view of the new evidence that has been adduced, I take it that the Official Receiver will want an adjournment – "

Mr Bloom signified that this was exactly what he did want. He also looked as if he could have done with a stiff drink.

The court accordingly recessed.

14

Assorted Acts of Violence
with Surprising Results

As soon as they got ouside, into the passage, Lord Cedarbrook seized Jenny's arm, motioned to Nap to follow, and set off at a great pace.

They went up the corridor, climbed a flight of stairs, went along another corridor, and turned into a room. From its appearance and furnishing it seemed to Nap that it was probably a Judge's private apartments, but Lord Cedarbrook seemed to be perfectly at home. To an aged clerk who looked through an inner door he merely said, "It's all right, Bignold, I'll slip the catch when I've finished," whereupon the aged clerk vanished.

Lord Cedarbrook saw Jenny to a chair, then turned to Nap and said, "Here's a pretty kettle of fish."

"Why," said Nap, "what's wrong? Where have you been all this time?"

"Never mind where I've been, but just tell me this. Did you know that that was Legate sitting next to you in Court?"

"Was it though? It did cross my mind that it might be – towards the end, I mean, when he reacted so strongly. Actually I've never met him."

"He knew you all right," said His Lordship grimly. "I never for one moment imagined he'd come into court himself. He's a good hater, isn't he?"

"Why should it matter," said Nap. "Even if he hadn't turned up. He could have read it all in the papers tomorrow."

"It throws out my timing," said Lord Cedarbrook. "I calculated that he'd know by tomorrow and react accordingly. Now everything's got to go back one day. There are certain precautions I meant to take. Never mind, we shall all have to improvise for twenty-four hours."

He looked so disgusted that if Nap hadn't known his uncle so well he might have felt like smiling.

"Do you mean that there's any danger," he asked.

"Of course."

"Golly," said Jenny. "When does the shooting start,"

"That's just it," said Lord Cedarbrook. "I don't think they can get anything going tonight. But it's better to be safe than sorry. Where's Paddy? I told him to come along."

"He couldn't make it. He said he might get along towards the end of it."

Lord Cedarbrook thought for a minute.

Then he said, "I expect I can find out where he's gone. I'll have some enquiries made. I think you had better take Miss Burke home, Nap. She'll have to spend the night with you."

"Uncle!"

"That's all right," said His Lordship. "Paddy'll be there too. I suppose you've got a spare bed haven't you? Or one of you can sleep on the sofa. That's fixed then. Tomorrow I'll make some better arrangements."

"But look here, uncle. Are you sure you're not making a – I mean – we're not actually being besieged or anything."

"I haven't time to explain everything, but I'll say two things. First, did you look at Legate's face when he went out of that Courtroom? No? Well I did. He was raw, I tell you, Nap, this was to have been the culminating moment of his career. This was one of the things that he'd been working for for thirty years – to see Bairsted squirming on the hook. And then – we get hold of one fact – a fact that he'd have given his right hand to keep hidden

– and not only use it but use it for Bairsted's protection. He won't be satisfied with anything short of blood."

"Let's be quite clear about it," said Nap. "Would he risk murder?"

"Up till yesterday afternoon, I should have said no. But now I'm not sure. I think that our Mr Legate is very near to the end of his rope. He knows that I know what he's up to. That's bad enough. But the stakes are higher than I thought."

Lord Cedarbrook paused. Then he said quietly: "Colonel Vassilev is in England."

Jenny caught the note in his voice and looked up quickly. Although the name meant nothing to her it clearly meant something to both men.

"I thought he was in Canada," said Nap.

"So did I," said Lord Cedarbrook. "And you can imagine my surprise yesterday when I met him on the platform of an Underground station. It was a brief but rather poignant meeting. We knew each other very well indeed. I once tried to murder him in Poland."

"How did you run across him yesterday?"

"I fished for him," said Lord Cedarbrook. "Or to be quite accurate, I set a line for him, with myself as the bait. I fooled round London with a two days' growth of beard and a rather doubtful Scots accent until I'd attracted the right sort of publicity. I had a bit of official help, of course. I sold myself, in the end, through a left-wing journalist – the Special Branch have had their eye on him for some time – and a communist agent who acts as his go-between. It was all great fun up to a point – and I'll tell you about it sometime. The moment when it ceased to be funny was the moment when I saw the old pike, Vassilev, swim up out of the pool."

"You didn't actually do anything?"

"There was nothing to do. God dammit, you can't shoot a man on a tube station platform."

"I suppose not," said Nap. "You're sure that he's in this particular show."

"Yes. I tell you, I *know* now what Legate's up to. And it's just the sort of mischief Vassilev must be up to the eyes in. Don't forget Legate's political history. He was a communist from before the last war. And he had a ready-made grudge against the capitalist class."

"Although he is now a member of it himself."

"That made him all the more useful."

"Then you mean – "

"I mean," said Lord Cedarbrook, "that when Legate has finished his work here – and he's very nearly finished it – he's got a back door to get out by. The arms of the Law may be a very formidable thing – but it's no use blinking facts. It doesn't stretch through the Iron Curtain."

"I see," said Nap. "Yes, that does make it awkward, doesn't it."

"Well, never mind about that now. For the moment the thing is to look after yourselves, and take care of Miss Burke. I think your young lady's safe enough. Warn her to stay in the hospital and take no notice of telephone calls or telegrams. I'll get hold of Paddy as soon as I can contact him. There's the devil of a lot to do."

Nap and Jenny walked thoughtfully into Carey Street. It was a perfect evening. The pavements still reflected a pleasant, tar-smelling heat and the trees in the precincts of the court looked grey-green in the twilight. On Nap's suggestion they turned left-handed and strolled through Portugal Street into Kingsway. It was difficult in such surroundings to tune the mind to melodrama. They had their evening meal in a little restaurant in Duke Street, which Nap sometimes used. It was a silent meal. Then, as the street lights were coming out, they walked back to the Temple.

As they were turning into the building which housed Nap's chambers, Jenny said a little guiltily, "I wonder what kept Paddy. I hope nothing's happened to him."

"He'll be all right," said Nap absently. "Uncle Alfred seemed certain that nothing could happen tonight. Damn this hall light.

It's always going off. Wait here a moment, Jenny, and I'll turn the sitting-room light on."

As he felt for the handle of the door he heard the beginning of a scream and swung round.

A torch came on, and Nap could see that there were at least three men in the hall.

"You keep quiet, yes," said a voice which he recognized.

It was evident that Uncle Alfred had underestimated the speed and organizing power of Luciano Capelli.

"Now everybody will keep very quiet," said Capelli.

In fact, after Jenny's first involuntary cry, no one else had spoken. Everyone stood for some minutes in the dusk of the hall listening.

Footsteps came up the stairs, paused, and went up on to the landing above.

Nap appreciated the hopelessness of the position. They were crowded together in a tiny space. He was in the light, his enemies were in the shadow. Even by himself he could have attempted nothing. With Jenny in baulk he was doubly helpless.

"Now listen," said Capelli. "When I give the say-so go outside. Tony, you go first. Then Rudi, with the girl. You will hold arms, please, we don't want trouble, eh? I am warning you that if – "

"That's all right," said Nap hurriedly – he didn't want Jenny to be frightened unnecessarily. "There's not going to be any trouble."

"That's right," said Luciano, "that's right. No trouble. You come last of all with me. *Andiamo.*"

In that order they went down the stairs, along the hall and out into the yard.

There was a car parked there. It was a French model, Nap saw, a Chaussée-six, one of those family cars, built on American lines, with a back seat which would take three easily, and a long undivided front seat which could take three more.

Luciano had evidently given some thought to the seating arrangements of his party.

"You go in the back, Rudi. The girl next, then Tony. So. That is comfortable."

Nap held his breath.

A good deal turned on the next few seconds. When he had noticed the make of the car a tiny hope had flickered up.

A driver was already seated at the wheel.

Nap moved towards the car.

"I'd better get in next," he said, casually. Perhaps a little too casually.

"No. No," said Luciano. "I do not like that. How awkward it would be for all of us if you were to interfere with the driver as we were going along, We might even be involved in an accident. We do not want that, do we? So. I get in first. Then you. Right?"

The car swung up through the narrow passage, under the arch and out into the Strand.

Nap could scarcely refrain from smiling. Everything would depend on the next few seconds but fate, combined with Luciano's excessive caution, had presented him with the chance he had been angling for.

Nap had remembered a device which had once saved the life of a friend of his during the Occupation. And it turned on the peculiar design of the Chausée motor car.

In most cars the autovac is on the passenger's side of the front seat – as indeed it was in this one – but in a normally constituted car the feed-pipe which joins it at the base runs away into the dashboard at some distance above floor level.

The makers of the Chausée, however, for some reason best known to themselves, have led this pipe right down to footboard level before returning it to the engine. It is a stout enough pipe, but is only made of copper, and copper is not the most resistant of materials.

Nap shifted carelessly in his seat, and to cover the movement, said to Luciano – "Where are you taking us?"

"You will see," said Luciano.

The car turned into Kingsway.

Nap had the iron-tipped toe of his shoe against the copper downpipe, and levering slightly forward on the ball of his foot, he exerted pressure.

Nothing happened. Nap could feel his shoe slipping.

It was terribly difficult to put the necessary force into his thrust without drawing any attention to what he was doing. Fortunately at this moment the car turned left again, rather sharply, and everyone heeled over slightly.

Under cover of this movement Nap again shifted his left foot. He now had it wedged with the heel firmly against the steel running rail under the seat.

Again he levered his leg forward – increased the pressure.

Then a number of things happened.

The pipe gave way. The car swung left again, and then right. The autovac spluttered wildly, and the car skidded to a halt.

Nap looked out of the window and gave vent to a silent but most bitter curse.

Of all the million streets in London he had chosen to engineer his breakdown in the only one which was useless to his plan.

They were in the middle of Covent Garden Market.

There are times of day, of course, when Covent Garden would have been a good place to break down in. In the early morning, and even later in the afternoon, it is thronged with large and law-abiding citizens. But from five o'clock onwards it is a desert.

"What's wrong?" demanded Luciano. He added an opinion of the driver which fortunately, perhaps, was expressed in Italian.

"Swipe me," said the driver. "You tell me. The engine's cut out. It's out of petrol!"

Nap could have told him what was happening to his petrol. It was coming out in a steady stream over his left foot, Luciano would be bound to spot it. The reek was overpowering. It was only a matter of seconds.

Thank God, here came two men.

Two large figures, in the working dress of market porters, had approached from behind and were now standing watching the car with the interest and sympathy which Londoners always find time to accord to a broken-down vehicle.

Nap uttered a prayer, seized the handle of the door, and stepped out.

He saw Luciano's hand go into his pocket.

"I don't think he dare," he thought. "I only hope I'm right."

"Thank you very much for the lift," he said loudly. "Come on, Jenny."

He had the rear door open.

The two porters had evidently decided that it wasn't a breakdown after all. They started to move away.

Tony and Rudi obviously had very little idea what they were meant to do. In the indecision the one man with a clear plan was at an advantage. A second later Jenny was out of the car.

The porters were ten yards away.

"Run," said Nap.

His first and urgent idea was to put a corner between themselves and the men, whom he could hear tumbling out of the car behind them.

In his hurry he took the first that offered and had run ten yards before he realized his mistake.

What he was in was not a street, it was one of the private ways of the market. It ran between two tall colonnades. On either side he could see the shuttered stalls. And ahead, unless he was mistaken –

"Damnation, Jenny," he said. "It's a dead end."

The way was blocked by a steel mesh gate.

The pursuit had turned the corner and was coming up fast.

Nap seized Jenny by the arm and dragged her behind a pile of something – half-seen in the dark –

The movement was evidently spotted.

There was a noise like the breaking of a violin string and something smacked into the front of the pile.

It was then that Nap realized that the men meant to kill them. The thought was a sobering one.

He put his mouth close to Jenny's ear and whispered.

"They're using a silenced gun, so keep your head down. Move along behind this stack, and see if you can feel your way round into the next bay."

Another shot hit the stack behind them.

Nap put up his hand, felt in one of the sacks and identified a turnip.

"That should keep the bullets out all right," he reflected.

"We've got to get moving all the same. We can't go back, because we shall show up against the light at the end of the passage. If we stay here they'll rush us. Can't think why they haven't already. Perhaps they think I've got a gun."

Jenny seemed to have found a way past the end of the stack so he followed her.

They found themselves in a similar bay.

"Try that door," whispered Nap. It was almost bound to be locked. At that moment he heard one of the men. He was coming round the end of the first bay they had entered. There – he was using his torch. It flashed on for a moment, then off.

It was a matter of seconds now. He felt rather sick.

Jenny was whispering something.

"Nap – the door's open – a lot of men – "

He couldn't make out the last bit, but the first sounded hopeful.

He tiptoed back after her, and saw that the door, which led into a sort of shop front, was ajar.

He eased in.

Jenny was there all right, and he realized with a bit of a shock that she was not alone. Several men were moving softly in the darkness. They were making no attempt to molest him, and as his eyes got used to the dark he thought they looked like market porters.

Nap sat down on a crate and waited. There was nothing else to do. The men must know they were there.

In the darkness he made out Jenny sitting beside him, so he held her hand. That seemed quite logical too.

They were in a sort of greengrocer's shop or selling room. The door through which they had come was rather an ill-fitting affair. Through the chinks they could see the flashes as Luciano's men hunted outside among the sacks and bales. They seemed to have lost the trail.

Presently they heard the mutter of voices in conference.

Then someone came up to the door of the shop in which they were sitting.

The handle rattled, and the door swung open. A torch flashed in the room, and Nap heard a startled exclamation in Italian from the man who was holding it.

Then every light in the place came on.

The scene which followed will always remain sharply etched on Nap's memory.

It was Luciano himself who was standing just inside the room, a big torch in one hand – its light dimmed to nothing by the blaze of the overhead arc lamps – in the other hand a gun. Behind him, crowding the doorway, were his two henchmen. But it was the figure in the middle of the room which seized Nap's attention. He was an immensely tall, broad man, with a big white gloomy face. He stood in an attitude which was at once loose and drooping, yet alert – rather like a heron fishing, thought Nap. He was dressed in black: not the black of the stage villain but the respectable black of a suburban householder. The black of a churchgoing worthy.

Nap had never seen him before but he recognized him at once from Major McCann's description.

Luciano apparently knew him.

He put away his gun, snapped off his torch, and walked a step or two further into the room. In a voice which sounded faintly conciliatory he said, "Well, Birdy, this is a surprise."

Birdy McLaughlan said nothing. Perhaps he felt that he was in a strong position. There were at least six of his men in the room, and Nap felt there were probably more at call. He recognized two of them. They were the men who had come up and stood beside the car when it had broken down.

"I did not know," with a well executed smile, "that this lady and this gentleman were friends of yours."

"They aren't," said Birdy.

Luciano was plainly at a loss.

"Well then," he said, "perhaps they had better come along with me and the boys."

"And perhaps they hadn't," said Birdy.

Nap felt that he was making things rather difficult for Luciano. So, evidently, did Luciano, who, after shooting a dirty look at Nap, decided that the only thing to do was to withdraw with what dignity was left to him.

"Well," he said, "I'll be going."

"Not yet you won't," said Birdy. "Not until I've said what I want to say." He spat with great precision, nine inches to the left of Luciano's neat dancing shoe.

"The last time we met," he went on, "I told you that I didn't like you. I said that I had no use for you. I stood up in that so-called eating house that you run and said it to you. And I gave you my reasons. Now that you've been so good as to come and visit me, perhaps you'll do the same."

When Luciano had ignored this opening – wisely Nap felt – Birdy McLaughlan went on:

"Now here are two more reasons for you. I don't like people who come into my territory and start shooting. I don't like people who come into my territory at all. When they start shooting I like them even less. That's one thing. The other thing is that from what I've heard you've been getting into bad company. Perhaps you'll tell me this. What's the *colour* of the money you've been taking?"

He put such a degree of unexpected emphasis into these last few words that everybody present looked at Luciano to see what his reply would be.

Apparently he understood the innuendo only too well. He looked quite horrible, Nap thought. Both venomous and impotent.

"It wouldn't be red, would it?" went on Birdy. "It wouldn't be a dirty filthy red?"

Without a word Luciano turned and left the room. His two men went with him. They heard their footsteps echoing along the empty colonnade.

"They've got a good walk home," said Nap. "I've wrecked their car."

"Serve the bastards right," said Birdy. "Give them five minutes and you can go too." He seemed to have lost interest in Nap and Jenny and his men had long ago resumed what they were doing. It was something to do with tins and packing cases, but Nap took care not to appear too inquisitive. As far as he was concerned Birdy could have robbed the Bank of England.

Five minutes later he and Jenny were walking quietly up the Strand. One of Birdy's men had seen them as far as the corner of Henrietta Street and had then left them without a word.

They weren't a chatty crowd.

Nor were Nap and Jenny feeling talkative.

Logically they should have been bubbling over with excitement and relief. In fact, neither of them seemed inclined to talk. They were both absorbed with their own thoughts, and when Nap's hand accidentally touched Jenny's he apologized with quite unnecessary fervour.

As a matter of form Nap asked the Temple porter to come up with them, but there was no one in his rooms. Not even Paddy, though the clock on the mantelshelf showed that it was long past midnight.

When the porter had been rewarded for his efforts and had returned to his lair below stairs, Jenny sat down on the sofa whilst Nap revived the fire.

"I wonder where Paddy is," said Jenny. "Do you think those men – some of the others have been sent after him – "

"If only he had told us where he was going," said Nap crossly, "then we might ring up and find out whether – Jenny, will you marry me?"

"Yes," said Jenny.

About an hour later, rather guiltily, they started thinking about Paddy again.

"We might try the police," said Nap. "But it seems so silly. He's probably just making a night of it – "

"Nearly two o'clock, darling."

"Yes, sweet, but you know what Paddy is."

"I don't think I ever really knew him," said Jenny. "That was half the trouble. You're different."

"I'm easy to see through, I suppose," said Nap.

"Don't be silly."

Another half-hour passed.

"Look here," said Nap. "We must do something. We can't just go to bed – I mean – you know what I mean."

"Of course," said Jenny gravely. "The proprieties must at all costs be preserved. Let's make up the fire and then we'll sit in this chair and wait for something to happen. We're bound to get news soon."

It was half past three when the telephone bell woke them.

Nap jumped to the receiver and a very polite woman's voice at the other end said, "Mr Rumbold?"

"Yes – who is it?"

"This is Night Sister in Charge. I'm speaking from Raheres. We have a Mr Yeatman-Carter here – "

"Paddy Yeatman-Carter – yes. Is he hurt?"

"He has some minor injuries. A broken collarbone. Nothing to worry about. There are two other gentlemen with him. One has a broken wrist – "

"Two other – what's it all about, Sister."

"He can tell you himself in the morning, Mr Rumbold. He wants you to come round and see him. Not before nine o'clock, please."

"It's Paddy," said Nap. "He seems to have got involved in an accident. He's in hospital. I'm to see him tomorrow."

"Someone will have to tell him – about us."

"Yes," said Nap thoughtfully. "I think you'd better explain."

"When you see Patricia you'll have some explaining to do yourself, darling."

2

At nine o'clock next morning Nap was walking along one of the spotless chlorodol-smelling corridors of Rahere's Hospital. It had been agreed that he should have the duty of breaking the news – with the proviso that he might exercise discretion if the patient's situation seemed too serious to withstand the anticipated shock.

Paddy was apparently in a private room.

When he arrived outside the door Nap stood for a moment rehearsing an appropriate opening to what was likely to be one of the most embarrassing speeches of his short life.

From the complete silence reigning on the other side of the door he imagined that Paddy must be alone.

Well he couldn't stand there for ever.

Summoning up his courage he seized the handle, opened the door and walked in.

Paddy was sitting up in bed, but he was not alone. Nurse Patricia Goodbody was sitting beside him, and they were holding hands.

It took Nap about half a second to grasp what he had seen and then the pure rich humour of it hit him between the eyes and he threw back his head and gave a great roar of laughter.

"Really, Rumbold," said Paddy in his stiffest voice. "I can't see that this is a laughing matter. It's a bit unfortunate you should have come in when you did, but believe me, I should have broken the news to you in a proper way at the first opportunity – "

He had not let go of Patricia's hand and was looking as dignified as anyone can look with his shoulder in plaster, his hair on end, and a day's growth of beard on his face.

"Nap," said Patricia, "this is going to be a bit of a shock for you, I expect."

"When did this – er – when did it happen?" asked Nap.

"The first moment I saw Patricia this morning," said Paddy. "I knew – we knew."

"It's just not possible," said Nap. "I know all about hospitals. I've been in them. Nurses come round at six o'clock. Love at first sight is a very beautiful thing, but not at six in the morning."

"Nap, you're being horrid," said Patricia.

"Really, Rumbold, making due allowances for the shock it must have been for you – "

"All right," said Nap. "It would serve you right if I kept it back for a bit longer, but I can't. Just let me tell you what I came here this morning to say – "

He told them, and one way and another it was some time before they could get down to the business in hand.

"Look here," he said at last, "we can't go on like this all morning. There's work to be done. First of all, do you mind telling me how you come to be lying here looking like a casualty clearing station – "

"It really was the most amazing show," said Paddy. "I still don't quite know how it all happened. It all started with the Hornet's Rugger Club – "

"Rugger," said Nap. "In this weather!"

"Not playing Rugger. It was the club dinner. The Hornets always have their annual dinner at the beginning of June. Of course, I don't often play now, but I like to get along to the old functions and keep things going. I keep in touch with a lot of the chaps I used to know before the war. Ronnie Selden – you remember him, Nap. He joined the Hyde Parks at the same time as you did and got a Company just before you left. And Duggie Malcolmson and little Harry Sparkes. And a lot more, too. A damn fine crowd.

"Well, the dinner was a pretty good show. We always have it in the Bell out at Winchmore Hill. The proprietor's a supporter of the club from way back, and he always puts on a good party. There was jugs of beer and Chris Carter made a most amusing speech – you should have heard some of the things he said about the government – pretty caustic, I can tell you. And then we sang a few songs. As I said, it was a good evening. But I think everything would have gone off quietly enough if it hadn't been for the Crusaders – "

"The who?"

"Crusaders. You must have heard of them. Another Rugger club. They have the ground just across the way from ours, and of course there's a good deal of healthy rivalry. I forget how it started. You know how these things are. I believe one of their forwards brought a hammer on to the field back in 1890, or something of the sort. Anyhow we always have a match on Boxing Day and it's a bit of a local derby. Well, getting on towards closing time somebody noticed that one or two types from the Crusaders were drinking our beer. They'd infiltrated into the party. I don't suppose that would have mattered, either, in the ordinary way. You get pretty laissez-aller at that time of night, and there's nothing wrong with the Crusader types – they're very decent citizens, off the rugger field. But unfortunately they had one big fat fellow there – a back row forward called Gumboil – or some name like that – who got pretty tight and climbed up on the bar and started shouting things. Well, Ronnie Selden – you know Ronnie – he got a bit tired of this and in the end he leant across and pushed him over backwards – absolutely smack-o in among all the beer barrels.

"After that things really did hot up.

"Well, I didn't want to get involved. I don't think I'd had as much to drink as some of the others, and I can't say I really care for these free-for-alls. So when the tankards started to fly I slipped out and made tracks for home.

"It's about a couple of hundred yards from the Bell down to the trolleybus stop – quite a lonely bit of road. I was strolling along, enjoying the night air and thinking about nothing in particular when a man stepped out of a side turning and stopped me. There was another chap with him. The first man asked me if I could oblige him with a light. Of course, I said yes, why not, and started to put my hand in my pocket. Well, it's odd how things occur to you, but suddenly I realized that the man with him was smoking, and a little voice in my brain said 'something phoney here. If he wanted a light for his cigarette why didn't he get it off his pal. Why did he have to stop me?' Then something else happened. We were all standing near a lamp standard, and I could see both these chaps' faces quite clearly. And by a fluke I recognized them. Yes. I'd seen them both before, and I'd seen them together. They were the two men who had been sitting, with a middle-aged woman, at the next table to me, in the smoking-room at the Pike and Eels, that night I went there with Mr Britten. All this has taken a bit of time to explain, but it didn't take a second to happen. One minute I was standing under the lamp, feeling for a box of matches. The next moment I was running. If I'd been taken entirely unawares, I'd have been sunk. It was just the chance in a million of my recognizing them that startled me. I only just moved in time.

"Number two had moved up behind me whilst number one was talking to me, and the cosh or whatever it was he was using only missed my head, and nearly broke my shoulder, and at the same time number one kicked me in the groin.

"The next minute I was running up the road and they were running after me. I think I knew that I was for it, because I was pretty dazed, and they were both fitter than I was. Luckily, without thinking, I had turned round and was running back towards the Bell, and we ran full tilt into Ronnie and Harry and Duggie coming out.

"That really must have been worth watching. The funny part was they all jumped to the conclusion that the chaps who were chasing me were Crusaders or Crusader supporters, so they weighed into them with the best will in the world. Then one of the types kicked Duggie on the knee, and Duggie got angry. Well, you know what Duggie's like.

"There was a most terrific schemozzle, which was complicated by half a dozen more people coming out of the pub and joining in on both sides. My shoulder was hurting like hell, and what with one thing and another I spent most of the time sitting quietly in the gutter being sick, but it was a first-class show, viewed from any angle."

"And they got the two men," said Nap. "That's excellent."

Paddy looked a bit surprised and said, "What do you mean –"

"They told me on the phone last night," said Nap, "that two men had been brought with you to hospital."

"Lord, no," said Paddy. "That's Duggie and Ronnie. I told you – they thought the whole thing was a rag. All we've got of the other two types is their trousers – the silly asses debagged them."

15

Lord Cedarbrook at Home

The third member of the trio was in action that evening as well.

Lord Cedarbrook, when he left the Bankruptcy Buildings, made his way straight to Pall Mall, to the more respectable of his two clubs.

It is probable that he was being followed.

Condemn the fellow, he thought. Who would have imagined that he would come to court himself. And yet – one ought to have foreseen it. It was so well in character. One knew a good deal about Legate now and really almost his most salient characteristic was that he was a good hater. A man who nursed his dislikes almost to the point of madness. No – that was the wrong word. There was nothing in the least mad about Legate. To the point of fanaticism. But you had to hand it to him. He was a brilliant organizer, and had shown himself desperately quick on the riposte.

With such an opponent, the loss of twenty-four hours might be serious.

Lord Cedarbrook took possession of one of the private telephone rooms at the club and asked for a line to be put through.

First he rang up the legal assistant to the Director of Public Prosecutions, missed him at his office, and found him at home, changing for dinner. He talked to him for nearly half an hour, and finished by making an appointment for eleven o'clock on the following morning.

Then he tried Hazlerigg's code number, and found the Inspector at his desk. Here the conversation was shorter, and it, also, concluded with the arrangement of a rendezvous.

Finally he telephoned his own house and told Cluttersley that he would be dining at his club.

Cluttersley said in a resigned voice, "The dinner is already in the hoven."

"Then heat it – I mean, eat it – yourself," said His Lordship. "And – oh – Cluttersley – "

"Yes, my Lord."

"Have you got someone you could take out to the cinema."

"Not to the cinema, my Lord. The housekeeper at number five shares with myself a taste for the classical in music – "

"Then this is your opportunity to gratify it," said Lord Cedarbrook. "Take her to a concert. Take a box at the Albert Hall. Only I must have you out of the house by eight – and don't come back before midnight. I'll let myself in."

"Very good, my Lord. I will connect the electric coffee percolator to the plug in the library."

After a solitary dinner, Lord Cedarbrook left the club, and took a taxi to Charing Cross Station. Before he got into the taxi he considerably astonished its driver by making a very careful test of the door handle to ascertain that it was not one of those cabs, well-known to readers of thrillers, the doors of which only open from the outside.

From Maze Hill station he walked home, keeping conscientiously to the middle of the road.

It was not that he anticipated any immediate trouble but he had had very considerable experience of violence and he had learnt that it never paid to take obvious and avoidable risks.

He reached his house as the church clock on the corner struck nine and made his way straight to the library. This was the room into which Nap had been shown when he had come to visit his uncle some months before. It was a finely proportioned room, and occupied the full depth of the building. Its northern windows looked down to the river, while at the other end its French windows opened on to the terrace and the strip of garden behind the house.

Cluttersley had left the curtains open, but now, although it was not yet quite dusk, Lord Cedarbrook drew them across.

Then he turned on the desk lamp which was so arranged that it also acted as reading light to the big leather armchair beside the fireplace.

Finally he switched on the coffee percolator, and made a cup of strong coffee, which he drank slowly, black and sugarless.

Then he settled down in his chair to wait. His face was in shadow, and it was not possible to be certain, but he seemed to be smiling. Possibly he was thinking of the time only three days before – it seemed much longer – when Mr Watson alias Wilson had sat in very different surroundings, also waiting on providence.

Ten struck, and eleven, before he heard the sound he had been listening for.

It was a light slurring of metal on metal, followed by a tiny click.

Then, for some minutes, nothing more. But he knew that there were men in the house.

So deft and quiet were they that he never heard the handle of the door turning.

Then, quite suddenly, he seemed to become aware that two men were in the room.

As they moved towards him, Lord Cedarbrook got to his feet. He saw that they were young men. The front one, with his clipped hair and light blue eyes, had the unmistakable look of a soldier. He was grinning. His companion, Lord Cedarbrook thought, was a plain lout.

"Who are you?" he said.

"District visitors," said the front one. "You're Lord Muck-a-muck, I take it."

His Lordship had a sudden inspiration.

"And you," he said, "are Conlan, I think."

"S' right," said Conlan. He seemed unperturbed that his identity was known, and Lord Cedarbrook realized that this was a very bad sign indeed. "You all alone?" he went on.

"There's no one else in the house."

"Keep an eye on His Lordship, Ted. If he gets restless, sing to him."

Ted grinned.

Really, thought Lord Cedarbrook, Ted was one of the most unpleasant-looking persons he had ever seen. He had a large, raw face, pinhead eyes, and a mouth with an underslung lower lip like a pike. As a boy he had, no doubt, enjoyed pulling the wings off butterflies.

Patsy Conlan went out, and a few seconds later they heard his footsteps as he left the carpeted hall and went down the service stairs which led to the kitchen and to Cluttersley's domain.

"Well, Ted," said Lord Cedarbrook, "you haven't introduced yourself."

Ted neither replied to this, nor moved from where he was standing.

"You're Bates, aren't you?"

"And what if I am," said the other. He seemed a little less sure of himself now that Conlan was gone.

'Nothing," said His Lordship. "Nothing. A fine old English name – really quite Shakespearian. One of your ancestors was at Agincourt. Are you an admirer of Henry the Fifth?"

Bates came a step or two nearer and said, "Do you want a slap on the kisser?"

Even at that distance Lord Cedarbrook could smell that he had been drinking. He wondered where he managed to get the whisky from. He thought that he ought to prod him a little further: bring him perhaps one step nearer.

"Wasn't it you and Conlan," he said very gently, "who killed poor old Doctor Potts."

"Doctor – look here, what are you calling me – "

"I'm calling you a murderer."

Bates hit Lord Cedarbrook a chopping slap across the face.

Then Lord Cedarbrook hit Bates.

It was a magnificent blow. It came straight up from the floor, not swung, but pushed, as an upper cut should be, with a last second curl to it, brought about by a twist of the elbow. It had every pound of weight and strength which Lord Cedarbrook possessed, and Lord Cedarbrook had boxed with Lonsdale.

Bates folded up.

It all happened so smoothly that an onlooker might have wondered whether it had taken place at all. At one moment Bates was on his feet, the next moment he was lying on the Axminster carpet, his great red face cradled over his arm in an absurdly childlike attitude of repose.

Lord Cedarbrook stood over him for some seconds, listening hard. Then he walked over to the desk, opened the middle drawer, and picked out a revolver. It was a huge weapon, of .455 calibre, and a last-war model; but it had obviously been tenderly cared for. After a little thought Lord Cedarbrook broke the gun, inserted one bullet, rotated the cylinder until the round lay next to be fired, clicked it shut again and laid it ready on the desk.

Bates had not stirred. From the sound of his breathing it seemed probable that it would be some time yet before he started to sit up and take notice.

Conlan came back along the passage. Confident, it seemed, that the house was unoccupied, he was no longer troubling to walk quietly – in fact he was whistling happily to himself.

He was well inside the room before he quite grasped the changes which had taken place during his absence. Then he stopped whistling.

"Come in," said Lord Cedarbrook. "Don't trouble to shut the door. Just keep walking forward."

The gun in his hand was a powerful argument. But it was not the gun alone. Patsy Conlan was used to guns. It was something altogether different. Something in the size and authority of the man who held it. Something in the unpromising lines of the mouth. More than anything it was the voice. Patsy had once attended in the gallery at the Old Bailey and had heard the judge say, "That you be taken hence to the place from which you came, thence to a place of execution – "

"All right. Now stop."

Conlan stood still.

"I've got three questions to ask you. Whether you answer them or not is entirely your own affair."

"You're telling me."

"But before you indulge in any more pert answers I'd better perhaps explain to you that you're not in a very happy position. You and Bates broke into my house tonight. The Law entitles me to protect my property. Not to put too fine a point on it, it entitles me to shoot you – if I must."

"You can't shoot me if I don't attack you," said Conlan. But he didn't sound very confident.

"Exactly," said Lord Cedarbrook gently. "But who is to say whether you attacked me or not – once you yourself are no longer with us."

There was a short silence before he went on:

"I don't know why I should tell you this, and I doubt if you'll understand it. I've had a lot of loves in my life but only one of them's lasted. That's my love for England. I'd shoot you gladly, now, and risk hanging if I thought it would help her in any way at all. That's the mistake you people make. You sell yourselves for the first dirty money that offers. Well, that's all right as far as it goes, but when you've done it once or twice you begin to think that nothing else matters except money. And the joke is, if you choose to think of it, that time and time again, throughout this affair, you've come to grief by running against people who weren't working for money at all. I hope you'll find the thought a comfort in the long days that lie ahead. Now. First, did you know where the money came from that you've been getting for these jobs?"

"And suppose I don't want to answer your questions."

"It will be my sad duty," said Lord Cedarbrook, "to shoot you in the right knee. A .455 bullet at this range is going to make a horrible mess of your kneecap. The pain will be exquisite and I guarantee that you will never walk unaided again."

The barrel of the revolver descended slowly.

"No," said Conlan thickly.

"No what?"

"No. I don't know where the money was coming from. We got paid by Capelli. He got the money from someone called Legate. That's all I know."

"Very well. Was tonight to be the last of these particular jobs?"

"Yes, it was. We got five hundred each. You had to be hurt – you and the other two – then that was the end of it."

"I see." Lord Cedarbrook was under no delusion as to what 'hurt' meant.

"A last and most important question. Was it to be any part of your job, you or your friends, to help Mr Legate to get away?"

"No. He had it all fixed. It was nothing to do with us. I don't know anything about it. I just did what I was told. I don't know anything more."

"All right," said Lord Cedarbrook. He touched the desk lamp off and on again and the room suddenly seemed to be full of policemen. There must have been a dozen waiting in the garden.

When Bates and Conlan had been taken away, Lord Cedarbrook said to Chief Inspector Hazlerigg, "I don't know how much you managed to overhear of those last exchanges but it seems obvious enough that Legate's preparing to run."

"I think," said Hazlerigg cautiously, "that he has already flitted. He never went home tonight. He was last seen leaving the Stalagmite building at half past two."

"He spent the afternoon at the Bankruptcy Court." Lord Cedarbrook gave the Chief Inspector a brief résumé of what had passed.

"He's a quick mover, isn't he?" said Hazlerigg. "I mean, up to the moment he saw you in court he probably thought he was pretty safe. I think he'd been preparing his getaway for some time, but until this afternoon he had no idea the red light was showing. And on that subject, what about your nephew and his friend – "

"I expect they can look after themselves," said His Lordship. "They both took bigger risks during the war. No. It's Legate I'm worried about. He's got six hours start, and for a man with his political connections that's six hours too much."

"We shall catch him," said Hazlerigg with conviction. "He can't fly, you know."

"Can't he, though," said Lord Cedarbrook slowly. "Can't he, by God? I knew there was something – it happened when I was playing at Watson – Wilson. On the last day. I told you how I went out on the Underground to meet a certain Mr Bernard Rose who turned out to be Colonel Vassilev. And I told you how we waited on the platform for him. Well, that was when it happened. I asked Rubinstein, the fellow with me, 'How will he come?' and Rubinstein said 'By train. Did you think he was going to – ' and then he broke off. It was obvious that he had meant to say 'Did you think he was going to fly'; but it suddenly struck him that it might be – well, perhaps an injudicious expression. You see?"

"You mean," said Hazlerigg, "that Colonel Vassilev *does* fly? He keeps a private plane somewhere?"

"Well, he must have got into the country somehow. I don't think that he passed the ports – not after his Canadian efforts. He was an ace pilot during he war. In the first two years of the war – before he turned to special service – he was credited with thirty-two 'certains'. Suppose he came in by plane. It would need some arranging, but it could be managed. Suppose also that it's a two-seater. And remember that even for a small civilian plane it's only about four hours' flying time to Russian-occupied Germany."

16

The Political Angle

In spite of the fact that it was after two o'clock before he finally got to bed, Lord Cedarbrook was up again, and had dressed and breakfasted by eight.

He had a busy day in front of him.

At nine o'clock he was shown into Hazlerigg's office, where he found the Chief Inspector in conference with Inspector Roberts.

Inspector Roberts looked as happy as a professional policeman is capable of looking.

"It's a funny thing," he was saying as Lord Cedarbrook came in, "but these crowds are all the same. For years and years they go on being ultra-cautious, and looking before they leap and taking one step forward and two back and so on, and then suddenly they go crackpot. Just look at last night's effort!"

"I've spoken with my nephew," said Lord Cedarbrook, "and I gather that he is all right. Yeatman-Carter is in hospital, but not badly hurt. What exactly happened?"

"So far as we know," said Inspector Roberts, "Legate, through Brandison, paid Luciano three thousand pounds in cash. I'm not sure how the money was to be split, and I don't know, and I don't suppose we ever shall know, exactly what they had to do to earn it. They say, of course, that they were told to 'treat 'em rough' – I gather that meant all three of you. Personally, I've got my doubts. I think they meant murder."

"I'm certain that Legate meant murder," agreed Lord Cedarbrook. "And he could well afford to mean murder – since he wasn't staying behind to suffer the consequences. But whether Luciano and his assistants meant to carry out their instructions quite so literally – well, the point is now academic."

"They've finished their run," agreed Inspector Roberts. "Last night – well, it wasn't their lucky night. Two away defeats and one draw. You didn't hear what happened up at Winchmore Hill. Apparently two of them went after Yeatman-Carter and got involved with some of the Rugby boys. Something midway between boat-race night and a country dance. One of them, Bell, left his trousers behind. Unfortunately for him he has the American habit of keeping his wallet in his hip pocket, so we've got plenty of identification there. Then Rumbold and Miss Burke can give us enough evidence to put away Luciano and three others. We haven't caught them yet, but we soon will. Bates and Conlan are inside already. It's a clean sweep."

Lord Cedarbrook noticed that so far Inspector Hazlerigg had allowed Roberts to do all the talking, and he guessed the reason. In the last analysis, Luciano's crowd were secondary.

Behind Luciano was Legate, and his financial game. And behind Legate there was opening a yet wider vista, a barren and violent region, where Harry Hyde, the left-wing journalist joined hands with the philanthropic Jones brothers. And behind them, Colonel Vassilev.

Hazlerigg said: "I don't think I've ever known a more curious case. Consider this. It opened, so far as we were concerned, six months ago, when Mr Britten went into the Thames at Staines. For five and a half out of these six months we've had practically nothing to go on at all. At times, I haven't even been sure there was a case. Now we've got so much – why, we hardly know where to start."

Sensing Lord Cedarbrook's surprise he added: "The Rats' Chorus is beginning. First thing this morning we had Gould in. He was that agency chap you employed to find Potts. No doubt his contacts had told him that Luciano was finito and Legate was on the run, and the result was he just couldn't talk fast enough. Apparently they had some frame on him over the Potts killing. That's why he wouldn't talk before. Actually he didn't tell us much that we hadn't guessed but his evidence links Legate with Doctor Potts in a very satisfactory way. We'd no sooner finished with Gould than I heard that Bates had decided to talk. He's got it into his head that last night's fiasco up at your house was all Conlan's fault. We encouraged the idea and let him think that Conlan had already started talking to us himself. It's a corny device, but it's surprising how often it works. If we accept his evidence and put him in the stand we've an even chance of hanging Conlan for the murder of Doctor Potts. But that's not all. Do you know who we've got next door?"

"Legate," said Lord Cedarbrook with a sudden wild hope.

"No. But the next best thing, Brandison. He came in this morning, as soon as he heard Legate had bunked. His nerve is all to pieces, I think, among other reasons, because he's out of cocaine. The Luciano supply has dried up and he hasn't had time to arrange another one. But he was ripe to talk. Perhaps you'd like to see this first report."

Lord Cedarbrook read through the three pages and then, turning back to the beginning, read through them again. Hazlerigg waited patiently.

"Embezzlement," said His Lordship at last, "or False Pretences – or both. There's quite enough there for a warrant. I expect your lawyers will worry out the technicalities for you – if you catch your man."

"When we catch our man – " amended Hazlerigg.

Lord Cedarbrook looked up for a moment, and then resumed his study of the papers.

"ABC CBA," he said, "that's clever. I don't think I should ever have spotted that. And the etching – that's a nice little point too. I suppose Sherlock Holmes would have based a whole train of deduction on it."

"I expect he would," said Hazlerigg, "but it wouldn't have helped him to find Legate."

"What actually happened about that?"

"Immediately we got your telephone message last night I sent a man round to keep an eye on him. He lives in a service flat in Kensington. The man got there at seven o'clock. According to a porter Legate wasn't back, so he waited for him. He's still waiting."

"I see. Then he never went home from the Bankruptcy Court. It's annoying, but you can't help admiring a bit of clear thinking. As soon as he heard that we'd troubled to unearth his early life he must have known that we probably knew it all. And then Vassilev would have told him about my meeting with him, and he'd only got to put two and two together."

Hazlerigg said: "I must confess that the political angle has me worried. I think I have grasped the financial side. In fact, it's really very simple. It'll mean at least one criminal prosecution – if we put Brandison into the dock instead of the witness box. And perhaps a big civil action. But the other business – I hardly know what to make of it. It's really more a job for our Special Branch, or even for you MI folk."

"Colonel Vassilev," said Lord Cedarbrook, "is the stormy petrel of the USSR. He was in Italy when they nearly came off the rails in the spring of 1946 and he was in Canada at the time of the Atomic Secrets enquiry. He's a unique person. I mean that. I don't think there's another like him inside or outside Russia. He's a professional trouble-encourager, a fanner of flames. It's important to bear in mind that he doesn't start things. His technique is always the same. When he visits a country he makes his contacts through the extreme left wing of the left wing. The pro-Russia-at-all-costs boys. They show him the little fires. Some they may have started, some may be other people's work. He provides them with petrol to pour on the flames. Money – yes, and advice and encouragement. But chiefly money. That's how he's backing Legate and that's why he's backing him. He spotted the political possibilities of what he was doing – if it could be properly exploited. I agree with you. It's not Legate's side that we have to worry about. I'm taking Curtis from the DPP's office to see the Stalagmite Board at twelve o'clock. What's been done can't be completely undone, but I think we can plug the leak. There's bound to be a scandal, but now that we're warned it can be kept within bounds. It's the political exploitation that's going to cause big trouble. Imagine our position with Legate the other side of the Iron Curtain making a series of carefully inspired statements. That's why he's got to be found. And quickly."

"If he tries any of the ordinary ways out," said Hazlerigg, "I think we shall get him. I had a closure on the ports by eight thirty last night and there's no possible combination of boat and train or car and train which could have got him out before that time. We've got your photographs, and a very good description with accurate measurements – we got those from his tailor, by the way."

"And if he tries to go by air?"

"Yes. That's not so easy. The passenger airlines will be closed to him, of course. But there are two further chances. A certain number of private planes are kept at the different airports and a certain number of private licences have been issued since the war – mostly to businessmen. I'm having a very careful check made of these. The trouble is that there's very little to prevent one of these owners – if his sympathies lay that way – *allowing* his plane to be stolen. We should know about it almost at once, of course – "

"Almost at once might be too late."

"Exactly. The other chance, of course, is that he may not go from an airport at all. There are a few places left, even today, where a man could land a plane, and take off again, without attracting too much notice."

"Baron Childerpath's Melsetshire estate," suggested His Lordship.

"No names no pack drill," said Hazlerigg hastily. "I don't say that it could have been done during the war," he went on, "when people were security conscious and we had the spotting service organized. But nowadays – well, who takes any notice of aeroplanes nowadays? People don't even bother to look up when one goes over."

2

At half past ten Lord Cedarbrook visited Paddy at Rahere's. Although the results of Paddy's investigations had been passed on to him, in summary form, this was really the first opportunity that he had had of seeing him for some weeks.

There were certain aspects of the connection between *Market News* and the Stalagmite and the operations of Moody and Van Bright on which he was not yet quite clear, and Paddy did his best to enlighten him. His Lordship was also particularly interested in the identification of the two men who had sat in the smoking-room of the Pike and Eels on the night of Mr Britten's decease.

He was mildly surprised to find that Paddy appeared to be on terms of considerable intimacy with Nurse Goodbody. Not that he had any objection to Nurse Goodbody, whom he thought a most sensible, old-fashioned girl. But he had had the impression that she was engaged to his nephew. He made up his mind to ask Nap about it next time he saw him.

Lord Cedarbrook was not really a lady's man.

As he was going Paddy said: "You know this is rather an opportunity for me. I like the paper I'm working for, and I'm staying on permanently. If I can give McAndrews – that's my copy chief – the low-down on this, I'm made for life – "

"Forty-eight hours," said Lord Cedarbrook, "and even then he'll be ahead of the field. He can publish what he likes, on the morning of the day after tomorrow."

His next move was to Whitehall where, at eleven o'clock, he kept his appointment with the legal Mr Curtis. Here he encountered a degree of official opposition, but a telephone call to the Director of Public Prosecutions (with whom Lord Cedarbrook had been at Winchester) removed the obstacle and his plan was agreed.

3

The message which summoned the Directors of the Stalagmite to a general meeting at twelve o'clock had been carefully worded so as not to alarm. It mentioned that a matter of policy had arisen which called for immediate decision. It was signed by Mr Lloyd, an inoffensive person who was head of the Life section and was generally accepted as Mr Legate's second-in-command.

Sir George Burroughs and Hewson-Collet came together in a taxi. Sir Hubert Fosdick and Andrew Chattell arrived in their chauffeur-driven cars. Charles Bedell Atkinson strolled across from the headquarters of the Home Counties Bank. And old Lord Stallybrowe, who had his long hooked fingers in a hundred financial pies, came up from his soundly mortgaged acres at Sunningdale by Southern to Waterloo – he always travelled third class – and from Waterloo he caught a bus, carefully alighting two stops short of his destination in order not to exceed the three-halfpenny fare.

On their arrival in the boardroom the six directors were equally surprised by the absence of Mr Legate and by the presence of two outsiders – though one of these appeared to be known to some of their number. For Sir Hubert Fosdick said: "Good Heavens, Alfred, what are you doing here? Have they co-opted you on to the board," and Lord Stallybrowe grunted and said something which sounded unfriendly. Hewson-Collet took a quick look at the second of the two strangers and seemed to be on the point of addressing him, but refrained. As he took his seat with the others, it was noticeable that he looked thoughtful.

"Gentlemen," said Mr Lloyd. "If you are all ready, I think – that is, would you be seated."

He looked like a young and nervous mother forced against her sounder instincts, to give a tea party to a lot of obstreperous children.

"I say, Lloyd," said Sir George Burroughs, "where's Legate?"

"What's this all about?" asked Mr Chattell.

"I hope this isn't going to take too long," said Hewson-Collet. "I've got an appointment for lunch. What's the trouble, Lloyd?"

Mr Lloyd shot a glance of appeal at Lord Cedarbrook, who rose to his feet.

He said, "I called this meeting. You were enquiring where Mr Legate was. I wish I could tell you. The police, too, would be interested to know."

Just so must it have been with Perseus, who with a quick turn of his wrist, twitched the cloth from the Gorgon's head. The nobles and counsellors sat silent and turned to stone.

There was not a man present who did not fully understand every implication of Lord Cedarbrook's words.

Having delivered the coup His Lordship seemed unwilling to follow it up. He stood at the top of the table, his massive shoulders stooped forward, his head turning slowly as he surveyed the company. The hardest hit were Lord Stallybrowe and old Sir Hubert Fosdick. The consternation of the former, indeed, was so extreme as to be almost ludicrous. Sir George Burroughs seemed suddenly to have aged. Andrew Chattell had ceased to look pompous and was beginning to look plainly frightened. Hewson-Collet managed to retain an appearance of professional composure, but his hands betrayed him. Of all six men only little Charles Bedell Atkinson, the banker, seemed unmoved. Lord Cedarbrook had found the man he wanted, and it was to Mr Atkinson that he now addressed himself.

"It will undoubtedly have occurred to you to wonder," he said, "what my standing in this matter may be. However, if you are prepared, for the time being, to take that on trust, I will merely mention that this gentleman with me here is Mr Curtis, one of the legal advisers to the Director of Public Prosecutions. And it is with the consent of the Director that I am taking this course." He paused for a moment, then went on, picking his words carefully: "You must all of you be aware, from what I have already told you, that the great corporation whose interests you represent stands in danger. But if you are to appreciate the real gravity of the position, I shall have to go back some years, and tell you something about your General Manager.

"It is the history of a young communist, a single-minded enthusiast, a drinker of the undiluted waters of Marx, who joined the great steel firm of Impeys at Deptford, at the beginning of this century, and quickly made his mark – in more ways than one. As an active and intelligent worker, and as a political organizer. He became, at a very early age, a shop steward – or what passed for one in those days – and he organized and took part in a series of strikes and demonstrations which culminated in his dismissal by the firm. The matter, unfortunately, did not end there. There was a scene in the staff manager's office, a policeman was called in, and Legate – or Lake, as he called himself in those days – struck him. As a result, he got a prison sentence.

"Incidentally, it was suggested at the time that he may not have been entirely responsible for his actions. On the previous day he had been involved in an affair in Hyde Park and had suffered a sort of delayed concussion from a truncheon blow. I don't think we shall ever know the real truth about that, but there is a certain amount of evidence that Legate regarded that day as the turning point in his life. When he was suffering the effects of concussion he talked in the most lucid way about his life's plans and ambitions to a doctor who happened to be attending to him. Whether or not they were exactly those plans which he eventually followed up we do not, of course, know. But in view of the fact that he later thought it necessary to have this doctor traced, and later still, when his plans were very near to fruition – to have him murdered – well, it seems probable. For make no mistake about it, gentlemen, he was a very patient, very determined, very far-seeing man, infinitely capable of subordinating himself to an objective.

"He had the weakness of his strength, too. He was a great hater. He didn't forget things. I suppose you must have noticed that he had an etching of the north-west corner of Hyde Park hanging in his office. I am told that it went with him wherever he worked. Well, that sort of thing was typical, and in the end it brought him down. However, I am getting ahead of myself.

"When Lake came out of prison he changed his name – a reasonable enough action in a man who wished to live down his one criminal indiscretion – and he joined the army. He had an undistinguished career, but he got what he wanted – commissioned rank – and a few contacts. After the war he went into his CO's firm, and soon made his mark. He was the type who gets on, and he had the additional advantage of knowing exactly where he was going. He changed firms, joining Moody and Van Bright in, I think, about 1926. They were a smaller business, and he was very soon in virtual control. When he made his money, during and after the 1931 financial crisis, he bought out the existing partners and put in young Philip Van Bright as his nominee. So that when he came to you as General Manager he retained – although of course you weren't to know it – the control of that firm."

"No wonder we did such a lot of business through them," said Mr Atkinson drily.

"And they hold most of our securities," squeaked Mr Chattell, appearing for a moment above the surface.

"Yes, we're coming to that. But there's one thing I should like to clear up first. When Lake joined you – did you ask *him* to take the post, or did he apply for it?"

"He applied for it," said Sir George Burroughs. "But even if he hadn't we should probably have asked him. There wasn't another man of his standing or special knowledge available. We congratulated ourselves that we had made a very good bargain. Even now I can hardly see – "

"Don't be silly, George," said Lord Stallybrowe. "He joined us to ruin us. To ruin us. And he has ruined us."

The solvent of personal danger was quickly reducing each of them to primary elements.

"Personally," said Mr Atkinson coolly, "I'd welcome a few more details about this 'ruining'. We've got very good auditors and the last balance sheet looked healthy enough to me."

"Right," said Lord Cedarbrook. "I hoped you'd say that, because it brings me to my next point. When Legate joined this corporation his objects, as I see them, were twofold. To get his own back on the world of big business, and to line his pockets in the process. It is difficult to weigh the Marxist against the rogue and say which object was the more important. Possibly they seemed to him equally so. For a number of years he worked steadily, to gain your confidence and to get the feel of his position. Also he had some preparations to make. He needed at least one confederate. If necessary, I think he would have installed him. But it wasn't necessary. He found Brandison, whom he promoted to chief cashier, just the man for the job. Brandison was a drug addict – "

"Drugs," moaned Sir Hubert Fosdick.

"Also there were certain outside agencies which had to be prepared. But when he was ready he wasted no time. About a year ago he set to work, on three distinct lines. First, on one pretext or another he lodged a good many of your soundest securities with Moody and Van Bright. An auditor, as you know, will accept a certificate from a reputable firm of brokers as to what stocks and shares they hold on behalf of a client, without actually bothering to see the share certificates. In your last three quarterly audits you will see, I fancy, that an increasing number of your most valuable securities are described as 'lodged with Moody and Bright'. In effect, of course, that certification came not from Moody and Van Bright but from Legate. I think that a number of those securities may be regarded as non-existent. They have been quietly sold over a period of months. The total loss under that head alone may amount to something like three-quarters of a million pounds."

No one seemed disposed to break the silence that ensued, so Lord Cedarbrook went on:

"Now the second matter. Recently, as you must have noticed, you have been placing your money in a number of rather speculative concerns. I will mention one – Syn-ol Company – "

"But, Cedarbrook," – Mr Chattell seemed to have found his voice. "I was present at the Directors' Meeting when the purchase was discussed. I resent the word 'speculative'. We went into it very thoroughly. Why, I remember an article in *Market News* by their City Expert which gave the most convincing reasons – "

"Exactly," said Lord Cedarbrook drily. "I suppose you know that Legate owned *Market News*. He probably contributed the article himself." He went on: "There's no evading the conclusion, gentlemen, that with his own brokers, his own financial press and your unbounded confidence in his judgement, he had you in blinkers. He had you hypnotized. I'm not blaming you – I'm just stating the fact. If you look now with a fresh and unbiased eye on some of your recent purchases – Syn-ol, West African Hostels, those Czechoslovakian Bonds, Factory Fitments – I'll say more about them in a moment – Syndicat Universal – and a dozen others."

"You're right about the hypnotism," said Mr Atkinson. "Recently, about nine months ago that is, we formed a finance sub-committee. Myself, Chattell and Sir George, with Legate as a permanent member. Any three of us to form a quorum. This committee approved all those purchases you have mentioned – and I must have sat on most of the committees. And yet the matters were so cleverly presented that I, for one, never questioned them."

Lord Cedarbrook said: "If it's any comfort to you, it was, I think, the formation of that committee which caused Legate his biggest headache – and in a way, it led to his discovery. You see, until very recently he tended to be a bit short of money. Until the last moment he couldn't actually realize too many of the securities which Moody and Van Bright were holding. And I must emphasize again that any actual stealing of money from the Corporation was out of the question. Your internal security measures were too good. So what he did was, like all his tactics, very simple. He got you to authorize double and treble his salary and allowances. It wasn't too difficult. As you know, he had a basic salary, and on top of that you paid him a commission on profits, on a sliding scale, with a bonus on certain big deals, and there was an arrangement by which he could draw lump sums against this money. I think that's correct, isn't it?"

"Yes," said Mr Chattell, "but the cheques had to be signed by a director. Surely we should have noticed – "

"Not if he was careful, where he drew money twice, that the duplicate cheques were signed by different directors. That was where Brandison came in. He used to make out lists of cheques for your signature at each meeting. Three months ago, for example, you allowed Legate an advance of two thousand five hundred pounds against accrued bonus. Do you realize that you paid it him no less than three times? One cheque was signed by Mr Atkinson, one by Mr Chattell and one by Sir George Burroughs. Of course, that was an extreme example – in the earlier days he didn't overreach himself to that extent. Besides, as I said, in the early days, when he might have been dealing with any two out of six directors it was easy. Latterly, with only three of you on the finance committee, it got more difficult."

"Look here, Cedarbrook," said Lord Stallybrowe, "is this true? Where did you hear it. It sounds far-fetched."

"I heard most of it from Brandison this morning. But if you want a practical example of the cheque business let me tell you what happened in January. At the beginning of this year, as you may remember, Brandison was ill. Your second cashier was away, too. So the duty of preparing the list of cheques for your signature devolved on Mr Britten, one of your junior cashiers. Legate gave him the original list – and told him to have four or five copies made – one for each director and one or two spare. Britten was incurably careless. He typed out the copies himself, and – I think entirely by mistake – instead of leaving the cheques as they were, he put both Legate's duplicate pay cheques – a small matter of a thousand pounds each on account of salary – into your column, Sir George."

Sir George Burroughs went very red and said, "Do you mean to say that I signed the same cheque twice over."

"A different cheque, of course," said Lord Cedarbrook, "but the same payee and the same amount. Legate was in the room when you did it. I suppose he would have explained it away somehow, if you had noticed it. But it must have given him a bad five minutes. But the remedy was worse than the malady. Because he got it into his head that Mr Britten had done this on purpose. There I think he was entirely wrong. I think it was just an example of Britten's usual inefficiency and muddle-headedness. But the implications were alarming. If Britten had done it on purpose, then Britten knew what Legate was up to. Legate was too far committed by this time to draw back. I must say, he acted very quickly. First he had Britten sacked – not only to get him out of the way, but in order to create a convincing motive for suicide. Then, on Britten's last night with the firm, he hired two men to follow him home, knock him on the head, and push him into the river – first searching his pockets and afterwards his house in order to make sure that he had left no documentary evidence behind. They were professional murderers, and they did their work in a very neat and professional way and Legate must have been very pleased with them. But unknown to him fate had already dealt another hand into the game."

Lord Cedarbrook explained the part played by Paddy on that memorable night and finished by saying: "When Yeatman-Carter turned up a few days later and actually outlined to Legate the whole truth of the crime – with a few important exceptions – well, it must have been a ticklish moment. Carter, remember, had seen that very list, with Mr Chattell's initials and Mr Atkinson's and yours, Sir George. He remembered the first two – ABC and CBA. If he'd once realized what they signified the whole game would have been up.

"Legate improvised brilliantly. But at the end of the interview one of those silly things happened which confirm one's belief in Providence. Carter said something uncomplimentary about communists and this casual remark touched Legate on the raw. He must have been mad enough in a general way with this young fellow who had blundered in and was threatening to upset his carefully stacked apple-cart. Here was the last straw. As soon as Carter had left, Legate sat down to think out how he could hurt him most effectively. And since Carter was a very junior member of a firm of accountants which depended on your goodwill for a lot of their work – well, it didn't take him long to think out a stupid little piece of retaliation.

"And that was really the beginning of the end. First Britten, then Carter. Two unimportant people, who incurred Legate's displeasure. And two of the proximate causes of his failure. The third was Bairsted. Some of you know that story, so I won't waste your time with it now. Enough to say that as soon as we heard that Legate was on Henry Bairsted's trail, we tracked back and we found Lake. And when we found Lake, we knew all about Legate. An inefficient cashier, a sacked accountant, a bankrupt industrialist. How shall the small confound the great."

"Some time ago," said Mr Atkinson, "you said that Legate's object was to make money and to ruin us. Was there anything more to it than that?"

"At first," said Lord Cedarbrook, "possibly not. Unfortunately for all concerned, the facts of the case became known to a certain Power – I needn't elaborate the matter – a Power which has always thrived on the misfortunes of its neighbours – and for some reason is able to reap particular advantage if it can promote a really stinking financial scandal. You remember the Mont de Piété revelations which nearly brought down the French Government in the thirties – or more recently the Vatican currency-smuggling scandal which might have had a decisive effect on the Italian elections."

"Admitted," said Hewson-Collet, "that any financial embarrassment on our part is a cause of rejoicing to a certain Power whom we're all too gentlemanly to mention by name. But was there, in fact, much in this for them. The only villain of the piece is Legate. We may be stung or we may be sunk – probably shall be. But it isn't a criminal offence to be fooled – not yet."

Lord Cedarbrook looked faintly surprised. "I'm afraid you haven't got the idea at all," he said. "Look it at this way. Suppose that we hadn't got on to Legate's game. Suppose he had wound up the business in a blaze of well-organized publicity – as he no doubt meant to. He'd have got rid of all your soundest holdings – and your shaky ones would have dropped through the floor. Your total loss would have run into millions. The public aren't financial wizards, but that's the sort of thing they *can* understand. The Stalagmite has lost two or three million pounds – *somebody* must have pocketed it. The suggestion, of course, is that *you* have done so. Then why haven't you been prosecuted? Well, there's a suggestion for that, too. Sir George has got a brother-in-law in the Cabinet and your cousin, Lord Stallybrowe, is a Parliamentary Under-secretary. We know it's nonsense, of course, but that sort of thing's meat and drink to the left wing. It was a perfectly lovely weapon. But, as I said, it was a weapon which needed the nicest timing in its use. And it is that timing which they have just failed to achieve. If Legate could have got clear away before you had any idea of what was happening you would have gone down without a struggle. As it is, you've got a chance."

"There is a chance," said Mr Atkinson slowly, "if you will hold your hand for a day or two. We can put an immediate distringas on any securities that Van Bright hasn't actually sold. And where he has sold, we may be able to impugn the sale for lack of good faith. Then we shall need to float off some of those doubtful securities. It all depends on how long you can give us. If you upset the market now we shall get about a farthing in the pound."

Lord Cedarbrook looked at Mr Curtis who said: "The Director has had to consider his duty to the public as well as to your shareholders and yourselves. But in the special circumstances he is prepared to suspend all action for forty-eight hours – "

"We shall have to get a move on," said Mr Atkinson. "There's only one thing to do. We shall have to form a private company to buy every single Stalagmite share which is offered for sale. When the news becomes public that ought to prevent a general run on our credit. I'd better see to the details – "

"Then we'd better have a test audit at once to find where we stand."

"Mr Lloyd can take Legate's place for the time being. If anyone wants to know where Legate is, say that he's ill – "

"The police hunt will have to go on," said Curtis. "We can't guarantee that we shall be able to keep the public in the dark even for forty-eight hours. Something may get out."

"Then the sooner we start the better," said Mr Atkinson, who seemed quite cheerful now that there was action in prospect. "If you will leave the immediate steps to myself and Hewson-Collet I suggest we adjourn and meet again in two hours' time."

Lord Stallybrowe was last to go. He seemed to move in a daze. When he left the building he made instinctively for the modest café at which it was his custom to lunch on Board-meeting days.

In the middle of the road he changed his mind, and by vigorously waving, succeeded in stopping a taxi.

"Where to, sir," said the taxi driver.

"The Ritz Hotel," said Lord Stallybrowe.

It was the gesture of a lifetime.

17

Curtains

And so for forty-eight hours.

The directors, under the inspired leadership of Charles Bedell Atkinson (Sir Charles now, of course), wrought to save the Stalagmite. And though no one will ever know what it cost them personally, it is a matter of history that they did save it; and with it a small but definite part of England's financial credit. And at that time she was living on her credit and on not much else.

The police spread their invisible net, the unostentatious net of the man-to-man enquiry, and thousands of uniformed policemen and thousands of plain-clothes detectives and even more thousands of Specials and railway police and dock police and customs operatives and airport officials received a Description and a Name.

And reports came flowing in, and were sifted and scrutinized and analysed – and about one in ten seemed promising enough to be followed up.

And the trouble taken was infinite, and the success achieved was nil.

Appropriately it was Lord Cedarbrook who made the final suggestion. He made it to Chief Inspector Hazlerigg on the morning of the second day of the great search.

They were talking about the character of the Russian – or Lord Cedarbrook was talking, for it was a subject about which he knew a great deal, and Hazlerigg was listening with one ear cocked for the telephone.

"They're diffcult to grasp," said His Lordship, "because it's always difficult to understand an alliance between fire and ice. On the one hand they are devastatingly practical – they subordinate the means to the end to a degree which frightens a Western European. On that side of the medal, you know, Legate was pure Russian. I expect that's why they understood him so well. And then, when you think you've understood that part of their character you strike this extraordinary vein of sentimentality. It takes a lot of different forms – a secret respect for convention, an exaggerated hero worship – "

Hazlerigg waited patiently. He guessed that some practical suggestion might eventually emerge from this theorizing. When it did come it surprised him.

"I should look for Vassilev," said Lord Cedarbrook at last. "If you find Vassilev he'll lead you to Legate."

"Quite so. Where do we look?"

"It's only a suggestion," said His Lordship. "But why not start with Highgate? I can't give you very convincing reasons, but such as they are, they seem to point there. First, when I met Vassilev he was in a tube train going in the direction of Highgate. Of course, the train was going to the centre of London as well, but I don't think he'd be living there. And then again, he may have been bluffing. But that's where the Russian character comes in. If he had been a German I should have guessed he lived in Edgware – the place the train was coming from. The German is by nature a double bluffer. The Russian is a treble bluffer. Therefore, since he was going towards Highgate, I think he lives in Highgate. And that fits in with his respect for convention, too. You'll find that most prominent Russian anarchists have lived in Highgate or Hampstead. Peter Kropotkin, Felix Volkhovsky, Rankow. Karl Marx was buried in Highgate Cemetery."

"That's all very well," said Hazlerigg. "It's an interesting theory. You talk of Highgate and Hampstead, but have you got any idea of their size? Together they form one of the biggest residential areas in London. We may have a lot of men on the job but strike me down, I can't authorize a house to house search throughout the whole N6 and NW6, postal districts."

"Nor am I suggesting that you should," said Lord Cedarbrook. "This is where my lecture on the Russian respect for the great men of the past comes in. I'll get the Department to give you a list of a dozen houses where heroes of the Revolution have lived in exile. It would be so completely in character for Vassilev to pick one of those."

"We can try it," said Hazlerigg. In his philosophy police work largely consisted in trying anything. It was the longest shots which sometimes came off.

At the third attempt – it was at the corner house in Nansen Hill, where Oralov the nihilist poet had spent seven hectic years before returning to Russia and martyrdom in 1918 – Sergeant Crabbe struck a very warm trail. He telephoned Hazlerigg, who said, "That sounds like Vassilev all right. Left yesterday afternoon, did he? I'll get a search warrant and come along myself. You stay there and watch the house. Oh, and see if you can pick up anything from the neighbours."

Colonel Vassilev was a thorough man, as Hazlerigg and his professional searchers realized when they had finished their first quick survey of the house. But he had left in a hurry, and in a hurry even the most experienced agents make mistakes; sometimes quite obvious mistakes.

"He cleared his desk and his wastepaper basket," said Hazlerigg. "And the blotter's clean. But – wait a minute – look here." He pulled out the thick pad of blotting paper – a dozen double sheets together. The outside ones were blank, but at some time the whole pad had been refolded, and the inside sheets showed criss-cross lines of spidery writing.

"It's Russian, all right," said Lord Cedarbrook to Nap, who seemed to have attached himself to the party. "Something about an 'uncle' with a house in the country. And look, here's a place name in capital letters, and there it is again – Blampford."

"That's near Salisbury," said Sergeat Crabbe. "It was an Air Force station. I think there's a small airport there now. I was in the village at the beginning of the war."

Hazlerigg said, "This is beginning to look solemn. It might be a matter of hours – or even minutes. I don't suppose he'd have been in time to get off last night, but this morning – he may be in the air now."

Nap never forgot that last scene. The shabby little over-furnished room, the bulk of Lord Cedarbrook. Hazlerigg in front of the fire, his grey eyes very anxious. Sergeant Crabbe and the two police searchers; the landlady fluttering in the doorway.

"Have you got a telephone?"

"Yes, sir. There's one in the hall."

"Get on to headquarters," said Hazlerigg to Sergeant Crabbe, "and tell them to clear me a priority to the Air Ministry. Tell them I'll be at my office to use it in eight – no – seven minutes. Then see if you can get a line to Blampford. It mayn't be easy on this phone but try. Come on."

The drive was a memory, too. There were two police drivers, and they knew their way about; but to get from Highgate to Westminster in seven minutes is a feat.

2

Sergeant Crabbe's call to Blampford got through at the same time as Hazlerigg's – and both of them crossed a message from Blampford police station. This was brief and to the point. It said "A small civil Auster type monoplane Registration GAWG left Blampford without permission from Control Tower at 1100 hours this morning. Control Tower sent us this information at 1105."

"Not bad," said Hazlerigg. "1115. We've still got a chance. Hello. Yes. Group Captain Maine, please. Yes. Extremely urgent."

"Another message from Blampford, sir," said Inspector Pickup. "The chap in the plane – it's not Vassilev. It's Legate. There's no doubt about it at all. They had our description in the routine way. They are quite positive."

"Legate. I thought it was a monoplane."

"That's correct, sir. It seems he's flying it himself."

"Can he fly?"

"He was in the RFC for two years," said Lord Cedarbrook. "And he had a peacetime 'A' licence at Hatfield. An Auster isn't difficult."

"Hello," said Hazlerigg, turning back to his telephone. "Is that Group Captain Maine? Look here, can you put any fighters into the air. Yes. Now. What? I see. Yes, of course it's operational. You could. How long?"

After a few seconds Hazlerigg said, "I see," and put down the receiver quietly.

"It'll take two hours," he said, "to get a fighter up."

"An Auster's a slowish plane," said Lord Cedarbrook. "And its cruising speed's not much over ninety. All the same – two hours!"

"He was heading North-East," said Pickup. "He'll cross the coast between the Thames Estuary and the Wash. A hundred and forty-sixty – a hundred and sixty miles as the crow flies."

"He took off at eleven," said Lord Cedarbrook. "It's eleven twenty-five now. He'll be over the sea by one o'clock."

"Then there's only one thing for it," said Hazlerigg. He sounded almost cheerful. "But it's not a decision I can take myself – thank goodness for that."

He dialled a number and when he spoke it was to the Commissioner of Police for the Metropolis.

Then they all sat in the office, with the June sun pouring in at the window, and waited whilst the minutes ticked away.

It was five past twelve when the telephone rang again and Hazlerigg picked up the receiver.

"I've been up to the top." It was the Commissioner's voice. "They've passed orders to the War Office. I hope to Heaven you're not making any mistake about this, Hazlerigg."

3

Lance-Bombardier Smith (Gertrude) had just told her friend Sergeant Evans (Florence) that she was bored.

Annual camp was all right, she said, as far as it went. But with seven and a half girls to every chap, well, one hadn't much chance, had one. And as for Dummy Targets – well she, Gertie, had sat at a predictor on the South Coast during the last three years of the war where anti-aircraft gunnery was anti-aircraft gunnery and you shot at things which shot back at you, and she had assisted in bringing down German fighters and German bombers, and V-ones and V-twos and V-everything elses, and once, for a bet, she'd laid on a seagull at five thousand and hit that.

Cromer was all right, it was a nice place for a camp, whilst the weather kept fine. And Captain Berry was a good sport – and knew his stuff, too. Married, of course, but you couldn't have everything.

There he was, now, talking on the field telephone,

"Hullo," said Flossie, "he seems excited about something."

"He's running," said Gertie. "This is going to be good. That's the first time I've seen him run this week. I expect he's heard that the Brigadier's on his way. Now for a bit of bull."

Captain Berry was observed to be talking into the R/T head-set. Evidently he was giving orders to the aeroplane which was cruising in a desultory way overhead towing a sleeve target; for it turned about and made for its landing ground.

"Attention, everybody." Captain Berry had picked up the loud-speaker microphone. "I have just had orders from Group. I understand that they come direct from Command. All ack-ack batteries on Coastal practice have been ordered to open fire on an Auster aircraft, green fuselage with silver wings. Registration GAWG. Flying North-East. Expected to be flying low."

Captain Berry paused. So far so good. But he felt that the occasion called for something more.

"I think," he said, "that this is probably some sort of operational Readiness Test. The plane is probably a Robot. I want you to be very careful in your laying. If it appears in our zone it must be destroyed. I rely on you."

All the same Captain Berry was both worried and intrigued. His instructions had said nothing about the plane being radio-controlled. And his orders had sounded very definite.

A shout from the Spotters interrupted his thoughts. There it was, all right. Pat on its cue, like the demon in the Pantomime. An Auster. Too far to read the identification letters.

"Plane," he pointed. "Flying North-East."

Thank God his NCOs in charge of the guns and Radar were veterans. And the predictor sergeant was a good girl too, though new to the game.

He thought he'd try it with his glasses again. It was going to pass to the North of the Battery, over the sea, but quite close.

"Predictor steady. Target in range," said Sergeant Evans non-committally.

Ten seconds. Twenty seconds. Thirty seconds.

GAWG. Quite plain.

Captain Berry lowered his glasses and took a last look round. The target plane had gone. Apart from the Auster the sky was empty. Unconsciously he took a deep breath.

"Fire."

It was easy enough. A crossing target, flying low and not very fast. For a few seconds it seemed to bear a charmed life.

Then the tell-tale plume of smoke. The fan of orange flame. The deadly comet's tail of fire.

"Cease loading."

As he spoke the Auster went plunging seaward down the parabola of its own velocity. The white wave tips rose up to meet it. The spray covered everything.

"Sweet shooting," said Gertie softly.

MICHAEL GILBERT

BLOOD AND JUDGEMENT

A Patrick Petrella mystery

When the wife of a recently escaped prisoner is found murdered and partially buried near a reservoir, Patrick Petrella, a Metropolitan Police Inspector, is called in. Suspicion falls on the escaped convict, but what could have been his motive? Petrella meets resistance from top detectives at the Yard who would prefer to keep the Inspector out of the limelight, but he is determined to solve the mystery with or without their approval.

> 'A crafty jigsaw puzzle of many parts put together by meticulous detection.' – *Chicago Sunday Tribune*

CLOSE QUARTERS

An Inspector Hazlerigg mystery

It has been more than a year since Canon Whyte fell 103 feet from the cathedral gallery, yet unease still casts a shadow over the peaceful lives of the Close's inhabitants. In an apparently separate incident, head verger Appledown is being persecuted: a spate of anonymous letters imply that he is inefficient and immoral. When Appledown is found dead, investigations suggest that someone directly connected to the cathedral is responsible, and it is up to Hazlerigg to get to the heart of the corruption.

> '…brings crime into a cathedral close. Give it to the vicar, but don't fail to read it first.' – *Daily Express*

MICHAEL GILBERT

THE DUST AND THE HEAT

Oliver Nugent is a young Armoured Corps officer in the year 1945. Taking on a near derelict pharmaceutical firm, he determines to rebuild it and make it a success. He encounters ruthless opposition, and counteracts with some fairly unscrupulous methods of his own. It seems no one is above blackmail and all is deemed fair in big business battles. Then a threat: apparently from German sources it alludes to a time when Oliver was in charge of an SS camp, jeopardizing his company and all that he has worked for.

'Mr Gilbert is a first-rate storyteller.' – *The Guardian*

THE ETRUSCAN NET

Robert Broke runs a small gallery on the Via de Benci and is an authority on Etruscan terracotta. A man who keeps himself to himself, he is the last person to become mixed up in anything risky. But when two men arrive in Florence, Broke's world turns upside down as he becomes involved in a ring of spies, the Mafiosi, and fraud involving Etruscan antiques. When he finds himself in prison on a charge of manslaughter, the net appears to be tightening, and Broke must fight for his innocence and his life.

'Neat plotting, impeccable expertize and the usual shapeliness combine to make this one of Mr Gilbert's best.'
– *The Sunday Times*

Michael Gilbert

Flash Point

Will Dylan is an electoral favourite – intelligent, sharp and good-looking, he is the government's new golden boy.

Jonas Killey is a small-time solicitor – single-minded, uncompromising and obsessed, he is hounding Dylan in the hope of bringing him into disrepute.

Believing he has information that can connect Dylan with an illegal procedure during a trade union merger, he starts to spread the word, provoking a top-level fluttering. At the crucial time of a general election, Jonas finds himself pursued by those who are determined to keep him quiet.

'Michael Gilbert tells a story almost better than anyone else.'
    – *The Times Literary Supplement*

The Night of the Twelfth

Two children have been murdered. When a third is discovered – the tortured body of ten-year-old Ted Lister – the Home Counties police are compelled to escalate their search for the killer, and Operation Huntsman is intensified.

Meanwhile, a new master arrives at Trenchard House School. Kenneth Manifold, a man with a penchant for discipline, keeps a close eye on the boys, particularly Jared Sacher, son of the Israeli ambassador…

'One of the best detective writers to appear
since the war.' – BBC